Mariposa Writers
Anthology
Volume II

Mariposa Writers
Anthology 2014

ISBN-13: 978-1494497811
ISBN-10: 1494497816

Published by Plettstone
Box 5008 128
Mariposa, CA 95338

Michelle Stone

I intend to evoke emotions. I'm a formally trained electrical engineer and have dabbled in amateur astronomy for years. I've hiked a thousand miles in the Sierra range and even learned hang gliding. My favorite genre for writing is science fiction. I truly enjoy giving my imagination a worthy workout. Yet, good science fiction requires great story and character development to begin with. As exercises, I like to write fictional shorts to develop new characters or recreate an anecdotal piece of something I've heard in passing.

In the all fictional pieces I've submitted this year, I think I've created vignettes most people can connect with... all without pulling out a single laser pistol or shunting off to some far flung star system to fight hairy green aliens with big teeth.

The Messenger

I felt like an unwanted wet dog sitting there. My wife, her six siblings, and I scooted up to the old table in her mother's old Tucson, Arizona storage shed to divvy up her mother's remaining possessions. I've never dealt well with death. I wish I could just ignore it at times like this. It's not that I didn't care for the old gal. She was such a sweetheart. I'd only been able to visit with her a few times in the past four years after Sherry and I married in Portland. On each occasion, she graced me with immense gratitude and every courtesy.

Sherry, the youngest of the seven children, came along late in her mother's life. She was a most fortunate unplanned 'accident'... at least for me. After all, I married her. Our marriage had alienated some in her family for a while. We didn't announce the wedding in advance. We invited no one from either side of the family. Yes, my family, in Denver, was equally offended. To us, at the time, it seemed like a great idea. Simple, easy, and cheap.

Two of her sisters kept glaring at me. I was the *only* spouse here. I hadn't met them until this very day. Their scowls forced my eyes to the tabletop as the group sorted through trinkets, jewelry, religious icons, and 70's artwork. Mom didn't have much and I certainly wanted nothing from the estate. We were doing just fine financially and this visit really wasn't necessary as far as I was concerned. I felt terribly uncomfortable and self-conscious.

The table must have been made for dining some time in the ancient past. The old flat top kept tilting back and forth under each person's elbows as though one of the legs were shorter than the others. Sherry told me it sat in this storage shed for as long as she could remember. The family used it to support stacks of treasured detritus. The timeworn patina, scratches, old water stains, and the worn finish belied its age. As a hobbyist woodworker, I realized that the wood must be cherry. Its warm and dark brown hue enticingly glowed to my relatively experienced eye. The grain indicated quarter-sawn wood, almost impossible to come by these days and must have been very expensive even when the table was made.

"Parker, would you like this St. Christopher medal?" Sherry asked me.

No one else seemed to want it. I knew of her mother's love for the Catholic Church and the extreme reverence and faith she held. Of all the trinkets on the table, I probably would have chosen this very piece.

"Sure," I said as my eyes charted lines in the top of the table. The grain was incredibly tight with a beautiful figure, also most uncommon in cherry wood. The Shaker styled top, in its simplicity, exemplified the very finest artisanship.

"Parker, are you interested in this daisy print?" Sherry asked.

I glanced up at the gaudy thing. It was her turn for first selection of a piece. I couldn't believe how civilized her siblings acted in this process. Events like this tended to evolve into full-scale wars, from what I'd heard. "If you like it, love," I said somewhat uncommitted. I was more interested in the table than the business at hand.

I pushed my chair back a bit to see the support structure. The Shaker top seemed mismatched with the rest of the piece. Shaker furniture exhibits simplicity in every detail of construction with modest straight lines... yet, delicately carved roses graced the ends of the rails where they met the legs. The legs were round and fluted. Upon careful inspection, I noticed that no two carvings, no two legs were exactly the same. People don't normally notice such things, but I have an uncanny eye in spotting such differences. Someone had clearly made this table by hand. Really by hand... with handsaws, chisels, and hand planes. I slouched down in my seat and scooted to the floor, hoping no one would miss me as I took a peek underneath.

"Oh Parker's just looking at the table," Sherry explained to her questioning brother and sisters. "He has this thing with wood."

I was not surprised to sense the working of a long hand plane as I traced my fingers across the underside's surface. The ridges were so slight, I doubt that anyone would notice even if this side had been flipped and used on the top. I felt some words or numbers carved into the underside, but the light was so poor, I couldn't make them out. I *was* shocked to see hidden drop drawers on each end. I could see well enough to release the latch on the drawer near my chair.

"Have a nice nap?" one of Sherry's sisters

asked as my head popped up from under the table. She replaced her previous glower with a captivating smile, injecting some levity into the solemn occasion.

"Uh, yeah, sure," I replied and forced a smile in return as I lifted myself back into my seat.

Sherry's family sorted through some silver dollars and paid me no heed. I peered into the drop drawer and found only one object, a small four by six inch notebook. No one noticed as I snatched it and opened it to the first yellowed page. This looked like a diary. The author had superb penmanship and entered his name on the inside cover… Joseph Kinze. I skimmed through the first few pages.

Writing from a hospital in Paris France… first entry dated July 1, 1919… can't wait to see my family… miss them so much… wounded in the Battle of Reims July 18, 1918… gut wound and knee shot to hell… captured by Germans… wounds not properly treated… malnourished… serious infections… delivered to the French after the war… almost dead.

And there, after these few pages, he had carefully folded and inserted an onion skin letter dated May 20, 1918, dated over five weeks before his first entry. I carefully unfolded the thin fragile paper.

"Dearest Joe, I just heard you were alive. I'd given up hope when you were officially declared dead. Over a year passed with no news of you. I've remarried. The children are well. I'm very sorry, Joe, but…."

I didn't need to read the whole letter. I've heard enough tragic stories to know how this relationship ended. A lonely crippled veteran lost his family with a tragically brief one-page letter. I carefully folded the letter and returned it to its original location. When I glanced up, the family sorted through Mom's jewelry. I knew of only one piece with any real value, her wedding band. It went to Sherry's eldest sister. Yes, she should get that. I started browsing the journal again.

Returning home…watched children from afar… rented a shack on the north side of town… dirt floor… no work for someone with a bad knee… selling newspapers… apples… then finally a job in a lumber yard… great depression… lost his job at the yard in 1930 … no money for back pay… accepted a stack of cherry lumber in trade for five months' labor.

Poor guy, I thought. He had it tough. This entire history consumed only twelve pages in the small diary. He didn't write anything about his ex-wife or children after that. I had a hunch it was too painful for him to consider. Specifics of this table sitting right in front of me filled the rest of the book. He sketched several excellent freehand drawings, dimensions, and details. He explained how he learned the skills to build this piece of furniture. He cut the wood by hand, learned how to use a borrowed plane, found someone who taught him joinery, someone else taught him how to carve the delicate roses.

His last entry, dated December 25, 1940, contained only one sentence: "I have finished the table."

The sibs still sorted through the coins when I blurted out, "Who was Joseph Kinze?"

Sherry's eldest sister, Mary, in her early sixties asked, "Why?"

"I've just discovered a journal of sorts in a hidden drawer in this table. He's the author," I answered.

"Oh he was some crazy uncle or something. He lived in a shack out on the north side of town, from the stories I recall."

Noting my interest, she rummaged through her box of memories and pulled out the old leather bound family Bible. She opened it to the family tree. "Hmm. Let's see if he's in here. Oh, here it is… oh my! Our great grandmother Clara was married to him, then remarried Robert when Joseph was declared killed in action. I thought Robert was my great grandfather but it was really Joseph Kinze." She paused to collect her thoughts, sort through new emotions, and reconcile her personal slot in her family's life. After a few deep breaths, she regained her composure and continued. "A side note indicates he actually died on December 25, 1940. I'm afraid there's nothing else, Parker."

He died the very day he finished the table. I could picture him short of breath, rubbing out the last coat of finish, straining to complete this project before he died. What pushed him so hard?

A blanket of silence crushed the chatter in the sweltering Tucson heat as Mary passed the Bible around to share this new revelation. I was surprised none of them had ever bothered to look at the family tree. This was fascinating stuff. I passed around the notebook journal. The family gave it a cursory glance when they discovered it mostly contained details of the table's construction. Sadly, no one noticed the old letter concealed in the early pages. If they did, they expressed no interest. I didn't want to be the outsider shedding negative light on their great grandmother by pulling it out for show and tell.

The session lasted another two hours. I told Sherry to make up her own mind rather than ask me about the rest of the trinkets. My mind wandered elsewhere as I studied the table. Imagine a ten-year project, all with hand tools. Although the style was a little odd, it majestically bore its age with grace and beauty. The old scars of a long life gave it considerable character. When the family finished their solemn duties, I asked, "What about this table?"

"Oh that's just a piece of junk. I don't want that old thing. Besides, it doesn't even sit right," Mary said as she tilted the corner up and down by applying pressure with her fingers on one corner.

Others offered similar opinions. No one wanted it. "I want it," I firmly blurted out. I noticed the floor of the shed was slightly off kilter and the table would likely sit flat and sound on a level foundation.

Sherry's eyes opened wide as if to say, "I don't want that thing either."

I gave her my grin with which I won my first date. She relented and gave me her look of approval. She can say so much with a smile and bright sparkle in her eyes.

"You will refinish it won't you?" she pleaded.

"Nah. We'll take this home and I'll give it a good wax and buff it up, Sherry. It has too much character to refinish. Look at that patina and grain. You'll be able to drown yourself in its depths when I'm done." She had nothing else to say. Her trust in me was all that mattered. Her facial cues agreed.

I carefully lay down a shipping blanket in our pickup and Sherry's elder brother helped me load up. We turned the table upside down onto the tailgate and easily slid it in. It fit, just barely. I thanked him for the help and then noticed the lettered carving on the underside of the table's top. Fortunately, it lay before me near the end where I had been sitting. The late afternoon sun light forced a deep shadow into the crevices making the characters clearly stand out. Sherry joined me as we read the text together.

"For my children. Joseph Kinze Dec 25, 1940"

The old man's poverty worn face and crackled skinned hands impressed his very soul into every cut, plane mark, carving, and once fine hand-rubbed finish. The essence of his voice, his years of longing and suffering, clearly spoke to both of us.

I love you, my children. Please don't forget me.

Sherry's eyes immediately welled with tears and mine quickly followed. My voice fractured with overwhelming emotion. "Grandpa, this is your great granddaughter, Sherry. I'm Parker, her husband and your new great grandson. We shall never forget you."

Mental Health Day

The beach was white and the waves lopped gently at my feet as he bent over me to gently slip his fingers through my long blonde hair. His deep brown eyes always pulled me in. They had an inviting glow that showed his passion for me and me alone. He brought his lips towards mine and stroked my hair.

"I love you Marie." He said and kissed me gently.

And then I woke up. Richard stroked my hair and gave me a good morning kiss. "Wakey, wakey, my love," he said. I glanced at the bedside clock. He'd let me sleep in. He noticed my instant panic. "Don't worry, love. I made breakfast for the boys and got them ready for school. We're on our way out. Have a pleasant day off."

I lay comfortably between the crisp sheets for a moment to plan the day. Richard and the boys left singing "Roxanne, you don't have to turn on the red light..." He could never remember more than the first line of a song. He'd repeat it over and over. The kids would always join in, no matter what he was singing. I often got frustrated that he could never complete a song, but in this case, I was grateful.

We had three boys, Theodore, Trevis, and Stephen. Aged eight, seven, and six respectively. They came 14 months apart. Now before you ask... don't. Don't get me started. Like any mother, I loved them dearly but I was thankful we had only three. Today, Friday was my mental health day. I worked as a VP at our small local bank and they were very good at letting me take a day off from time to time. I worked hard and they paid attention. Although I must admit, work can be a lot less stressful than most of my time at home. But today was special. Charlotte Grossman had just published another bestseller romance. I hadn't read any of her books since my college days. I remember squeezing romance reading between classes and homework. I'd even sneak a flashlight into my dorm room to catch a few chapters.

I snatched a quick shower, even though a long gracious respite was in order. I wanted to get a few things done before I sat down with *my* good book. I went to the closet to get out my old comfy sweats which I hadn't worn for months. It's called a walk-in closet. This was anything but. Richard had so much of his camping and sports gear stacked, there wasn't even enough space to step into the tiny room. He had promised to get rid of it and had built some closets in the garage over a month before, but had neglected to finish the job. I climbed over the pile to grab my sweats from the back top shelf. The pile below me sucked me in like a sand monster. I climbed back up, grabbed my clothes, and something below turned skiwampus. I took a tumble backwards into the bedroom. I hadn't been hurt, but I was mad. When I get mad, I organize. *How much time could this take?* All I had to do was take all this stuff into the garage and toss it into the cabinet drawers. I put on my sweats and sneakers and attacked the pile, throwing everything that didn't belong in *my* closet out onto the bedroom floor.

You know how a project can suck you in? The closet carpet was filthy. So, before hauling out the huge pile of stuff, I filled up my carpet cleaner with hot water and soap. I love that machine. It made short work of the carpet. After two passes, I glanced at the clock. I'd already spent two hours on this mess. I decided to rearrange all the clothes. It did need to be done. Richard's clothes were all over the place so I organized his suits, shirts, ties, and occasional wear in order. Then I remembered he liked to organize his stuff by color. Crap. I was not going to spend time reorganizing. That could wait. Of course, the baseboards need dusting and washing. Three hours gone.

I took the first load of stuff out to the garage. Our three dogs, Brownie, Blackie, and Spartacus were thrilled to charge in through the doorway, knocking me down to get inside. It was raining outside and there's a doggie door to the garage, but getting inside is much more fun on a rainy day, I suppose. At least they hadn't been out in the rain and came in dry. Richard bought each of the boys a dog to take care of on their fifth birthday. It really was good for them and they all took their assigned tasks very seriously... except picking up their droppings. If you ask Richard about the dogs' names, he'll tell you that his grandfather always named his brown dogs Brownie and his black dogs Blackie. If you ask him about white Spartacus.... well, don't. Don't get him started. He'll first tell you that his grandfather never owned a white dog and then start into some story that has no ending. I still don't know why Spartacus got his name.

It took me another hour to haul all the stuff out and put it away. Perhaps I should have just thrown it on his workbench, but it's not in my nature to do that. I had to put it away. I only had a couple hours left before Richard brought the boys home. I wouldn't have time to use part of my mental health day to read even a couple of chapters of the new novel. I had special plans to make an exceptional dinner for my family and that was more important than the book. A special neighborhood friend had given me a secret family recipe. She'd been a long time friend ever since we came to the area.

Richard and I moved into the neighborhood when he set up his law practice. I'd just finished my degree and landed a good job at the bank. To celebrate we went to town to find a unique dining experience. In the tiny outdoor mall space, a new restaurant had opened. The grand opening of the place hadn't been advertised and no brightly lit sign adorned its entrance. A simple A-frame white plywood sign sat on the sidewalk: "Phuc Yu Family Oriental Dining." Richard turned to me and smiled, I grinned back to answer yes. We stepped inside. The proprietor eagerly met us as we entered.

"My name Fook Yu. I make veddy good mee fo you." (My name is Phuc Yu. I'll make a very good meal for you.)

I could see tears of laughter forming in Richard's eyes. "That's a very interesting name. Can you tell me where you are from?" Richard asked.

"I brom Biet Nam bud hab Tinese padda."

(I'm from Viet Nam but have a Chinese Father.) Phuc explained

I assumed this explanation served as an explanation for his mixed Chinese and Vietnamese name. He led us to a table and pulled out a chair for me. He. was overly gracious and prepared for every detail of our dining experience. After taking our order and leaving for the kitchen, I asked Richard, "Do you think we should tell him about the name of his place?"

"I don't know," answered Richard. "If he changed the name, he'd have to refile all his paperwork and pay some legal fees. It looks like he's running on a shoe string as it is."

"But Richard," I whined, "everyone will be making fun of him within days. And there's no telling what he'll get from the high school aged kids. You have to tell him."

When we finished, Richard paid the bill and gave him a generous tip.

"Mr. Yu," Richard said as he stood to introduce himself. I'm Richard Sterling and this is my wife Marie. I must say that I enjoyed my dining experience immensely and wish wholeheartedly for you to succeed. I'm not sure that this is appropriate but the name for your restaurant may garner a negative response from the community"

"I don und a dan," he said in reply.

"Mr. Yu, here in America there is a derogative slang word that phonetically looks like your first name," Richard tried again.

"I don und a dan," Yu answered the second

time.

"Stand aside, lawyer, let me give it a go," I advised Richard and wedged myself into the conversation. "Mr. Yu, your first name means this in America as I poked my right index finger back and forth through the loop made by my left index finger and thumb. You should change your restaurant's name."

Shock, awe, and disbelief washed Yu's face followed by an embarrassed curtain of red. "Oh no!" he cried. "I not know. Bad lawwa not tell me. Whad I do now? No mo money. I paid all to lawwa fo bidnu lizu. No monney lebt." (I paid it all to the lawyer for the business license, there is no money left)

We weren't well off by any means back then but Richard promised that he'd take care of it. Richard was good to his word, and within days changed the name of Yu's restaurant to "Yu's Fine Oriental Dining," paid all the legal fees with the county, helped pay for a proper restaurant sign, and became Phuc's instant lifelong friend. And mine too. After that, we'd never get a bill dining there. But Richard would always leave a hefty tip to cover the price of the meal and a good tip for our server.

The Yu's were a kind and gracious family. Sheila Yu, who had grown up in the US, was teaching me how to make some of the recipes not offered on their restaurant's menu. Often, when we stopped in to the restaurant, we'd ask what the Yu's were eating as a family that night and ask for the same thing. It was fun to experiment with their recipes that hadn't been adjusted for American tastes. Usually it was quite exotic, occasionally it smelled a little off, and once in a while it stared back at us. Still, our family learned about another culture as we shared meals with them and family outings.

Today's experiment was a favorite chicken curry I'd never prepared before. Sheila freely gave me her secret recipe and I was excited to cut and chop everything ready to cook. The dogs had to go out before I'd do anything in the kitchen. I opened the door to the garage. "Outside." I commanded. They obeyed... what luck.

Cutting up the chicken is the most distasteful part for me. I wish I could buy it all cut up in neat little cubes rather than crack bones and strip skin... yuch. After that, I prepared the marinade, threw in the chicken, covered it and in the fridge it went. I spent another twenty minutes dicing the vegetables and preparing the other odds and ends. I set the table and put the wok and other pots on the stove so I'd be ready to go.

Brownie, Blackie, and Spartacus appeared at the long window of the back door to the dining nook soaked with the onslaught of rain. "Please let us in....... please...." You know the look. But no way was I going to let three wet dogs into the house. They'd have to dry off first in the garage. I'd get the boys to towel them down when Richard brought them home which was about... She looked at the clock... *Well, there goes my special reading time for sure.*

"Once there was a little old ant, thought

he'd move a rubber tree plant...." The first line of the song echoed over and over and grew stronger as my family approached the front door. The children burst in throwing their wet coats on the kitchen chairs, dowsing my carefully placed napkins.

"Oh poor doggies!" Stephen wailed as he opened the back door. Spartacus charged in with the two others right behind.

They ran wild with happiness pausing to sniff each of the family and shaking their coats dry. What a rollicking mess. Thankfully, Richard ordered the dogs back into the garage and locked the doggie door so they'd dry off. We surveyed the damage. The dogs had spread mud throughout the kitchen, the set table was a wreck, all of my cookware had rain and dog hair in it.... and the kids were laughing their heads off.

I wanted to be mad. I really did. The most I could offer was a false frown and then I couldn't refrain myself from giggling with the children. "I'm sorry hon," Richard said. "I know you were planning something special. If you'd like, I'll take the boys and get some take out while you.... ah..."

I could see his lawyer's mental gears turning, wondering if he was going to get himself in trouble by escaping clean up duty. Honestly, it was easier to take care of by myself. Help in my household usually doubled the work, especially if one of the boys was involved. Somehow finger-painting with butter, soap, or some other goo would creep into the task. "No, get out of here, go get something good. It will only take me twenty to thirty minutes to clean up.

"Ding dong, the witch is dead the wicked witch, the witch is dead…." My four men donned their coats repeating the first line of the song and marched out the door. Fortunately, my new novel had been spared by the dog storm. I snatched it from the lamp stand and placed it on my bedroom dresser. Cleaning up was a mess but didn't take a whole lot of time. All the dishes went in the dishwasher, I mopped the kitchen floor, and wiped up the kitchen surfaces. By the time I had finished, I felt like I'd had a great workout at the gym.

"Ding dong, fook you, ding dong, fook you…." sing song from the car. It was barely audible at first and then clattered through the house as soon as the door opened. Richard gave me a look pleading, "please, can you handle this?"

"What happened?" I asked.

"Mr. Yu introduced himself to the kids and gave them all business cards," Richard answered. All three boys proudly waved their cards in the air. "It was Stephen who phonetically analyzed his first name and spouted the new word at 80 decibels in the lobby. Mr. Yu taught them how to pronounce his name properly. He was very gracious. But the kids won't let it go and I can't stop them."

"You could tell them to cut it out, Richard."

"I know but, you are so much better at this sort of thing.

We sent visual cues back and forth, smiles, and quirked up lips and finally a wink from him. Okay, it was my problem now. "Boys," I yelled. "Listen up!" They quit their singing. "Come here, please," I commanded.

"Are we in trouble?" Trev asked with a tremulous voice.

"No, kids, but I want to explain two things to you. First, what is Mister Hanson's name who lives next door?"

Ted answered proudly, "Mister!"

"And so it is with Mr. Yu. Until you are grownups, his first name is Mister and I don't ever want to hear otherwise," I explained. They all mumbled an "okay" in unison.

The boys felt like they were getting off the hook pretty easy. I could sense their anxiety level drop. "Now, the second thing I want to talk about is this word you are making fun with. Do you know what it means?"

"It's when you and daddy go in your bedroom and lock the door," Stephen offered.

"Na, uh," Trevis expounded. "They also take off their clothes and do things."

Well, it was a start. "Okay boys, everyone goes in their bedrooms and take their clothes off before they go to bed. What you are thinking about is love. That's how mommies and daddies make babies." I paused for effect. Great, no questions. That would be up to Richard someday. I continued, "The word you have learned from who knows where isn't a dirty word, it's a trashy word. It means I don't know how to talk properly. I can't read. I am not a very smart person. The correct word for making love is copulation. Now I want you all to say the word once with me so you remember it. One, two, three... "copulation,." Everyone said in unison. Richard looked at me like

I had just escaped the loony bin. His eyes asked why in the world would you teach them that?

"Wake up, mister lawyer. They'll forget it in ten minutes."

The kids let the now sort of dry mutts in and tried very hard to separate the dogs from their tails all the while singing and adapting their new song. "Ding dong, compensate you" to "Ding dong, update you" to Ding dong, I'll date you." Richard soon settled into the couch and tried to separate the roof from the house with his new sound system and a football game.

The take out he'd brought home was the very dish I was going to prepare. It was fabulous of course. I supposed we'd be having my version the next day. Dogs bouncing here and there. Barking and jousting. Young boys climbing the furniture, throwing pillows, the ruckus of the opening blows of the football game…. Well, it was too much for me. I crept into our bedroom and closed the door. I'd left the light on in the closet to help the carpet dry and ran my hand across the fibers to check. Yes, it was dry. Then it hit me. It was almost quiet in here. I ran to the bathroom and pulled a beach towel out of the cabinet. I laid it out carefully in the closet, threw in one of my bed pillows, grabbed the novel, and closed the door.

I lay down all comfy and a sense of calmness surrounded me. It was at least an hour before the boys would need to go to bed and Richard would be involved with the game. I had private time at last! I had a secret place to hide and I was determined to crack that book's spine. I eagerly opened to the first page. YES this is what I craved. A good romance story, perhaps something to help me remember my college days, or just a great escape. The principal characters were a cruise ship captain and a New York financier, both married and by the third chapter, they were "compensating" with each other. Did I really like this trash when I was younger? I suppose I did. No, I didn't need to escape into a world where people cheated on each other, told lies, and ran around in the shadows. I had MY family and it was perfect. Every challenge was a new adventure. I didn't need a trashy book to make my life look good.

I popped out of the closet and threw the novel in the trash. The booming and all the noise had stopped. I put on my nightgown and brushed my teeth. Richard opened the door to the bedroom as I stepped out of the bath.

"I put the kids to bed, sweetie," he said.

"What about your game?"

"Oh, it wasn't my team so I lost interest, I think I'll just turn in with you."

"I'll go take my vitamins and I'll be right back," I said.

"I'll be here, he promised."

Blackie and Brownie had both laid down on their little beds and snoring puppy dreams. Spartacus followed me into the kitchen. "What's a matter, Spartacus, don't you have any slaves to lead?" He gruffed in response. I gave him a treat. That trick would come in handy the next time someone asked Richard to explain his name. Spartacus and I shared a secret.

I retired to the bedroom, turned off the light and slipped into bed. I cozied up to Richard and gave him a warm embrace. "You want to compensate?" I asked grinning wildly? He was already fast asleep. I suppose that I could wake him, but I decided against it. Instead, I laid there amazed at the wonder of my life and how fortunate I was. Then a great thought came sharply into view. *Tomorrow is Saturday and I'll go out and buy a really good book. I'll read it in my new private place, the walk in closet.*

Odd Ducks

"Ah... Wednesday," she thought. It felt like a Friday. Not the light hearted 'here comes the weekend' sort of way but in a heavy-handed 'weight of the world' feeling. She sat on an old sun bleached green park bench as she fed 'her' Mallard ducks. Spring brought the green, the color in flowers, and the Mallards to Central Park. She loved coming here to wile away the few minutes she had for her lunch hour. But, she was no longer constrained by time.

"How's your ankle, doing?" Clint asked as he approached from behind.

Clint introduced himself in the most unpretentious manner just after she sprained her ankle two months prior. She'd been coming to the park for years to walk and explore during this time of her work days. After the injury, she settled for the seat on the bench close to her office instead. At 42, she felt too young to be so hampered by such a silly excuse to get out and walk or jog. She also felt very self-conscious about dragging her foot around as she tried to manage a set of crutches, her lunch, and current Smithsonian magazine. Of course, she felt self-conscious about everything, from her somewhat plain face, to her too curly hair, and slightly odd design in general. She always knew her legs were too long. The sprained ankle was merely proof of that point. She was clumsy too.

"Oh, I'm coming along fine. How are you today?"

"Good," he said as he handed her another

piece of bread for the ducks.

Clint was not one for words. At first, she'd been frightened to meet someone new, especially in the park. She was a transplant from North Dakota to the big city and heard far too many rumors to trust someone new. But as the days and weeks wore on, she'd become accustomed to his visits and the time shared as he sat down on the opposite end of the bench. He'd never treated her anything but the lady she'd always wished she could have been. But Clint was a bit odd. After all, who ironed a crease down the front of their jeans? She wouldn't say that he was all that handsome, but she had to give him credit. He was very clean and did his best to not look a slouch in his modest clothing.

A pregnant pause hung in the air. Neither one had much to say at times like this. What was there to say? How could you ever get to know someone if you couldn't talk to them? Clarice wriggled in her seat and figured that Clint must feel the same way. He seemed like he could be affable enough but caught a hint of a trained away stutter over the past weeks.

"Today was my last day at work," Clarice blurted out. "I got handed my papers just before lunch."

"Oh, my, what are you going to do?"

"Well, I've saved enough to retire, so I might do just that. I'd like to travel and write the great American novel, but I'm afraid I'll only be able to do the novel part. I don't think I have enough money to travel much." Most would decidedly think her to be far too young to retire.

But Clarice learned life's lessons well. There was more to life than a stupid career and living for the next paycheck. She had saved and invested well.

"Are you going to st... st... stay in the city?" he asked as color drained from his face.

More than a hint now, his stuttering was all too clear. Clarice felt genuine fear in his voice. *Why is he afraid?*

"I don't have to decide now. My lease isn't up for another ten months. But I suppose that I'll move on after that to reduce my monthly expenses," she answered.

"Oh," Clint sighed with relief.

She looked at him, reexamining the kindness he had shown her during their short visits. She broke up his offered slice of bread into pieces and passed back half of the pile to him. He accepted the small offering and threw out two pieces to the pair of Mallards begging at the bank. He really was a nice looking man in his own way. Why had she not noticed before? Had she been that involved with her career and personal finances to notice? Or had it been his presentation... one that wasn't all that different from her own. She certainly screamed 'leave me alone!' in her outdated hairstyle and manner of dress.

"Clint," she said.

"Ah, yeah?"

"I hope you don't think me too forward, but will you take me to lunch?"

His eyes brightened. Indeed the hairs on his head seemed to light with joy. And for some reason, he lost his stutter.

"I've been trying to work up the nerve to ask you that ever since I first saw you here in the park. Yes, of course, I'd love to!"

Boring Life with Jane

I wish that I could tell you that I had a long recovery from alcohol and drugs. Perhaps a sexual addiction might be more engrossing. How about a sordid affair with a movie star? No one ever listens to a story anymore unless you start with something like that. Now I have your attention, I can tell you the truth. Friends tell me I'm so dull that I bore life itself.

My phone rang right in the middle of my favorite dog training show. I had hoped that it would be an invitation for dinner. No, it was some angry guy selling insurance and he didn't even ask me out. I'd paused the TV during our conversation. Those slice and dicer ads can be so annoying. When I hung up the phone, a cartoon lettered sign painted the screen; "BUT WAIT!" You know, they tell you to wait before they lower the price or add some extra goodies to the sale. For some reason, I felt amused with fired irony. Should I leave the television waiting as instructed? What would it do? Would it make a decision if I waited? No, it wasn't all that humorous, but I felt my facial muscles pull a devious grin across my face. Yes, this is the way I think.

Distraction pulled me from musing thought. Sam, my Shep, danced around the room to tell me emphatically that it was time for her walk. I never ignore her. That can be bad, you know? I left the machine paused. It needed some space while I took my grin and dog out for a walk.

She serves as point for me on my boring

path, every lousy morning. Deaf and dumb as a rock, she is. Sam's a useless watch dog too. Her lips move and nothing comes out. But she does have a nose for dead things. It's usually a dead cat, that even the buzzards won't touch, cause it's so putrid. She'll find it and cozy up to it to get that pukey smell all over her coat. Senior dogs do that, I heard just yesterday on the nature channel.

Well, this morning, she kept wandering off trail. We always follow the same track every morning of every day, week in and week out. She usually does her 'cozy up to some dead thing' when I'm not looking so I always watch her real close when we walk. Yeah. I look at her hiney. She walks in front to scout out snakes. That's what I tell my friends. People think it's cool that my dog protects me from snakes. But I know she only hunts puppy dream snakes when she's napping on the front porch.

To tell the truth, I think she doesn't want to walk behind me. She'd have to look at *my* hiney. I have my own sct of problems. I break wind. It's pretty bad when your dog loves to wrap herself around some old dead carcass but can't stand the smell of her best friend. I truly think that if she found a real snake, she'd just step aside, raise her paw and say, "This way please." No, that would never happen. *Only I* think she can talk. She doesn't know I do. Don't tell her, 'cause I don't want her to think I'm crazy.

Yes, she went off track. I could not bring her back. I could not get her to slow. No, she'd found a big doe.

The doe was hanging out next to the creek and 'deaf N dumb' Sam decided she needed to go say hi. Did I tell you this dog is also afraid of rocks? No kidding. If one pops out of the trees, she tails it to the front porch... and takes a nap. No, rocks don't pop out of the trees. I know that. They just sit there. She's afraid of that kind too. So, I was wondering why this deer begged her attention.

Now, *I* was curious. Same led me down to the stream. The deer rested on the high bank, just below us and to the left. I shouldn't have been thinking about the deer, I know, cause as I was stepping down the slope, oh so careful, SHE, yes Sam, broke wind. O M G. No more pastrami for Sam. I stopped in my tracks, or I tried to. Trying to stop sudden like that, my feet slipped right out from under me and I slid down the hill on my hiney.

Did I mention we have poison oak? I didn't know.

The short stop at the bank sent me flying. When you're launched like that, an eternity can flash before your eyes as you contemplate the landing, and I was thinking, "It could be worse. I could fall on a rock. This is a nice flat ditch of soft mud." I came to a jarring stop in the middle of the stream. It's not a big stream. There's just enough water for the animals to get a drink and to make a lot of mud. Did you know that rocks live in mud? I think they breed in there along with dead cats.

After I turned over to a sitting position, I examined myself for damage. I was beat up real bad. I had bruises, scratches, mud all over me, and

I didn't even know I'd been drug through poison oak yet. But I didn't have it as bad as that doe. She just laid there, above me, all sick looking. There was some blood around her too. It wasn't the right time of the year for fawning. How do I know? Smart couch potatoes watch nature shows. Deer are about the dumbest animals around they say, right next to my dog, and they run from their own shadow. She just laid there and stared at me with glazed over eyes. I decided to get my neighbor to help. He's our neighborhood's great big hunter.

I pulled myself out of the muck, back up on to the bank, and then up the hill, hand over hand, hanging on to those little baby trees, and walked over to Bill's place. That's Bill pronounced William. He's got this thing about his name. I think he believes it's magical cause he *can't* tell if it has two or three syllables and he's like some kid with a new engine from the junk yard. He loves to show it off.

Don't ever call him Bill. He has a gun. It comes with a badge.

"What happened to you, Jane?"

Yes, Jane is a boring name too. It fits the rest of my geeky life. Not only was I dirty, I was all scuffed up, out of breath, and smelled like a dead cat. Secretly, I hoped he figured someone had been trying to chase me, 'cause he had his gun in hand before he stepped out on to his porch. In reality, I bet he thought I'd just fallen down in my creek and didn't want me to dirty up his house. Nobody'd ever be caught dead chasing me, a dead cat being the exception.

I told him I had a deer down by my creek and it probably needed to be put down. He asked me to show him the way. I turned to my dog to take the lead.

"Sam?"

"I thought your dog was deaf," he said

"Yeah, but she's real smart. She can read lips," I answered. I covered my mouth so Sam couldn't exercise her craft, "but don't say anything to her about sign language. She can't do that on a count that she doesn't have thumbs. I don't want to hurt her feelings about that."

And wouldn't you know it? Some rock popped up right out of the trees and scared the wits out of her. She bolted off, straight back to the house, with her tail between her legs.

"What's wrong with her?"

I'm never good with words, on the spot like that, in a time that demands a clever response. It wasn't in me to tell him that she was just scared by a rock.

"She needs to go. If she hurries, she just might make it back in time," I answered.

"In time for what?"

"To scare off that snake on my front porch." I said. She was probably already asleep by the time I got the words out. Yeah, not only am I boring, but my neighbors think I'm bat crap crazy.

"You sure there's a deer down by your creek, Jane?"

I could tell he wasn't on board with me. "Ya. I was just down there with Sam. I can show you the way."

"Okay," was all he said as he grabbed a holster belt from his hat stand, and reluctantly followed.

We got to the top of the hill. "Now it's really steep here," I explained, "If you think you might lose your balance, you can just hold on to these baby trees."

William laughed and hooted as he gave me a botany lesson.

That's when I learned I was farming poison oak.

"She's right down here," I told him and pointed out the deer on the bank of my creek.

He unfolded his sleeves and pulled a pair of gloves from his back pocket. As he was putting on his gloves, he asked. "You went down here, Jane? Really?"

"Right here, straight down the hill."

"Why didn't you just take that game trail down, Jane?" he asked as pointed to my right.

I rolled my eyes and followed him. It was a lot easier trip down this time, for sure.

"Jane, it smells really bad down here. Is Elmer dumping his septic into your creek again? He used to do that before you moved in."

That's when I learned about my other neighbor's septic system. I didn't even know he had one. Now I do.

"She's over there," I said as I pointed to the doe.

"Ain't that a shame?" he asked.

"Yeah, she is kind of pretty."

"No, it's a shame I'll only get the flank meat. I can't take a chance on the rest of it." And then he shot her and pulled out a big knife from his belt to carve her up. As he worked, William explained that she'd likely been hit by a car and wandered down from the road to die. "Jane, I'm sorry. Are you crying?"

"No, I just smell like a dead cat, William. It brings tears to my eyes."

"That's no dead cat, sweetheart."

"I know, I'm just being polite, William!" I really had thought it was a dead cat. I was so embarrassed. What else it could be? I didn't know what a septic system was. Now I do.

"Jane, when you clean yourself up, you might want to put some lotion on your hands and arms for that poison oak."

I broke wind. It's one of those things I can't control. I shied away, and said, "Thanks for the help William." I didn't want him to see me turn red with shame.

Sam started howling from the porch.

I didn't know that Sam had fibbed to me about being dumb. Now I do. Maybe one of her snake dreams brought her voice back. Or, maybe the flatulence heard round the world shock cured her.

I said, "I gotta go. If I hurry, I just might make it back in time."

"In time for what?" William asked.

"Maybe my TV has decided what it wants."

Snowfall

Out on the porch we sat, gazing at the blue gray pre-dawn light. Seven inches of heavy snow blanketed the ground and still fell in the still clarity of morning soundlessness. A comfortable little redwood bench in the sheltered cove served as an ideal place to study nature. No better place could protect us as we gazed out to the large oak trees yielding their branches low to support the heavy snowfall.

I looked down at my little girl as I suspected what must be a touch of fear and amazement. Breathless, she stared intently out into that scary place. New. Cold. White. Strange.

"Well, what do you think?" I asked her.

She stared back with fear in her eyes and turned back ogling the strange sight. She gulped a breath of frigid air. To say she was adorable would be a severe understatement. She was the one so excited to wake me up and now she didn't know what to do.

"Do you want to go out there or not?" I queried.

She stared back with questioning eyes. Maybe she was too scared. Perhaps she just wanted to go back inside. The eerie quietness generated a certain level of spookiness after all.

"Go on," I encouraged her, "You'll like it."

She looked back up at me and ventured forward. One foot gently offered a cautious step forward and fell silently through the thick cloud of white. The next followed and she gained new confidence as she soon stepped gingerly towards the nearest tree.

"You'll not find any messages this morning," I said with an evil grin. But she is nothing but a small package of stubbornness. After three minutes searching, she found what I had neglected to see far in the distance. A large tree had managed to shelter the brunt of the storm and a few inches of bared winter grass stood proudly around its base.

It was there she found her p-mail. Her ears perked and tail wagged as she quickly replied.

Christmas Coal

Have you ever heard of a little girl who *wanted* a lump of coal for Christmas?

"Good little girls and boys get gifts from Santa," Mom reminded us all too often when we were small. I think that she directed most of her comments to my brother who needed that sort of coercion. His name was Brent, but to me he was Bugs. I was the only one who called him that.

I didn't behave just so I could get presents. I didn't pay attention to the obvious extortion during most of the year. Threats never could motivate me. Don't get me wrong. As a kid I loved Christmas presents and I could never sleep on Christmas Eve. But I tried to be good because it was the easiest thing to do. Whenever Bugs got in trouble, it was always a time consuming and emotional affair. I never wanted a piece of that demeaning ride. So I learned from his experience. I cleaned my room when asked. I was honest about most things. I confess… I really wanted to be a good girl because deep down inside, I knew I was very bad. I carried a deep-seated guilt ingrained upon me from my earliest years. I took my religious teachings quite literally.

At only five years old, I knew that I'd never be a mommy married to a daddy. It wasn't that I was physically attracted to other girls. I just knew I'd never have any interest in boys. People don't get that it doesn't have to be a sexual thing. After all, how can a five-year-old kid have sexual feelings? I can't tell you how I knew this at such a tender age. Some people usually don't figure stuff out like that until they're older. I had to figure out everything before my time. I'd already figured out the Santa secret. Mom and Dad told me I was too smart for my age. I didn't tell them about the lesbian thing. I didn't even know there was a word for it.

I remember going with my Dad to visit a fellow pigeon racer one day before Christmas when I was small. The old codger had a quiet flame in his fireplace and he slowly fed it coal. As he and Dad talked about breeding stock, I watched our host pack his pipe with wrinkled fingers, light it, suck in a mouthful of smoke, and put a piece of coal on the fire. Then, every few minutes, he'd relight his pipe, suck on it, stir the fire, and throw on another lump of coal. The bucket next to the fireplace overflowed with large shiny rocks of the fossil fuel. I loved its texture, its shine, and its dirtiness. I couldn't believe a rock could burn. My mind churned with the fascination for the peculiar substance.

It had a beauty that only I could appreciate. Coal held many secrets. I had a secret. Coal was dark and unwanted. I was dark on the inside where no one could see. And for most people, coal was ugly. Only a dirty ugly person could appreciate its beauty.

"Can I hold a piece?" I asked the old pigeon man.

He lit his pipe again and threw another chunk on the fire. "It's dirty, Judy. Aren't you afraid you'll get your hands and blouse dirty?" He sucked on his pipe and set his lighter on his side stand. He held the smoke in his mouth as if waiting for my answer.

I glanced at Dad with the unasked question.

"Go ahead, Judy. I'll deal with your mother if she gets upset."

For most things, Dad was very smart. He understood kids really well. I don't think he ever grew up. He worked at the railroad with industrial sludge all the time. He knew how to clean up when he got home. He wanted me to explore and learn.

I picked up the biggest chunk in the bucket. It was two Judy fists big. I held it in my two little hands. I considered its weight, set it on my lap, and passed my index finger across its oily colored smooth surfaces. I tested its strength by trying to break it with my batgirl Judy grip. The rock was strong. How could this stuff burn? Of course, my blouse and skirt were a mess when we left. Dad snuck me into the house and I changed. I don't know if Mom ever discovered the black dirt on my clothes. She was lousy with laundry.

While other secrets consumed my life, I now wanted a lump of coal for Christmas. Oh... I wanted all the other presents too. But I wanted a big piece of coal that I could look at and hold. I wanted a memento of the ancient past to put on my dresser. Oh yeah, I knew all about coal. I looked it up in the encyclopedia and asked Mom to read the entry. I was a budding dweeb, bookworm, a perfect nonsocial, non-essential, sit in the corner unperson.

When asked what I wanted for Christmas, I could never truly answer. "I want Lincoln Logs," I'd say blandly.

"But don't you want a dolly?" They'd ask.

Were they kidding? I had a perfect little baby brat sister. Sherry was better than a doll. She was the real thing. I got to help with the diapers too. Why would I want a doll? No, I figured out the doll thing real early too. It was training I didn't need.

"No, I want Lincoln Logs."

I don't know how many years I asked for Lincoln Logs. I can't remember how many dolls spent their existence rotting in the toy box.

More than anything else, I wanted a lump of coal. I was terrified to announce my real desire to my parents. Coal was cold, black, and filthy... just like my inner self. They could discover my cold dark heart secret if I ever asked. At the very least, they would surely know that I was weird. I gorged on the fetid guilt ordained on me every week in Sunday school. We never talked about the sins of my thoughts... We talked about the other things that children my age were consumed with... stealing candy, fighting, not sharing... you know, that sort of thing. Was it by osmosis that I knew my sinful nature? For some reason, that black rock was important. Deep within my childhood understanding, I felt it represented my nascent rebellion.

Like the Lincoln Logs, I never did get the lump of coal for Christmas. Mom and Dad did get me some precious yet modest things through the years as I grew up. Not every present was a doll. Other than the Lincoln Logs and the coal, I was pretty easy to please. I knew they had a limited budget. Dad didn't make much. In fact, he worked on most Christmas days and we'd get up at three in the morning to celebrate gift giving before he went to work. Of course that was just fine with me... the getting up part that is... since I never slept on Christmas Eve. My brother Bugs always got what he wanted. I was happy for him. I never, ever played with his toys. Little sis Sherry, always loved her dollies.

As soon as I turned eighteen, I moved away, far from the guilt dealers.

*****

A few years ago, my brother married Gabby, a beautiful caring young woman. It was early summer and the grass and flowers glowed fluorescent color in Dad's backyard. Bugs and Gabby got married there to save some money.

I showed up a day late and missed the ceremony. No one seemed to mind. I didn't have to mull it over, knowing the reason. They were happy I didn't show up. I was an embarrassment.

Bugsy's mother in law, Erika, came packaged with the marriage contract. She had injected herself and was already a close part of the family. She was an elegant single woman with a sharp wit. I hit it off with the new "mom" in law. She and I shared many of the same perspectives on life in a satirical way. We launched one-liners, jabs, and insults back and forth during a family lunch at a local restaurant. We instantly invented a new language without conspiracy. Our conversation seemed far-flung and unintelligible. To the others, we *were* speaking a foreign language.

Unfortunately, we didn't get to see each other again on that trip.

I usually didn't go home for Christmas, preferring to spend it with my friends who have nowhere else to go. It seems as though there was a never-ending supply of new friends who had lost their families for having a problem like mine. Anyway, that year for some reason, I decided to surprise Mom and Dad. I made the three day drive to Kansas City and showed up on their doorstop on Christmas Eve at 6PM. I know that it was rude. I should have at least called ahead under the current set of circumstances. They usually needed time to make sure that no one in the church was visiting… or would come to visit… when I came to stay for a couple days.

No one was visiting fortunately, and Mom was very excited to see me. In fact, she started to cry a little. She gave me a tender mom hug. Yeah, she still loved me. She stepped back and affectionately ran her fingers through the ends of my long black hair. It wasn't hard to figure out what she was thinking.

She gave my sibs a ring to let them know I was visiting. At this time in my life, not everyone knew about my "proclivities" and "chosen lifestyle."

"Judy, since Erika is now part of the family, I thought it was best that I tell her about your problem."

Ha! Erika probably figured it out in about a minute during the wedding visit. We never talked about it, I was just sure she got it. I just smirked at

Mom's revelation. Yeah, Mom and Dad still loved me, but I wasn't part of the family. It was too inconvenient.

Bugs called Erika to tell her I was in town and she immediately dropped everything to come see me. I felt like we were able to pick up the conversation right where we had left off several months before. We moved on to holiday talk and reminisced about our childhood Christmas mornings. To her, I revealed my long held secret to wake up on Christmas morning to discover the present I'd always dreamed of... a shiny black lump of coal. On that Christmas Eve, Erika was the first person I ever told about the coal. How is it you can know someone your whole life and never trust them... and then there are people who you meet for just a few minutes and you're ready to spill everything? I've never figured that out. Erika was an open door... just like that.

On Christmas morning, we exchanged gifts. After everyone opened all the presents, Erika pulled one last poorly wrapped package out from behind the couch and handed it to me. It was large and irregularly shaped. An understanding person she was, but she didn't have a clue as to how to wrap a lump of coal. I immediately knew what it was before she handed it to me. She knew I knew. She gave me a knowing smile. That did not lessen my surprise. I tore into the paper to reveal the huge piece of shiny coal.

"When did you get this?" I asked her. There had been very little time since our conversation the night before?

"Well, after we talked last night, I drove all around the old manufacturing district. I remembered that some of those old plants used to run on coal. I had to climb a fence to get it."

She went out late on Christmas Eve in the snow and ice, risked arrest for trespassing, and found a huge chunk of ancient carbon in a crumbling condemned building. Yes, I was in shock that someone would do this for me. It's easy to just buy a gift for someone... but risk arrest? Now, that *was* special.

I turned to the coal begging my attention. It was two Judy fists big. Its multi-faceted shiny black surfaces reflected the full spectrum of oily color. I hefted its weight in my hands and tried to break it with my batgirl Judy grip. The rock that was a dirty unwanted chunk of filth to most, was so precious to me. I squealed with delight. A special sparkle winked in Erika's eyes as she flashed a knowing grin. The rest of the family stared at us both, stupefied. No, they didn't get it. I don't think they ever will.

I felt overwhelmed with a pronounced and immediate release. I didn't really want a lump of coal. I never did. My soul took flight. I finally felt free. I knew Erika understood the significance of her gift. On that day, a beautiful white Christmas day with my new family, I no longer felt dirty. Erika's special gift gave me wings.

A What?

He was only three, well almost four years old. A little tow headed thoughtful type... if you can consider anyone to be of a certain type. No one is truly like another. So inquisitive and feeling, always asking questions and exploring the world. I only had to tell him once where my parameters were and he'd remember. Swimming blue eyes and the most adorable round face I'd ever seen in a child. He was my son.

"Guess what, Dad?" little Toby asked my husband Darian as we waited to pull out into traffic.

We'd been shopping for groceries and it was rush hour. the traffic was particularly bad at that time of day.

"Mathew showed me a penis."

Hubby had just pulled into traffic when the declaration sent him into rictus, an iron foot slammed down on the brake pedal. Our SUV slid sideways to a screeching halt in front of oncoming cars. Yes, Darian had been reared in what I would call a Victorian minded family. Such things were never spoken. I could see his blood boiling, his face turned a crimson red, and I swear his eyes were popping through his glasses.

I placed my hand on Darian's elbow. "Please, Darian," I said as angry drivers blared their horns at us. "Let me take care of this. Just drive."

I turned in my seat, the seat belt cutting into my shoulder screaming for me to turn back and face forward. I looked cautiously into my little man's eyes. "Where did he show you a penis," I asked.

"At his house."

"Okay," I responded. I rolled my tongue around in my mouth, a nervous habit I had, as I carefully considered what to say next. Mathew was his only friend in the neighborhood and was 18 months older than Toby. His parents were substantially more liberal than we were in such things. I had no idea what to do. My mind was frantic, hoping that nothing perverse had happened. "Where in his house?" I queried further.

"In his bedroom. He has a book with pictures."

Porn or medical? The question raced through my mind.

"Do you remember which book it was?" I asked.

"Yup. It was Greys Amotry."

His memory was pretty good, I thought, even if he didn't get the name quite right. Perhaps it was Grey's Anatomy they were looking at.

"Were they drawings or photographs?" I asked to clarify.

"Oh, they were drawings and they had all kindsa muscles and stuff. Mom, you can see all the way in, in that book."

My immediate concerns were assuaged. I was hoping that I'd be able to wait for another five years or so before we'd have this discussion. I'd not prepared properly, and besides, wasn't it the father's responsibility to instruct the sons in these matters? But Darian was fighting start and stop traffic. This was definitely the most awkward time to discuss birds and bees that I could imagine.

As a dozen loud motorcycles wove through traffic rattling my mind, I grasped frantically for the right words. I wasn't sure that there was any right way to deal with any sensitive subject such as this. I tried to think of real experiences he could relate to. After what seemed to be several minutes, but were really only seconds, I formed a strategy. "You've seen me change your little sister's diapers haven't you?" I asked.

"Yup. And she doesn't have one. Girls don't have them," he proudly announced.

"That's right, I said," wondering how I'd keep him from spouting this word all over the neighborhood. Shoot, I did when I was a kid and got walloped good by my Father. I wasn't about to spank my little Toby. Darian's smirk dared me to continue. I gave him a wicked smile in return and turned back, wrestling the uncomfortable seat belt, to where Toby sat. "Do you know what else boy's have that girls don't?" I asked. I figured that obfuscation was the best policy here. I'd smother him in facts and not allow him to see any embarrassment on my part.

"Uhm, beards?"

"Yep, they sure do, I said. "Boys also have a prostate. It's an inside part under your tummy," I furthered.

"Apostate?"

I wondered where he picked that one up...

probably in church. "No, Toby. Prostate."

I drew the word out slowly and asked him to repeat it several times. Now committed to memory for all time, I hoped we could finish up quickly.

"What does a prostate do, Mommy?"

I was surprised he didn't ask the same question about a penis. I quickly surmised that he'd already seen his in action and thought he knew everything there was to know. The rest could wait for a few years, I hoped. But the question about the prostate? All I knew about the prostate was that it caused all sorts of problems. Cancer and urinary problems flooded my mind. Quick, think girl, turn this around, I thought. I didn't want to throttle my three year old's development... too worried to grow up with information of that sort. I smiled at him and finally answered with the truth. "I don't know what it is supposed to do, honey. There are a lot of things I don't know about how people work. Doctors know about those sorts of things."

"I want to be a doctor," He proudly stated. "I can give shots to little kids."

I wondered if there was some sort of revenge cooked up in his momentary decision. "Doctors do only good, or at least they try to, Toby. Shots help people from getting sick."

"Oh," he said thoughtfully.

Finally we cleared the worst of the traffic and Darian cut in. "So, Toby, are you going to learn what the prostate does?"

Toby widened his eyes and stared in my

direction pleading me to help him avoid something bad.

"Perhaps you could ask your friend Mathew and you could look it up," I proffered. "You can use his anatomy book."

"Amotry book?" he asked.

"Yes the Grey's Anatomy book."

For the next several months, Mathew and Toby poured through the anatomy book. I'm sure that Mathew learned much more than little Toby, but I was astonished at what he'd come home with. Every other day, there'd be another new anatomy term he'd commit to memory. I doubt that he remembered the exact nomenclature correctly. But that wasn't the point.

For his fourth birthday, Darian and I gave him his own copy of Grey's Anatomy. He acquired a skill which most adults never seem to accomplish. Toby and Mathew soon learned to stretch out and do their own research. The two little boys, with a little encouragement, learned how to learn. And yes, they both became doctors.

Sam Hill

After 30 years Military Service in Special Operations as an Intelligence Officer, Sam Hill left the East Coast and retired to Mariposa California. Bad weather and recovery from serious injuries sustained in the Persian Gulf from an explosion led him to search for doctors who could assist in his recovery. After five years in a wheelchair, Sam found the right people to help him back on his feet, not the least of which was the soul mate he'd been searching for, now his wife, a new family and a great new community.

What should have been the end of his life turned into a rebirth. The path to recovery was full of obstacles, memories of his comrades, friends and soldiers who didn't come home and a long list of life lessons he was bound to relive if he didn't learn from them. The Blue Crab Syndrome is just one of many lessons Sam learned along the way that helped him connect the dots and learn not only about other people, but about his own deep inner self. Along the path of recovery and sixteen spinal reconstruction surgeries, Sam was told over and over, "You need to write a book" by people who learned of his situation. A chance meeting of the Mariposa Writer's Group was the spark that was needed and "Six Days To Zeus" is now being written. The introduction to that book is included.

The Blue Crab Syndrome

Out on the coastal waterways of North Carolina, I met a man who was 'crabbin.' Fishing for Blue Crabs. Hard telling how old the man was, but well into his seventies if I had to hazard a guess. Most likely a grade school education, or less. But wise in the ways of the world. You could tell he'd spent a lot of time on the beaches, pondering life. He watched more than spoke, sat still more than moving about, and seemed to just soak it all in. Somehow he could tell what a man was thinking just by looking for a few seconds. Natural instinct I guessed, but more likely years of experience. I could tell in a moment he was a man of few words. Mostly body language. He'd look you in the eye just long enough to get your attention, tip his head as if to say, "Hey, how ya doin?", then look away soon as you matched eye contact. He'd instantly sweep the horizon from left to right, look behind him for a second, then cautiously lean back on the bucket to pull a lighter out of his pocket. He knew everyone on the beach within a mile in every direction. He knew which ones were tourists, which were the locals and who they were just by where they were fishing. Most of the locals had staked out "special spots" that had been passed down from generation to generation. Some had small beach wood fires going, others just a cooler with some beer or wine coolers. But almost everyone had crab cages, a small container of chicken gizzards and leg parts, and a bamboo pole. While sometimes it could take a while for the crabs to home in on the bait, most folks would pass the time tipping a pole or two to catch a mix of local fish. Further up the river where the water wasn't so brackish, catfish was the catch everyone was waiting for. Red blood worms were the ticket in the dark muddy waters of the Cape Fear River. But out here on the inner coastal waterways, chicken parts were the way to go for catching crab. Gizzards and livers were used at first to gather the crabs into one area. The aroma would travel well on the current baiting crabs from all around the area and getting them to make their way to the waiting crab cages. Once the crabs got there, the competition was on to snatch the bait as quickly as possible, before the rest of the crabs got it. That's what crabbin was all about. Getting just one crab to take the bait with a vengeance. Once the rest of the crabs saw that one of them had a meal, they would pile on and try to get it too. The bait would be gone in no time if you used the wrong parts. Legs and other parts were used mostly as secondary bait cause the crabs couldn't consume it so quickly. This tactic kept more crabs in the area longer fighting for some of the bait. Crabbers could pull the cage out of the water, unload the crabs, re-bait if necessary and get the cage back into the water for another round much quicker than by using livers and gizzards all the time. The more experienced old timers would bring in a five gallon bucket of crabs in less than a half hour on a good day. Timing was everything, and you had to know when to pull the cage up. There were no "bobbers" like when you were fishing.

I watched half interested as he pulled a rope from the water. At the end was a collapsing cage made from stainless steel wire. The sides of the box fell away when he let it lay on the beach. Four individual lines went to four different sides that were hinged along the perimeter of the bottom screen. It was an ingenious device. When it laid on the bottom of the waterway, the sides fell away so the crabs could crawl onto the screening, and it stayed on the bottom as a flat screen. Attached to the middle was a piece of wire twisted around dried up pieces of chicken wing, turkey brisket or gristled up leg bones. Everyone had their secret weapon for bait. This guy preferred old chicken parts. I watched patiently as he tied another chicken wing to the cage bottom, then tossed it only several feet from the shore into the water, sat down on a flipped over bucket, and lit another "cigarette."

It was an epiphany from this man's mouth that led me to an understanding of people so deep, so profound; it stuck with me for the rest of my life. It had been one of those weeks. Hell, months I guess. Every single time I thought I was going to get through the muck, finally get to the light at the end of the tunnel, someone would pile more shit onto my head. It became almost comical.

"Ya eva notice ya never has to put a lid on a crab bucket?" the old timer asked me while I stood there pondering life, looking out across the gray water.

"Really? No, I never noticed. Why's that?" came my query before I even knew I was talking to the man. I was too deep in thought. Too wound up in my own head, trying to sort out WHY people were such assholes to each other. The old man began to speak, pulling a long drag on an unfiltered, hand rolled cigarette made from half tobacco and half marijuana. His favorite thing in the world at this stage in life was to smoke some grass, get a buzz on, sip on some 100 proof home made moon shine, and go crabbin.

He was thin. It was obvious this man lived off what he caught from the waters of his homeland. Wrinkled up skin testified to the years he'd spent in the sun. His white hair a testimony to his aged body, bright red blood shot eyes to years of alcohol and drug use. A plain white T-shirt, cut off work pants and bare feet told of his simple lifestyle. But something intrigued me about him too. There was a calm about him that ran deep. Like an old combat warrior who had seen it all, been through the mill a few times, and was willing to give some advice to those who would take heed. He didn't waste his breath on those who already knew the answers. Those who rushed by not even noticing the greatness in simplicity that defined the place in which they stood.

"Well, ya see...." came the explanation in that distinct southern accent. "Soon as wonna dem crab start out over the top of the bucket, wonna dem others grab onto a leg-a-hiz and pulls him back in. Soon as one of em gits ta peek over da edge, gits that quick smell of freedom, and has that split second a hope in is heart that he's gonna make it outta da soup..... da rest of em snatch him right back to the bottom a da bucket. Kinda like people does. Won't never have to worry bout any of em getting away, the rest of em ill make damn sure..."

That was the explanation I'd been looking for. Humans suffered from the Blue Crab Syndrome. I'd seen it from childhood when my miserable sisters would pull some bullshit that got me into trouble, got my ass beat because they wanted something or other, or just plain didn't have anything better to do in a day. The drama was unspeakable. Lies. Deceit. Then that look of satisfaction and laughter. After I left home, I still didn't see it coming. They often would pull some bullshit that I would end up shaking my head over. I couldn't understand how someone could live like that. I was born with a big heart, a forgiving heart, and I tried so many times to share my successes with the rest of the family. I often wondered why I did that. I guess I'd learned it from my grandmother....we were all in the same boat, and you took care of family. Problem was, you don't get to pick your family when you're a kid. You're stuck with what you get. So, you just do.....

Later on in life, I stuck to the same protocol simply because the military taught the exact same thing. Family is everything. The guy on your left and right is your family. There was no "I" in Team. Everything you did, was with "TEAM" in mind. You never left a man behind, you worked as a team, you thought as a team, and you were part of a team. So, it was second nature to share with my family the same concepts. What I hadn't known was that none of them took to heart what my grandmother had taught us. And no one else had been in the military. They'd been civilians all their lives and learned from early on that it was a dog eat dog world. Take what you can get before the other guy gets it. Just like blue crabs on chicken bait.

While I was trying to share with them, just to show them that there was a whole world out there waiting for them to explore, to engage in, to enjoy…..they were churning up inside. It would be years before I would understand the venom, the jealousy, the hatred that boiled up inside them. I should rephrase that. It took me years to recognize that they had the Blue Crab Syndrome. I still don't understand why they have it. But they do.

Instead of enjoying the company, the trips, part of my life, they took it as me rubbing their noses in it my successes and being mean to them. Showing off that I was better than them. It had never crossed my mind that anyone could look at it that way. I was more than naïve, I was stupid. How could I have missed it? That answer would come in time as well. I missed it because I didn't think that way. I had learned what honor felt like, what loyalty meant. Integrity was learned, practiced, and honed to perfection. The people I shared life with were all cut from the same cloth, understood and lived the concept of selfless service. That a man's word meant more than just words. It was about being a bigger person than the primal self that had gotten you through the early stages of life.

I was confused by what I was seeing, hearing, and the fallout of their actions when I returned home after 3o years of Military Service. When I finally saw it, I recognized it as the exact same syndrome I had seen in terrorists, in world dictators and bad guys we'd hunted the world over. It shocked me to my soul that the same hatred, the same distain and venom was in the very fabric of my own family. They were living with the Blue Crab Syndrome and had been pulling each other back into the bucket all their lives. God help them, cause no one else is going to!

Six Days To Zeus

Another 72 hours had transpired. Chief and his team were running on empty as usual. Barely 30 minutes after entering the air conditioned aircraft hangar, they were being briefed on yet *another* mission. The mission they just finished was a huge success no one in the free world would ever know about. Only those whose lives had been saved would know the real impact of the Team's professionalism. To the men of Team Six, that was all that mattered. The seven man team was barely awake, running on pure adrenaline and looking forward to some well deserved sleep, food and down time. They had dropped their gear in the secure fenced compound outside the hangar, slung their weapons and sensitive items on their backs and trudged into the hangar. Cautiously yet instinctively they let out a sigh of relief as they walked, allowing their unconscious to relax if only for a few seconds. Subconsciously they were taking inventory of what hurt, what was numb, what mattered, what didn't matter anymore and kept track of where their minds were teetering, keeping thoughts of home and loved ones at a distance. This wasn't the time. But then, there never was a good time to allow life back home to creep into their thoughts. Those thoughts were left idle in the darkest corners of the mind until such times that they mandated attention, or when boredom had to be dealt with. Those times that boredom prevailed was when talk of family, home, loved ones and each individuals favorite things in life were all allowed to come to the forefront.

The Team dropped their sweat encrusted, stinking uniforms on the concrete floor, sprayed their bodies with a garden hose hooked to a bathroom sink faucet and were choking down the remainder of the MREs they'd humped up and down the mountains of Afghanistan and Pakistan over the past three days as they made their way into the Sensitive Compartmented Information Facility (SCIF).

The SCIF was a "need to know" authority access area where Sensitive Intelligence information was discussed. The phones all had special filters on the incoming communications lines. The electricity was monitored for inadvertent bleed over of sensitive data and everything inside was special equipment used for Top Secret Compartmented and above intelligence conversations, communications and data transfer. This SCIF was basically a metal meat locker type of building that could be flown anywhere in the world and erected inside of building with it's own cypher locks, armed guards, computer systems and communications to all the higher echelon commands including the White House Situation Room, the Pentagon War Room, the CIA Operations Room, along with a number of other "Classified" consumers who were allowed to know what the "Intelligence Support Activity" was all about. ISA was a clandestine Intelligence organization that very few people ever knew existed.

Many Presidents had come and gone whose very lives, careers and Presidential legacies depended on the small number of highly trained professional intelligence personnel who were assigned to the "Activity" as it was known. The name changed so often that even those inside never knew what they were going to be called from month to month. It didn't really matter in the overall scheme of things since the mission always remained the same. Some referred to this unit as "the Farm", others just called it "that unit." FBI and CIA were constantly pissing on each other's turf, pointing fingers. The Activity didn't play politics. So, if no one knew what to call them, and never knew where they were, they could hardly be enveloped into that which eventually caused ineffectual impotence among those who defended America against all enemies, foreign and domestic! Very few of those Presidents or their cabinet members ever heard the name, but were highly grateful to those few men and women whose life were consumed with keeping continuity on elusive targets that were stated as Tier One threats. Warriors who owned the shadows and lived a lifestyle very few ever knew about.

Inside the "meat locker" the vast array of cutting edge technology struck awe into the hearts of those who were used to working with leading edge computers, communications gear and the latest in "high Technology" and encryption systems. The equipment changed constantly, even more so than the Activity changed it's name. But along with all the high tech stuff, there was one thing that remained constant no matter where the "meat locker" was deployed. Chief's desk.

The entire team was walking in a zombie state, a sort of comfort zone right next to being primal as they left the aircraft and headed into the hangar. Water was the only priority now. Every man acted in unison. Patient. Calm. As if a silent voice and familiar robotic routine urged them into perpetual action, feeding the body while their minds, numb and detached from the physical pain that was always there, absorbed the new mission particulars as they walked.

Chief was on year 26 with Joint Special Operations Intelligence, (JSOC-J2). He'd been there since the inception of "joint" operations, a result of absolute catastrophe in the deserts of Iran during the American Hostage Crisis of the early 1980s. Eight Special Operators had died that day, simply because no one in Aviation had checked the weather to see that a monster sand storm was on the horizon. Either they hadn't checked, or their lack of life experience in the Persian Gulf region kept them from understanding the devastating impact of what a real sand storm meant to an aircraft. Three meters of sand was coming straight down every half hour. The weight of that sand alone would crash any aircraft that flew in the vicinity, but in the case of Operation Eagle Claw, the C130s and Sea Stallion helicopters assigned to that mission flew directly into the storm and were consumed. A fuel tanker on the ground tried to take off and immediately met a fiery fate when a Sea Stallion helicopter crashed into it. Master Gunnery Sergeant Wilbur Campbell had also been on that fate filled mission and was now Chief's second in command with a total of 12 years experience in both Marine Force Recon and Delta Force, America's Premier Hostage Rescue Team.

These two men were the nucleus of the seven man team that worked together like a well oiled machine. A "Commander" would be assigned to this small team routinely, but would often transfer in and out just as routinely, staying six months or less on station. It wasn't that they couldn't take the physical stress, or that they didn't like the missions, it usually was the insane tempo of both training and real world operations that wore them out so quickly. Chief was the hub of the wheel. His years in Special Ops was the only real continuity in a chaotic high risk environment. Yet Chief was also considered the outrigger by the men who did the real work. All the other Commanders and officers were there for their own reasons, other agendas like a quick promotion, limited time in the driver's seat with limited experience. Then they hoped to be quickly reassigned and move on to bigger and better things. Bigger and Better things was "Enlisted speak" for desk duty and an easy cush future. Most of the men saw the officers who dashed in an out as politicians who were out to get the patches and badges to put on their "I love ME" wall. Chief was different. He didn't have an "I love ME" wall. All his medals, awards and recognition were in a box somewhere in storage. He had been there the longest with no end in sight. Literally hundreds of missions. Over sixty men had died while Chief had been working there. Some had died in training accidents, others on real world covert operations missions. Chief was a walking legend that carried things deeply and quietly. Those who had died that were "worth a shit" held a special place in Chief's heart. The rest who had died were just part of nature's inevitable herd thinning process.

If a person had their head on straight and spent enough time with Chief in a room they could come away with a treasure trove of wisdom and knowledge about life in general. Once there, a person could tell there was a lot more than met the eye when it came to big scary guy with the hard heart. He was a man of few words most of the time, and even less words when on a real Operation. But as with all things, a person had to be perceptive enough and present to find out. Chief didn't offer his experience, wisdom and life lessons for free, and not to just anyone. You had to pass the smell test and be on Chief's "Worth A Shit" list. There were very few who made that list, and several million who made the "not worth a shit" list.

This team of seven men had only been together a little more than a year. Their combined Special Operations experience was obvious and contributed immensely to the fluid mechanics and un-canny ability to predict what Chief was thinking. More times than not, someone would say, "I'm on it Chief" without any words being spoken. Just a look, a twitch in body language and everyone knew not only what needed to be done, but who's responsibility it was to get it done. Everyone was connected on a different plain, the unspoken communications plain of the Special Operations Warrior.

The selection process that Department of Defense used to find these Elite Warriors ensured they were highly motivated self starters. Thousands applied every year to get onto the Special Teams that America used to fight the War on Terror. But of those thousands, less than one percent would actually make it to training, and most of them would be weeded out. "Wannabes" was the name they were given. The ones who "Wanted to be" but just didn't' have the heart and soul required to become part of the inner circle. Once a man was selected, it was a given that any task that they perceived would be executed with the same immediacy and professional calm that any other task mandated. Taking out a terrorist, or taking out the garbage resulted in the same physiologic elements being present- a moderated heart rate, controlled slow breathing, attention to the smallest detail and execution with satisfactory result in the most efficient manner possible without drawing any attention to themselves. The only aspect that changed from one task to the next was the level of ferocity and ruthlessness required.

This mission would be double. Double everything. Double the length, double the danger. The standard mission set was three days. Some nerd, with all their medical and scientific studies had determined that the limits of human endurance was just more than 72 hours. But they had not taken into account the determination, the heart and shear perseverance of the Elite Warriors within the Special Operations world who were assigned to the Intelligence Support Activity. Without chemical or pharmaceutical assistance, these guys were literally head and shoulders above the rest of the Green Berets, Navy Seals and Marine Recon men. They were the best of the best, with no bravado, no flash, just silent efficiency and perfection with just the right touch of humility. This mission would take three days from wheels up to Zuess, the code word often used for mission completion.

Chief and his team had already been up for over 72 hours. But none of that counted now. It was someone else's turn, some other team's time to take a crack at it. But there was no one else. 28 Special Operators had been killed with one RPG strike less than three months earlier. It would take years to fill those slots, and decades more to fill their shoes. It was time to go again. They could sleep on the bird when they were wheels up. The clock would reset to zero when they lifted off.

Someone in the Chain of Command estimated this mission set would require six days. The radar in Chief's head went off. It was his internal compass, his personal "gut check" that had saved his life and that of his men on more than one occasion. For the longest time, he hadn't listened to that inner voice because he couldn't explain it. But years of real world experience had taught him to listen and listen well. This time it was telling him that something was wrong. He'd been on longer missions. Some as long as a year, others more than that. But this time there was an un-easy glitch that made him feel uncomfortable. He couldn't put his finger on it. But in the near future he would learn that "glitch" would change his life forever. Simply because the missions statement said, "SIX DAYS TO ZUES."

Jim Landis

WOW—Life is such a trip! I can't believe it. As if growing up in the Bronx wasn't exciting enough.

As a child, I often gazed at the moon; wondered what it was like and whether there were people living there. I even signed up for a trip to the moon at the New York World's Fair in 1939. Decades later I worked on the Apollo program—on the Lunar Lander no less. How wild is *that*?

I was a busy child. I made models of every plane (of that era). I ran around to the New York airports to watch and photograph the planes. Planes were my passion.

In sixth grade art class I made sketches of rockets and missiles. My art teacher laughed and said, derisively, "They can't fly, they don't have propellers." Twenty five years later I was a systems engineer on the Atlas Missile program (no propellers!). I also spent several years working on the B-52 bomber program.

While in the Air Force, I flew in many different types of aircraft. I crashed once, almost crashed on two other occasions, stayed away from anything with wings for the following eleven years.

In college, my English professor suggested that I quit engineering and take up journalism. I

scoffed at that. Here I am, many years later—and I'm writing!

During the preceding years, I married (twice), have two wonderful sons, have had fabulous women in my life (then), and now, along with precious friends—some of them from my early childhood in the Bronx.

The Bronx Zoo and Botanical Gardens were walking distance from my home. Today I live in Mariposa, California: Yosemite National Park is my "back yard."

So we never know what will happen next, or where we will be, or who will be with us. That is what makes life so exciting, challenging, and mysterious. Who knows: I might get that phone call tomorrow telling me my trip to the moon is scheduled for next Thursday. Would I go? You bet—if I can squeeze it into my busy schedule.

I hope you enjoy my writings. I send greetings, and wish you peace, love, joy, and bliss.

Sarah

She stood tall, over six foot, brunette, and stunningly gorgeous; a marvelous blend of Elizabeth Taylor and Ingrid Bergman. When she walked into a room ***everyone noticed***. I was in the Kona Lounge on Shelter Island, in San Diego. I watched as she strolled through the lounge. She sat next to me at the bar. I gulped, and downed my scotch and soda. We smiled a polite greeting to each other.

I immediately started searching for an opening line, wondering, *how do I get to know this beautiful woman?* I blurted out, "Do you know that you have great bone structure?" (probably the dumbest *line* ever spoken).

She laughed and said, "How would ***you*** know? That's not the part of me that you have been staring at since I arrived."

I acknowledged that, and said, "Certain things really stand out." She laughed. I ordered drinks.

We talked for many hours. I discovered she was not only gorgeous, but also brilliant; holding Masters Degrees in European art and history, and a Doctorate in Anthropology. She was also an accomplished pianist. I suggested that we go to a more exciting club on the Island. As we walked, Sarah said, "Don't you think I'm a little tall for you?"

I said, " I'm a really good climber."

She laughed and said, "So start climbing."

So I *did.*

Sarah's beauty left me breathless. When she stood in front of me, totally naked, (for the first time), I thought, *I'm dead. I died and went to heaven.* Then I heard her voice softly say, "Would you like to come to bed?" I thought, *Wow, so I'm not dead.* As I approached the bed, Sarah laughed and said, "Wouldn't it be better if you removed your clothes?"

Still in my breathless state, I answered, "Yes, yes, that's a good idea."

We enjoyed incredible sex; wild sex, and very tender sex, and everything in between. It was magnificent; so intense, so much passion, such a marvelous exchange of love and emotions. On one occasion, I was completely overwhelmed; I broke down and sobbed uncontrollably. Sarah held me close and showered me with kisses. I felt *her* tears.

When I awoke each morning, Sarah, this gorgeous, warm, soft, magnificent creature lay nestled in my arms; I thanked God and the angels for sharing this treasure with me. I kept saying (to myself), over and over, *Wow, what an incredible woman, what an incredible woman, what an incredible woman....*

We were not tourists. I was in San Diego on business with General Dynamics Astronautics, the prime contractor for the Atlas Missile. Sarah was visiting the recently established University of California, San Diego; exploring the possibility of joining the faculty as a professor of anthropology. We put those matters on hold; we had ***more important*** things to do.

We found that dining *out* took too much time away from *us*. We had room service arriving at all hours. The hotel restaurant provided an extensive menu. The food was excellent and carefully prepared. Sarah usually made the selections. Other than daily strolls on the beach, we did not leave the hotel for three days.

One evening, Sarah said, "Let's have a lot of special things with dinner tonight." In addition to the entrées, Sarah ordered cream puffs, strawberries, cookies, strawberry syrup, chocolate syrup, an assortment of pastries, ice cream, chips and various dips, banana cream pie, and lots of whipped cream. We fed *each other*. After dinner Sarah asked, "Have you ever been in a food fight?"

I laughed and said "No, never."

She laughed and said, *" Well, you're in one now,"* as she poured strawberry syrup over my head—and the fight was on.

I reciprocated with a wedge of banana cream pie right in her face—she screamed in delight and struck back with a fist full of whipped cream on my left ear. Our clothes came off, and the "goodies" kept flying. *No part* of our bodies went unscathed. I enjoyed French onion dip in some most unusual places. Sarah squealed with delight. Holding each other was a challenge—we were really slippery. Midst all this activity, the phone rang; it was the front desk inquiring whether everything was okay. Sarah answered and assured them that everything was absolutely wonderful. By midnight, all the food had either been eaten, was being *worn*, or had re-decorated the room.

As Sarah headed for the shower, she waved her arms straight up while her body swayed seductively. Watching her move gave me goose bumps everywhere. I threw a cream puff from across the room. It landed right on her back-side. She screamed and said, "Good Shot" and wiggled it off. I joined her in the shower. The rinse water swirled down the drain in a rainbow of colors. I suggested that a private piano recital would be the perfect ending for our day. Sarah agreed.

The hotel lounge was closed but showed just enough light on the Grand Piano. Sarah played, *Tenderly, Traumerei, Chopin's Piano Concert no.1, Adagio,* and *Over The Rainbow.* It was a brilliant performance—her playing was sensitive, passionate, and touching. I wanted more, but Sarah said, "We have had a long and exciting day. It's time for sleep."

We had not yet told each other about ourselves; who we were, where we came from, or what our lives were about. I held Sarah in my arms, looked into her eyes and gently, lovingly, and softly whispered, "Who *are* you?"

She smiled, placed her index finger over my lips and said, "I'm Sarah, the woman who loves you more than any other woman ever has, or ever will." She kissed me tenderly. We slept.

In the morning, we *did* talk about ourselves and our "history." Then Sarah announced it was time for her to return home. I asked, "Where *is* home?"

Once again, Sarah placed her index finger over my lips and said, "I have lived a lifetime in these three days with you. I know I will never experience anything even close to it ever again. You are a precious, loving man. I will love you for the rest of my life, and beyond. However, we each have other commitments. We must not let anything *tarnish* what we have shared here."

We held each other for what seemed an eternity. We did not want to let go. We kissed a lot. We cried a lot. We said many loving things, and then she was gone.

I watched as she walked toward her taxi. When Sarah walked, her body said, "Hey world, look! it's *me*, Sarah." She blew a kiss as the cab pulled away. What an incredible woman. What an incredible woman.

When I returned to my room, I knew instantly I could not stay there. Sarah's scent permeated the air and my senses. I struggled unsuccessfully to maintain control. I could not believe she was gone. I called the front desk, requested my invoice, and a reservation at the Town and Country Inn. I left contact information with them—*just in case....*

Our maid arrived to service the room. When she saw the condition of the room she smiled and said (in her broken Chinese/English), "Oh, big fun."

I said, "Yes, very big fun."

She asked, "Where lady?"

I answered, "Lady gone."

"So sad," she said.

I told her I was checking out, and asked her

to return later. I gave her one hundred dollars for the extra work she would have because of the food fight.

She thanked me and said, "You good man."

My reservation at the Town and Country Inn in Mission Valley was confirmed. My remaining three days in San Diego were awful. I was miserable without Sarah. I was an emotional wreck and it impaired my work. I prayed for relief; it arrived in one huge, emotional release, and then it was over. Again, I thanked God and the angels for sharing Sarah; that exquisite, precious, loving woman. My tears became tears of joy and gratitude. I love Sarah, and Sarah loves me; that's all that matters. That will not change. Life goes on. Endless blessings.

Gretchen Kemp said it all in her beautiful post script: "….See, there's this place in me where your fingerprints still rest, your kisses still linger, your whispers softly echo. It's the place where a part of you will forever be a part of me."

Epilogue

It has been 52 years since Sarah and I were together. My feelings today are as intense as they were then. I have often wondered why Sarah sat next to *me* that evening in the Kona Lounge; there were many other seats available. I have thought about Sarah on occasion, and wondered about her, and hoped she was well and enjoying life. I never told anyone about her; it was too painful to speak of it, as it is, in this writing.

The reader may wonder what precipitated

this writing after so many years. I never intended to write about Sarah. But then, ten days ago, I felt Sarah's *presence*. She was *here with me*. It was as intense, and as real, as when we last held each other. There were no words and no message; just an overwhelming feeling of love, joy, peace, and bliss; and then, once again, she was gone. My precious, loving, Sarah—how I love her. What an incredible woman.

Ultra-Sound

During a physical examination I told my doctor that I was having some discomfort in my legs. He did a visual examination and decided I should have an ultra-sound procedure. He arranged an appointment for me with El Portal Imaging in Merced.

After the usual preliminary paper-work, I was escorted to an examination room where two beautiful young female technicians were preparing the equipment. They asked me to remove my shoes, socks, and trousers, and to lie back on the examination table.They dimmed the lights and started the procedure. It was simple enough and not invasive; one technician moved a probe over my legs, while the other one watched the monitor and recorder. I thought about this scene and said, "I need to tell you something."

The technician asked, "What is it?" with some anxiety in her voice.

I assured her there was not a problem, and then said, "It has been a very long time since I was last in a darkened room,with two beautiful women, with my pants off." They started to laugh, and laugh, and laugh, uncontrollably. They were laughing so hard they had to stop the procedure and re-calibrate the equipment. We were all laughing during the remainder of the examination.

As I prepared to leave the facility, these two beautiful women hugged me and said, "Thanks, that was wonderful. Please come back again." How could I refuse such a request?

When Ya Gotta Go

We hear a lot about "road rage" and how nasty people are these days. I don't agree. I don't think it's that simple. Remember those TV commercials for the laxative that said, "It's *guaranteed* to work by 8 a.m." Well, on any given morning there are tens of thousands of cars jammed bumper to bumper, inching along on the L. A. freeways, and it's five minutes to eight. These drivers aren't nasty people. They're in a panic. They're stuck in traffic. They need to get to a bathroom—RIGHT NOW.

There's another area we hear a lot about on which I disagree: Smog. They blame automobiles, and farmers, and your fireplace, and your cat, and probably your Aunt Sue, for the smog. Frankly, I think it's the planes.

On any given day, there are 39,000 commercial aircraft flights in the U.S. With an average of two hundred passengers per flight, that means there are over seven million people up there in those planes. AND guess what? Most of them use the bathrooms at some point during the flight. You hear people (on the ground) complaining that the air is dirty; that it has brown streaks, or it's kinda yellow, or it smells funny. It's all of those—and it's from the planes! The airline people deny there is anything coming out of those planes, but consider this: fuel consumption is directly related to aircraft weight. The airlines are always looking to cut operating expenses. They're not gonna carry around any extra weight that they can get rid of.

Years ago there was a very popular song: *Pennies From Heaven*; part of the lyrics said, "Every time it rains, it rains, pennies from heaven..." Well, that was *then*. But that ain't what's coming down *now*.

Really Tired Today

By 1:00 a.m. (my usual bedtime) I was really tired; very sleepy. My bed felt good. I settled in, but found the covers were not "up" far enough. I grabbed the edge of the blanket and pulled; my hand slipped and punched me in the nose. Wide awake now! I felt something warm on my face. I turned on my light. There was blood all over my face, pillow, sheets and blanket. I got out of bed and did the first aid stuff. Then I had to change all the bedding; it was 3:00 a.m. by the time I finished. Back to bed at 3:30.

4:00 a.m.: The alarm clock rang; a left-over setting from my afternoon nap. Back to sleep.

4:45: The phone rang. I didn't answer. Back to sleep—*I think*.

6:00 a.m.: The fax machine rang and delivered a message. I didn't care. Wide awake again. Back to sleep at 6:15.

7:00 a.m.: Gorgeous and Jolee (our beautiful German Shepherds) showered me with kisses— time to get up!

Really tired today.

PS: The unsolicited fax message (at 6:00 a.m.) was an offer for a free booklet on how to get a good nights' sleep. I sent for it.

Ramblings

Stay close to those you love and hug them *today*—tomorrow is an illusion.

*****

So much to do—so little time. No time to waste—so many needs. Start in the morning—count your blessings in the evening.

*****

Take time to smell the roses. But before you stick your nose in the rose—check for bees.

*****

Every morning, Gorgeous, our magnificent German Shepherd, comes to my bedside and puts a smile on my face with his kisses. How could the rest of my day be anything but wonderful?

*****

Look around. Be aware. Many of our brothers and sisters are in pain and despair. Do what you can. A smile, a hug, a kind word, a piece of bread, a warm coat, can change, or even save a life—You may not know. You don't need to know now. Someday you will know.

*****

If you haven't laughed at yourself today—there's still time!

*****

Be kind and loving, even when you don't feel like it. Watch what happens!

*****

There are angels all around us—sometimes

you'll know it—other times you won't.

*****

In this land of plenty (and excess) there is no justification for leaving any person without food, shelter, or medical care. The Command is to love one another; it's unconditional; no exceptions, no excuses. Those who miss (or choose to ignore) that message, will always be "at war" with someone, about something.

*****

I went to summer camp in 1937. I was nine years old. It was somewhere in upstate New York. I had a good time. I found a dead bat in my cabin. I mailed it to my sister Rene with a note asking her to keep it for me. It was in a regular envelope—not a package. She received it. I asked her for it last week. She didn't have it.

*****

We all receive so many blessings. If we "give back" in equal measure, we can change the world.

*****

It takes so much patience to learn patience.

I Remember...

Haaren High School,
Manhattan, New York,

February, 1945:

In February,1945, I was in Mr. O'Ryan's American History class. He was very knowledgeable and relaxed. He also had a ready sense of humor, and an obvious bit of skepticism about some of the "facts" of American history.I liked the atmosphere in his class.

One day, the assistant principal came in during class and asked Mr. O'Ryan to excuse himself. We sat there wondering what was happening.A few minutes later,the bell rang and we were off to our next class.We had a substitute teacher the next morning and were informed that Mr.O'Ryan's' son (and only child) had been killed in action during the invasion of Iwo Jima.

Mr. O'Ryan returned to class two weeks later.The energy,the humor,and the spark, were all gone.He was as lifeless as his dead son.The bullet fired on Iwo Jima that day killed two people ten thousand miles apart. He resigned from teaching at the end of that semester.I often wondered what became of him.

Spring Semester 1945:

The Spring semester of our English class was devoted to the study of *Hamlet*. In a marvelous coincidence mid-way through the semester, Maurice Evans, the great Shakespearean actor arrived in New York with his spectacular production of *Hamlet*. The performances were held at the Columbus Circle Theatre, just four blocks from our school. There was a mid-week matinee, and we wanted to attend as a class project, but our teacher, Mrs. Sunsky, told us she could not obtain administrative approval. She hoped we would be able to attend one of the performances on our own. We all decided to cut class on the following Wednesday and attend the performance.

Maurice Evans and the production were exhilarating. It was the first time that sound effects and special lighting were included in a Shakespearean production. When the final curtain came down, and the applause ended, and the house lights came up, there was Mrs. Sunsky sitting nearby. She waved, and smiled, and said, "Class dismissed."

It's *Your* Life...

It's *your* life: Fix it. Change it. *You're* in charge. Break the routines: Don't set your alarm clock tonight. Get out of bed from the other side. Have your "morning coffee" at noon instead of 8:00 a.m. Take a different route to work. Better yet, don't go to work—call in, and if the boss gives you any crap, tell him to "shove it." You'll survive.

Have your breakfast at 2 p.m. Don't shave for three days. Stay up all night if that's what you feel like doing; go to bed at dawn. Play your favorite CD and crank the volume all the way up.

When the kids are ready to leave for school, surprise them: pack a lunch and take them to Yosemite for the day. Take your Sweetie for an ice cream cone. If you make a call and mis-dial and get a wrong number, don't say, "Sorry", and hang up. Maybe that person needed someone to talk to at that particular moment. Maybe there's a reason why you mis-dialed. Who knows, you may even save a life. Worst case: you might make a new, fabulous friend.

So relax, it's *your* life. Let it happen. It's gonna' happen *anyway*. You might as well enjoy it—*your way.*

It's *Your* Turn....

"By the rude bridge that arched the flood,
Their flag to April's breeze unfurled,
Here once the embattled farmers stood,
And fired the shot heard round the world."

Ralph Waldo Emerson

Yes, a handful of farmers took on the British army and marked the beginning of the end of the British Empire in America.

Nelson Mandela, after twenty six years in prison, "fired a shot heard round the world" and marked the beginning of the end of apartheid in South Africa.

Lech Walesa, an unknown shipyard electrician in Gdansk, Poland, "fired a shot heard round the world" and marked the beginning of the end of Communist rule in Poland.

Rosa Parks, a seamstress riding the bus home after a hard day at work, "fired a shot heard round the world" and marked the beginning of the end of racial segregation in the United States.

It's always *the people* that make the significant changes. Much remains to be done. IT'S *YOUR* TURN...

More Ramblings

Every day can be Valentines Day. It's up to you!

*****

During a physical examination my doctor asked, "How many times during the night do you get up to go pee?"

I replied, "Never."

He was incredulous and asked, "Never?"

I repeated, "Never."

He said, "I get up three or four times every night."

I responded, "You need to see a doctor."

*****

A woman is in a produce market in the Bronx. She looks around, picks up two apples and asks, "How much are the apples?"

"Two for 49" the clerk answered.

"So then one is 25 cents?" she asks.

"That's right" responds the clerk.

She says, "So I'll take the other one."

*****

The United States has more people in prison than any other nation. There are reports that at the present rate of incarceration, every man, woman, and child in the United States will be in prison by the year 2037.

*****

Misery is plentiful, and free. So is Joy—

your choice.

*****

I say my prayers when I get into bed at night. By the time I finish, it's time to get up.

*****

I heard that some of the Olympic badminton players were disqualified for trying to lose. How weird is that? So what's so difficult?

*****

They passed a law in Malawi against flatulence. It's a misdemeanor to "flatulate" in public. But I wonder, what does the arresting officer present to the judge as evidence of the crime? There's a lot of resistance to the new law, and the rate of public flatulence has skyrocketed. Most of the people think that things were better before the new law. You just did what you did, when you wanted to do it, and nobody *else* made a stink about it.

*****

So many opportunities to be kind and loving every day.

*****

It doesn't matter how long you, or your family have been in the United States. If you're not Native American, you're an immigrant or the descendent of immigrants.

*****

Aboard my recent flight to New York City were four Buddhist Monks resplendent in their saffron robes, a Rabbi, and a Jesuit Priest. So how could anything go wrong?

*****

Forgive everyone—for everything.

*****

I spent many hours in the Great Hall of the Metropolitan Museum of Art in New York City. I was mesmerized by the incredible sculptures of the ancient Greeks and Roman Emperors; works by Michelangelo, Bernini, Rodin, and others whose names may not be as well known, but whose works are equally magnificent. I marveled at the beauty of Sappho, Venus, and Hercules. I wondered what went on in the Great Hall during the night when all the visitors and staff were gone; I wanted to be there *then*.

*****

I felt an intense connection to those ancient Greeks. I decided that I must research my Greek lineage. I sent an e-mail to my friend Lowell: "Wondering whether I am a descendent of Plato, or Aristotle, or Sophocles, or just the millions of Greeks who have (throughout the ages) run greasy hamburger joints?" Lowell answered back: "I like my burgers well done, no pepper, and hold the onions?" That *was not* the response I was hoping for.

*****

Last Wednesday we stopped to pick up our mail. There was a package. Pandora asked, "What's in the package?"

I answered, "It's a book."

"What is it about?" Pandora asked.

"I think it's about eyes." I responded. When

we arrived home I opened the package. The title of the book is *Combating Memory Loss*. I forgot that I ordered it.

*****

In the United States we have:

> Forty nine million people on food stamps.
>
> Sixteen million children living in poverty.
>
> One million homeless children.
>
> Thirty one million high school drop-outs.
>
> What is happening to us?

*****

Scientists have concluded that the universe is male. After the "Big Bang" he wandered off and had nothing to say.

*****

Family, Friends, and Pets—So many blessings, I've lost count.

Goin' Home

In the Spring of 1949, I was just a few months from the end of my enlistment in the Air Force. Thousands of troops in Japan and Korea were in the same situation. When the Air Force high command in Washington realized they had a looming manpower shortage, they panicked.

Orders went out to all unit commanders in the Far East instructing them to personally interview each man in their unit and exert whatever pressure necessary to cause the individual to re-enlist. I met with my commanding officer. He laid it on pretty heavy.

He said, "Re-enlist today, and tomorrow you will be promoted to Tech Sergeant with a $300 re-enlistment bonus in your pocket. In six months you will be promoted to Master Sergeant, and you know that Master Sergeant is the sweetest deal in the Air Force." I acknowledged his offer was very attractive for someone who planned to stay in the service, but not for me. I told him I was accepted for admission to New York University commencing in September. I showed him their letter. He said, "That's very nice" and then resumed the pressure. I kept refusing his offers. In exasperation he said, "You know, I could declare you 'essential to the mission' and hold you here for two years."

I 'lost it' then and said, "Fuck you."

He turned red and angry-looking and I expected him to call the Military Police and have me dragged off to the stockade. He stared at me and then said, "You are dismissed, Sergeant."

I stood up, saluted and said, "Thank you sir."

I was in my barracks when the inter-com blared, *Landis, report to Orderly Room immediately.* I figured, here comes trouble. When I arrived, the First Sergeant was smiling and waving some papers. He said, "I *have* something for you." I assumed it was the papers for my courts martial for insubordination.

I scowled at him and said, "And fuck you, too."

He looked incredulous and said, "What's wrong with you?" I told him about my meeting with the C.O. He laughed and said, "Damn, I've been wanting to say that to him for years."

He handed me the papers—they were my orders back to the States. They read: Hdqtrs Air/ Airways Communication Service, USAF: Landis, J ames, S/Sgt, S/N RA13258772 report 48 hrs Replacement Depot Yokohama. Embark troopship General M.M. Patrick, Seattle/ Ft. Lewis, processing / transportation Ft. Slocum, N.Y. Separation From Service, Not Later Than 8/6/49. Wow—I'm going home!

I requested a meeting with my Commanding Officer. I apologized for my behavior. He apologized for the pressure. He said, "You are one of my best men---sorry to see you go.

Good luck. Have a great life." We exchanged salutes, and I was off to Yokohama.

When you run away from home....

When you decide to run away from home, you better have it all figured out, otherwise you're gonna' look really dumb. That's what happened to me.

I was a wild kid. I always wanted to go places and do things. That's why I played hooky so much; I couldn't stand to sit in that classroom, in the same seat all day. Lots of kids lived on my block and I wanted to be out playing all the time. During the winter when we could sleigh ride, I stayed out there after dark, sleigh-riding until I was soaking wet and freezing. In the summer it was warm all night and too nice to be indoors. I wanted to be out with my friends.

When Momma called me in for dinner, I usually didn't obey. My Uncle Gus lived with us. He had standing orders from Momma: "When you come home from work, and you see Sonny, don't ask questions, just pick him up and bring him upstairs for dinner." That's exactly what he did; he tucked me under his arm, while I screamed and kicked, and punched him all the way up the five flights of stairs to our apartment. He was big and very good-natured, and he would just laugh and carry me upstairs.

All I needed were two nickels and I could be anywhere in New York City: riding the Staten Island Ferry across New York harbor, at Coney Island, the Bronx Zoo, in Times Square, at the World's Fair on Long Island, at LaGuardia Airport, or just about anyplace. I was twelve years old and wasn't supposed to be running around by myself in New York City at all hours of the day and night. I got punished frequently for my excursions and for disobeying Momma. Getting my back-side spanked was one of the punishments.

Finally, I decided I had had enough. So—I announced to Momma that I was running away from home. I expected (and hoped) for resistance but received none. Instead, Momma said, "Oh, okay. Would you like me to make a sandwich for you to take along?"

I said, "Yes please." Momma made the sandwich and put it in a brown paper bag.

She said, "Here you go, be careful out there." I stood waiting for Momma or my sisters to urge me not to leave, but there was only silence.

I exclaimed in a raised voice, "I'm leaving now." Still only silence, so out the door and down the stairs I went.

On the ground floor, I met my best friend, Lenny Klein, coming out of his apartment. He said, "What's in the bag?"

I said, "It's a sandwich. I'm running away from home."

Lenny laughed and said, "Eh, remember, last year? I tried that already—it didn't work. My Mom and my sisters laughed and just said "Goodbye." I didn't go far."

I responded indignantly, "Well, *I'm really going.*"

Lenny said, "Yeah, sure, see ya later." So off I went. Crossing to the other side of our street, I looked up at our apartment. My sisters were at the window, laughing, and waving goodbye.

I started walking and wondering, *what do I do now?* I thought running away from home was a good idea until no one said, "Oh please don't leave." I wandered around for a while keeping out of sight of our building. Then I sat down by the bagel factory around the corner and ate my sandwich. I tried to figure out how I could go back home without looking really stupid. After several hours I still couldn't come up with a good plan, so I just went home.

Momma answered the door. Seeing me she said, "Oh, you're back."

I needed some reason to justify my return, so I said, "I ate my sandwich and I'm still hungry."

Momma said, "Well, you're just in time for dinner. Would you like to stay and have dinner with us?"

I replied, "Yes, I would."

My sisters and Uncle Gus were seated at the dinner table. Everyone said, "We're glad you're home, Sonny." We all had a good laugh with hugs and kisses all around. I really loved my family and was really happy to be back. Then I thought, wait till Lenny sees me tomorrow!

Would You Stop?

You're on a cross-country trip by car. You run into bad weather. It is a dark, stormy night, and you are hopelessly lost. You keep driving. Then, in the distance, you see a faint light. You drive toward it and the light becomes brighter. When you get closer you see that it is a sign. The sign reads, "BATES MOTEL." Would you stop?

Try To Do Nothing...

Sometimes you just have to stop, step back, stop thinking, and try to do nothing for awhile. It's not that easy to do. Last time I tried it I got a ticket for parking in the passing lane on Interstate 80. The Highway Patrol Officer came to my window and said, "What do you think you're doing?"

I replied, "I'm trying not to think."

He asked, "Where are you going.?"

I answered, "Nowhere, obviously, I'm parked."

In exasperation, he said, "I love a smart ass. License and Registration please." In keeping with 'my plan', I responded that I did not have a license or registration. He ordered me out of the vehicle, handcuffed me, and took me to jail.

The charges read: 'illegal parking, doing zero mph in a 65 mph zone, failure to produce a valid drivers license and vehicle registration, suspicion of mental impairment.' I pled guilty to all charges except the mental impairment. I argued that the police officer was not a trained clinician and therefore was not qualified to make that assessment. The judge agreed and fined me fifty bucks on the other charges. Then the judge asked, "Where are you going now?"

"Outside," I replied.

The judge shook his head in dismay and said, "Get outta here."

Spending five days in jail really helped me with "my plan", particularly the part about trying to do nothing for awhile.

The Dragonflies of Yosemite

How fortunate they are, those dragonflies of Yosemite. They circle, and dart, and glide, and skim the Merced River in their magical dance.

They come close and visit with us as if to say, "Who are you? And why are you here in our private preserve? You make too much noise with your talk and laughter, and with your rattling plastic bags of pretzels and Fritos. You seem nice enough, but we are always happy when evening arrives and you go home. However, you will probably come back again, so we might as well be friends."

We depart for home—thankful for our new friends, and for Theodore Roosevelt and John Muir, and all others since, who cared so much about Yosemite and its' dragonflies.

There Was a Time...

There was a time, long ago, when all we had was each other. Few phones, even fewer cars, no television. We were face to face all the time; at home, together at the dinner table, in school, in the street, at work. You knew who was who, and what was what. It was easy to tell which ones were really your friends---and which ones weren't; eye contact told you what you needed to know. Most significant: you *knew* your parents and your siblings. Sadly, it is an era gone forever.

My Father

My father, Peter Dimitri Landis was born in Sparta, Greece on December first,1897. At a very early age, he was sent to America to live with relatives. I don't know much about his early years. Unfortunately, I did not ask enough questions while the opportunity existed.

My father was a gentle soul with a great sense of humor. He was crazy about Momma from the day they met. They married in 1920 (he was 23 years old) and Momma was 25.

Dad was a great tease and he loved to tease Momma, and although she would try to dismiss his silliness, you could always see a slight, loving smile on her face, and you could tell that she really loved it all. Dad was always grabbing Mom and hugging her, and she would say, "Oh Pete, cut it out," always with that slight smile on her face. They were like newlyweds—always.

Mom and Dad had many difficult, stressful years, primarily because of finances. The 1930s were disastrous, however, they never allowed those circumstances to change their relationship to each other, nor did they "take it out" on me and my sisters. Despite the difficulties, we were a close, functioning family. We always had enough to eat, decent clothes, frequent extended family gatherings, exciting Christmas holidays and birthday celebrations. My sisters and I did not know how poor we were until years later. I don't know where, or how, my parents learned their parenting skills, but they could have written the book on what to do, and most important of all, what *not* to do when raising children. My parents were (and still are) my life's greatest gift.

My father was, indeed, a gentle soul and a gentleman. He never raised his voice to Momma, nor to us children, and God knows, there were many times when *I* certainly deserved to be yelled at. Dad always set an extra place at the dinner table in case someone arrived unexpectedly. He didn't want them to feel unwelcome. On many occasions, Dad brought people home; strangers—strangers who needed a meal and a place to stay for a few days. They came as strangers, and left as friends.

Dad lived his life with grace, gentleness, humor, and compassion. He set the example for us on how to live our lives and treat each other. What greater gift...?

"O Christmas Tree"

I have always had a fascination with Christmas trees. As a young child I would hang around the Italian market near our home in the Bronx, and help them show and sell the trees. I didn't get paid, I just wanted to be near the trees; I loved their shape, structure, and color, and not least of all—their scent.

Every Christmas season, Momma would take me downtown to Manhattan to see all the marvelous, huge, trees at Macy's, Bloomingdales, Gimbols, Wanamakers and Hearns, and the brilliantly lit trees stretching for miles along the center median on Park Avenue, and of course, the always breathtaking Christmas tree at Rockefeller Center.

I always had a Christmas tree at home; never had a Christmas without one. Even when I was in the Air Force in Japan, I would find a tree, cut it down, bring it into the barracks and decorate it with whatever was available. This year (2009) was no exception; at least that's how it started.

I bought an eight foot tall Noble Fir at the lot in Mariposa. It was gorgeous, perfect in every way, and it had a great scent. Pandora (my extremely significant life partner) and I, started to set the tree in place on the Saturday before Christmas. We had nothing but trouble. It usually takes just a few minutes to set a tree in the stand and lock it tight. This tree did not want to stand up; no matter what we did, it kept falling, or trying to fall. Minutes stretched into hours before we finally had the tree secured in the stand; with a nylon filament line tethering it to the ceiling, just in case...

Pandora, is six feet tall and is very adept at decorating the upper reaches of a Christmas tree. She got the light strings set on the tree and started decorating; working her way down starting with the smallest ornaments. Four hundred ornaments were laid out in the guest room, awaiting their 2009 "debut." Later that evening, Pandora said she felt as if she was getting a cold.

On Sunday morning, Pandora did indeed have a cold. We continued decorating the tree. Pandora's cold grew worse. On Monday, Pandora noted a correlation between how she felt and her proximity to the Christmas tree. It became apparent, she not only had a cold, but she was also having an intense allergic reaction to the tree. With great sadness and disappointment, we decided that the Christmas tree had to go. We stripped off all the decorations and lights and placed the tree outside on the deck. Pandora soon noticed an improvement in how she felt; now she was just dealing with a cold. I think the tree was relieved to be outside; it was standing straight, it looked "relaxed", and so beautiful.

We decided to donate the tree. We called St. Joseph's, Manna House, and Mountain Crisis Services. Mountain Crisis Services told us they had a family who could not afford a Christmas tree and their little boy was heart broken at not having one, so the tree went to them. What a great gift for them—and for us.

109

Maybe that tree knew something *we* didn't. Maybe it just didn't want to be with *us*. Maybe that's why we had so much trouble setting it up. Maybe (in frustration) it gave Pandora the allergy (which she *never* had in previous years), so that it could get out of *our* house and go where it needed to be.

That's a lot of maybe's.

From now on, we will probably have an artificial tree in our home. But I think I will still buy one gorgeous Noble Fir—for someone.

Questions, Questions---All the Time Questions.

What time is it? Is it still raining? Is today Tuesday? Who called at 7am this morning? What are we having for dinner? These are the everyday, mundane questions.

Here are the big ones. Questions that should have been asked a long time ago.

Questions to which I still want answers.

Mom: How did you and Dad meet? Were you introduced by a friend or…? What year was that?

Dad: Did your heart 'skip a beat' when you first saw Mom?'

Mom: Did you get 'tingly all over' when you first saw Dad?

How long after you met did you have a first date? Where did you go? Did you kiss on the first date? Did you have a second date soon after?

Mom: When did you know that 'He is *the one*?'

Dad: When did you know that 'She is *the one*?'

Mom/Dad: How long was your courtship? Were you doing *'it'* before you married?

Mom: How did Dad propose? Was he funny? Did you say 'Yes' right away? Were you sure that he was the 'right one?' Where were you married? Who else was there? Was it a 'grand party?'

Dad: I heard you really 'celebrated' a lot the day I was born. How long did the hang-over last?

Mom/Dad: I was your third and last child. Why? Was there something about *me* that made you decide you didn't want more kids? Wouldn't surprise me!

Mom/Dad: I know that you had many difficult and stressful years. How did you always stay so kind and loving to each other? You were always like young lovers. It made Marian, Rene, and me feel so loved, and safe, and secure.

Mom/Dad: We always hugged and kissed a lot and I am grateful for that, and the hugs and kisses were always special and meaningful to me— never routine. I hope you knew how much I love you, and how thankful I am (to this day), that you were my parents.

The three of us can stop crying now and relax. I'll have more questions later.

Meanwhile—keep in touch.

I love you both.

Jim

A Few More Rambles

Can you possibly imagine how desperately lonely the homeless must feel? On the street all day, and then evening falls, and the rest of us go home to our families and our warm homes, and they are still out there—in the dark, in the cold, all alone. Can you possibly imagine...?

*****

Every time you go to the market, buy one extra item that is not on your list. Be patient. Watch. You will see the need.

*****

The horrors in Tucson are numbing. I can't stop thinking about Christina Green, that beautiful little girl; shot and dying on the cold ground—without her loved ones. I hope she didn't feel the terror I feel. I can't stop my tears

*****

Wars will cease when the mothers of the world stand up and tell their leaders, "NO, you cannot have my child, to kill, or be killed, in your rich mans' "for profit wars."

*****

Always forgive your enemies—nothing pisses them off more.

*****

What makes life bearable midst all the deceptions, treachery, distortions, secrecy, fraud, brutality, and outright lies, is my firm conviction that sooner or later, and often in the most unexpected ways, *the truth always comes*

*****

So much suffering—so many ways to help.

*****

Step out into the light with your heart, mind, and soul. Weep for those needlessly killed. Speak out for those who are hungry, oppressed, and in danger. Speak out for the voiceless. They are all our brothers and sisters. Speak out and be visible for peace and justice at every opportunity. For what other purpose are we on this planet?

Procrastination

I have often said, "I must stop procrastinating," but I keep putting it off.

I think that procrastination is a disease—a very persistent disease. I decided to discus it with my doctor, so I made an appointment to see him. After sitting in his waiting room for two hours past my scheduled appointment time, and watching the doctor repeatedly flit from one examination room to another, I decided that he had the disease also, so I left. The doctor's nurse called the next day to see if I wanted to reschedule my appointment. I told her that I would as soon as I had time—that was four years ago. I haven't been back yet; all part of the disease.

For a while, I thought that "getting organized" was the solution for procrastination. I spent a lot of time getting organized. After two years, I came to the conclusion that getting organized was just another form of procrastination; nothing could get done until I got organized. The "getting organized" phase never ended, therefore I was not in danger; I could continue to procrastinate for the foreseeable future.

As evidence that procrastination truly is an incurable disease, I offer the following: I started writing this little treatise four years ago—and it isn't finished yet!

So laugh—already

Many wonderful things have happened to me during my lifetime. One of the most significant was being raised in a predominantly Jewish neighborhood. I lived on Boynton Avenue in the East Bronx for twenty years starting at age five.

Humor is a great part of the Jewish culture. The 1930s and the war years were dark times for Jews everywhere, but even then, they were sustained, and they sustained many others, with their ability to laugh when most of the people on this planet were in tears.

The sounds, the voices, and the expressions I heard all those years ago, are still with me. I still hear them. They still bring smiles to my face—and to my heart. Here are some of them:

A young Jewish man calls his mother in Florida and says, "Ma, how are you?"

"Not too good" she says. "I've been very weak."

The concerned son asks, "Ma, why are you so weak?"

"Because I haven't eaten in 38 days," she replies.

Shocked, the son responds, "That's terrible. Why haven't you eaten in 38 days?"

She answers, "Because I didn't want my mouth should be full of food if you should call."

*****

How many Jewish mothers does it take to change a light bulb? "(Sigh) Don't bother, I'll sit in the dark, I don't want I should be a nuisance to anybody."

*****

Jewish Telegram: "Start worrying. Details to follow."

*****

The Jewish view on when life begins: Actually there is no controversy on when life begins. In the Jewish tradition the fetus is not considered viable until after it graduates from medical school.

*****

Sam Goldberg is having his weekly poker game at the club house with his buddies. He loses five hundred dollars in one hand and falls over dead—heart attack. His friends stand for a moment of silence. Then Abe Schwartz says, "Somebody has to go tell his wife." Moe Ginsberg volunteers. Schwartz says, "This requires great tact."

Ginsberg says, "You shouldn't worry. Tact is my middle name." So Ginsberg goes and knocks on Goldbergs' door.

Mrs. Goldberg answers and says, "Whaddaya want?"

Ginberg replies, "Your husband just lost five hundred dollars playing poker."

Mrs. Goldberg says, "He should drop dead."

Ginsberg replies, "I'll go tell him."

*****

A lady goes to the butcher shop and tells the butcher, "I want a fresh chicken."

The butcher takes a chicken out of the case and throws it up on the counter and says, "This is a fresh chicken."

The lady picks up the chicken, sniffs it back and front, between the legs, under the wings, throws it back on the counter and says, "This chicken stinks."

The butcher says, "Lady, could you pass a test like that?"

*****

Another "chicken" joke.

A man goes to the movie theater with a live chicken in his arms. The theatre manager stops him and says, "You can't take a chicken to the movies."

The man leaves, goes around the corner and stuffs the chicken in his pants. He goes back to the movie house, buys a ticket and in he goes. He's sitting there watching the movie when the chicken starts gasping for air, so he unzips his fly and the chicken sticks it's head out. Velda is sitting in the next seat watching the chicken out of the corner of her eye.

Velda turns to her friend sitting to her left and says, "Bertha, look what's doing," tilting her head in the direction of the chicken.

Bertha looks and says, "What's to look? If you've seen one, you've seen them all."

Velda responds, "Yeah, but *this one's* eating my pop corn."

*****

A homeless man is sitting on the sidewalk in the Bronx. A well -dressed Jewish mother walks by. The man looks up at her and says, "Lady I haven't eaten in three days."

She looks down at him and says, "Force yourself."

*****

Abe Cohen is driving on the highway and gets pulled over by the cops. The police officer comes up to Abe's car and says, "Mister, do you know that your wife fell out of the car five miles back?

"Oh thank God" Abe responds. "I thought I had gone deaf."

Disposal

Despite my repeated assertions that I will be thirty four in September, Pandora takes a more realistic approach. She has asked, more than once, what I wanted done with my body when I "get my wings." The thought of being buried "six feet under" is suffocating, and ending up in an urn is just as unappealing. So, until they devise a method with which I am comfortable, I ain't leaving. All of this is, of course, my way of avoiding having to face my mortality.

My recent visit to the J.C. Fremont Hospital Emergency facility, and the Fresno Heart Hospital gave new vigor to Pandora's question. She told me that many universities and other medical institutions have "Body Donation Programs" and they will "come and get you" when the time comes. That kind of appeals to me. I want to go someplace warm, like San Diego. I always liked San Diego. I also want my body to go to an all-girls school. I hope that *they* have as much fun with my body as *I* have had.

Veterans Day

We set this day aside to honor and remember all veterans who have served our nation. We owe them a debt which can never be repaid. To those who died in battle, or have since passed on, we pray that they have found comfort and peace.

To those veterans who are still with us, we have a special obligation, not just today, but every day. For many of them, *their* war will never end. For many thousands, though their wounds are not visible, they suffer emotional trauma caused by the horrors witnessed, or the actions performed in combat.

Tens of thousands of veterans of Iraq and Afghanistan are unable to cope after returning to civilian life; unable to maintain employment, unable to maintain normal marriage or social relationships. Many are unable to obtain proper medical or psychological care from overwhelmed or inadequate government services. Many are unable to live with their nightmares; nightmares which make dying more attractive than living. More than eighteen veterans commit suicide every day— that's over six thousand each year. Thousands of others become homeless.

We have over 200,000 homeless veterans on the streets of America today; yes 200,000—that is not a misprint. That is a national disgrace.

The next time you encounter a homeless vet sleeping on the sidewalk, or pushing all his worldly possessions in a shopping cart, or sitting at a freeway off ramp begging for money, don't turn away. Don't avert your glance. Don't treat them as though they are invisible. They were young, and strong, and energetic, and full of hope when we sent them off to war. Look what *we* have done to them. God forgive us.

The homeless don't look good. They probably don't smell good either. Their clothes may be in tatters and ill fitting, some of them will probably freeze to death on the street next winter. Give them a dollar, or two, or whatever, and don't worry about whether they will spend it "wisely." Bring them a meal, or a cup of coffee, or a warm coat, or take a vet to a café for a meal and ignore the stares of the other diners. Look into the eyes of your new friend, and know that this is your brother or sister; if you don't see that, then perhaps you have missed the sole purpose for your existence on this planet.

THEY MADE A DIFFERENCE

Nelson Mandela
Eleanor Roosevelt
Raoul Wallenberg
Mahatma Ghandi
Maria Montessori
Cesar Chavez
Helen Keller
Booker T. Washington
Martin Luther King Jr.
Marian Wright Edelman
Mother Teresa
Archbishop Desmond Tutu
Mary Harris (Mother Jones)
Amelia Earhart
Ellie Weisel
Wangari Maathai
Fr. Daniel Berrigan
Rigoberta Menchu
Thomas Jefferson
Susan B. Anthony
Archbishop Oscar Romero
Maya Angelou
Rosa Parks
Abraham Lincoln
Sarah Winnemucca
Franklin Delano Roosevelt
Sojourner Truth
Rachel Carson

General George C. Marshall
Vaclav Havel
Marian Anderson
Frederick Douglass
Leonardo Da Vinci
Margaret Meade
Jackie Robinson
Oskar Schindler
Maggie Kuhn
Salvador Dali
Maria Callas
Barbara Jordan
Sandra Day O'Connor
Paul Robeson
Princess Diana
Marie Curie
William Shakespeare
Jimmy Carter
Margaret Bourke White
Lech Walesa
Jane Goodall
Thomas A. Edison
Harriet Tubman
Alice Walker
Hafiz
Beethoven
Winston Churchill
Albert Einstein
Carl Sagan
Sr. Helen Prejean
Madonna
Neil Armstrong

Sr. Joan Chittister
Ruth Bader Ginsberg
Sally Ride
The Beatles
Thomas Paine
Rosie The Riveter

The preceding is the *short list*. The full list fills scores of volumes, is endless, and awaits your contribution.

It is always the people that make the difference. Ordinary people doing extraordinary things; their courage, strength, determination, compassion, and love for each other have changed the world. Each of us has that gift; the power within waiting to be brought forth. It is *your* turn; each day in actions great or small, you have the opportunity to add your name to the list.

We need *your* gifts.

Donna Marks

Advice to Writers
"You will pardon my epitaphing,
But my fondest wish
Is to lie down and
Die laughing."

I have often repeated this wise and fun bit of advice authored by a favorite junior college instructor, C. K. Snyder. Life is too short not to find the funny side.

After ten years of marriage, my first husband announced that he had found someone new and wanted a divorce. I was lonely and depressed as I crossed the main street, Pacific Avenue, in Santa Cruz, California, later that day. A tall thin African-American walked up beside me and announced, "I is gonna cross da street wiz' you, cause den I knows I won't get run over!"

I could have kissed him for making me laugh when I was so depressed. That night I attended the film, "Zorba the Greek," and was further inspired by Alan Bates and Anthony Quinn as they overcame failure by dancing on the beach.

Sing, Dance, Laugh, Pray. Make life fun.

Dear Mrs. Robinson

Dear Garden Grove High School staff,

Please mail the enclosed letter to my former English teacher, Juanita Robinson. You have my permission to put it in your school newspaper or other publications. Hopefully, It will inspire others to write letters of gratitude to someone who has helped them to achieve their dreams. Mrs. Robinson helped me to enjoy a career that I loved, as an elementary teacher for 30 years.

Sincerely,

Donna Schurr Marks

Jan. 1, 2012

Dear Mrs. Robinson,

In 1953 I was a student in your junior English class. I am writing to thank you for bringing attention to a short story that I wrote while in your class, the first story I ever wrote. You had placed magazine pictures on a table, and invited each student to choose one and write a story about it. I chose a picture of a young soldier approaching the counter in the telephone office. My childhood playmate, Jimmy Randolph, three years older than I, had joined the Army and gone away to fight in Korea. We agreed to write to each other when he stopped to say good-bye. I was a freshman when he left. During my sophomore year, he phoned me. It was the first time in my life that anyone had phoned from overseas, an exciting event in the life of a 15-year-old. When I saw the picture on your table, I made a grab for it, happy to have an opportunity to record the romantic phone call in writing. We were both nervous, wondering what to say after a year and a half apart. I tried to be sensitive as I was fearful that my dear friend might not return alive. I changed both of our names when I wrote our conversation, writing as if the story were pure fiction. On the last page you wrote, "My heart is in my throat." I really appreciated that. Even more, I was grateful to you for reading my story to all of your English classes. Friends and strangers told me how much they liked my story that week. That meant a lot to me.

The experience helped me to gain recognition for my brains, a new event in my life. You

may or may not recall that I had won the "Miss Garden Grove" contest in between my freshman and sophomore years. The attention that the contest brought me was a bit

overwhelming and often made me feel uncomfortable. Being whistled at on my high

school campus was embarrassing. You helped me realize that I had other good qualities.

Thank you for shining a light on my academic abilities just when I needed it. Your encouragement helped to motivate me to attend two nearby colleges and earn a degree in elementary teaching.

God Bless You!

Sincerely,

Donna Schurr Marks

Kindergarten

My sister Lesandra, went to Mrs. Cook's first grade, so I followed her. We had always gone everywhere together. When two adults stepped into the classroom and led me out, I almost panicked. For the first five years of my life I had been watched over by my mother, my sister, or both. Even during the year following my father's death, while my mother was in an asylum, my sister was always with me at my Aunt Mary's house. As I was taken out of Mrs. Cook's first grade classroom, all the children were staring at me. Where were they taking me? I was scared. The hallway was dark and long. The double doors were heavy. The hinges made strange noises. The man and lady took me outside. The wind blew up my legs and I had the urge to wet my pants. "I mustn't do that," I thought. "I would get my shoes wet!" My heart was beating fast. I wanted my mother. Across the breezeway we entered another door. The two adults spoke with a young teacher, then left. The teacher told me her name was Miss Moon. She was small and pretty. I liked her. She told everybody that she would soon marry a soldier. That made everyone smile. We imagined them holding their wedding in our kindergarten room.

Each day we were asked to choose an activity. I liked to paint or play with big, smooth wooden blocks. One day I built my Aunt Mildred's farm, where I lived, with blocks. Then I built a freeway beside it. I told a friend that was Garden Grove Freeway. It was the only street name I knew at that time. I felt smart saying it. How do I remember? I don't know, but I do. It is amazing to me now that my block play was so prophetic. Garden Grove Blvd., less than one mile from our farm, was so rural in 1941, that there were more orange groves on either side than houses. Thirty years later it *did* become a freeway, the orange groves gone.

Not all the children in kindergarten knew how to print their name. I could. I painted "D O N" on the left side of a picture I made of my mother. I ran out of room, so I painted "N A" on the right. When it was my turn to talk about my painting, some of the kindergartners laughed at the way I had split my name. Miss Moon told them it was o.k. to do that. I really liked her a lot for taking my side.

On my Aunt Mildred's farm we raised goats. When they had babies, Lesandra and I could not drink their milk, so our mother gave us cow's milk. We did not like the taste, so she made it more palatable by adding sugar and vanilla. While I was in kindergarten she also added pink food coloring and froze the mixture in my thermos. The result was almost as tasty as a strawberry milkshake. The other children who were eating at my table said it looked good and asked if they could taste it. When I poured it into my cup, the icy pink chunks made a noisy splash, and the children listened. One girl offered to trade a cookie for a taste. "No, my mother told me not to trade," I lied. I drank it all myself while they watched. Something my mother had been trying to teach us was coming back to me; Exodus 20 in the Bible, the Commandments. "Thou shalt not covet thy neighbor's house." My sister had asked our mother, "What does covet mean?" She told us, "It means you are not supposed to want something that belongs to someone else." I guess those other kindergartners had mothers who did not make them sweet, icy, pink drinks or teach them the Ten Commandments as my mother did. I felt sorry for them and grateful for my many blessings.

There is one more thing I remember about kindergarten. There was one boy who was real mean. His name was Bobby. He often hit, kicked, and pushed the other children. Nobody liked him, but he didn't seem to care. He was bossy and he talked loud and fast. I was afraid of him. We were all afraid of him.

One day some of the children had to go to the nurse's office to get a shot. I was excused because my mother was a Christian Scientist. Some of the children came back to our room, rubbing their arm and looking unhappy. Others returned smiling and announcing bravely, "It didn't hurt!" We were all startled when we heard a boy loudly bawling all the way down the hall, and Bobby burst into our room, crying his eyes out. We all began giggling. It seemed so funny that the toughest boy in our class was acting like a big baby. After that, no one was afraid of Bobby again. And that is all I remember about kindergarten, seventy years ago.

The Magic carpet

My magic carpet is red, bright red. It measures two feet by three feet, just big enough for one person. Most of the fringe has been worn away by long years of use. When I bought it at a yard sale in Santa Cruz, California, I had no idea how much fun it would be to own. I just thought it was an elegant looking tapestry. I have wanted a magic carpet ever since I was ten, when I watched Sabu fly high above the city of Baghdad in the darkness of the Gem Theater in Garden Grove in 1946. Sabu was not much older than I when he waved goodbye to the crowd below in "The Thief of Baghdad." Without one flying lesson or a tank of gas, he was able to go wherever he wished, merely by whispering a magic word. After seeing the movie, I dreamed of being up there, flying away, with the wind in my hair, going wherever I wished. More than the rollercoaster, the merry-go-round, or the bumpcars at the Long Beach Pike. I yearned to be up there, like Sabu, riding on a magic carpet. I lay in bed for many nights imagining all the places I would visit as I whizzed through the air. That dream was almost forgotten when I spied my red velvet carpet at a yard sale twenty years later. I took it to my second grade classroom and laid it in front of the glamorous throne I had created for King Ferdinand and Queen Isabella to sit on in our drama about Christopher Columbus.

The royal throne was draped with shimmering blue-green brocade, purple velvet, and red tulle enhanced with gold flowers. The little red carpet provided the perfect spot on which Columbus stood as he followed my instructions about the proper way to bow graciously to the king and queen. Later, as I hung the Columbus costumes back in the closet, it occurred to me to convert the small red rug into a magic flying carpet during the week of Halloween. When the children entered the room after lunch on Monday, the magic carpet was waiting on the floor in the middle of the room. I announced, "I will choose someone who is quiet to ride on my magic flying carpet." Everyone was quiet. Everyone wanted to be chosen to go for a ride.

I instructed, "As you can see, I have provided the carpet with the steering wheel and a smaller carpet behind. That is a tandem for your dog or cat. Please wear the metal helmet to protect your head. (These three treasures were also yard sale finds.) You must think of all the magic words you know to make the carpet fly. If I tell you the magic word, it won't be magic anymore. It is not hokus-pokus or abra-cadabra. If you think of the correct word, the carpet will begin to rise slowly. Sit right in the middle so you won't tip. Do not fly higher than the desks. I don't want you to get hurt while you are learning. Do not go near the windows. You might break them. When the clock hand is on the four, I will choose someone else." After choosing a child to sit on the rug, I began to read a Halloween story. All eyes would watch the child on the carpet. The look of concentration on his or her face told us that all the magic words in their memory were being conjured up in an effort to glide free of the earth. After Ten minutes, I thanked that child for their good effort, and chose a new flyer. Halloween is in an ideal time to encourage imagination. Each of us has a magic flying carpet in our mind. It can be of help when dealing with stress. We can learn to close our eyes and visualize flying to a favored destination. We often do that while watching a movie or reading a book.

In one of Freud's letters to his beloved Marti, he included this romantic line, "The magic carpet that brings me to you is torn." As we age, it is important to keep the magic carpet in our mind in good repair. Imagination and creativity help to keep us young and emotionally healthy.

The poet, Louis Driscoll, expressed this idea well in the following poem.

"Hold fast to your dreams.
Within your heart
Keep one still, secret spot
Where dreams may go,
And sheltered so,
May thrive and grow-
Where doubt and fear are not.
Oh, keep a place apart
Within your heart,
For little dreams to go."

Happy New Year!

For fifty-seven years I have welcomed the new year with a very special wooden horn by blowing it at midnight. My first husband, Lloyd Brett, brought it back from France in 1954 and gave it to me after we were married, in 1956. It looks like a miniature green wine bottle with a fancy label. Many years later I bought another similar sounding horn for my husband, David Marks. This one this is a small bird, also made of wood. I treasure both.

During my 30 years as an elementary school teacher, I began each new year with a mock New Year's Party. A large bag of whistles came from a yard sale which I sanitized with alcohol on the preceding day of the party. These were passed to each student with the admonition, "If you use it, you lose it, until we are all ready." Ready meant counting together from ten to one, then shouting, "Happy New Year!" Everyone was then encouraged to hug a friend or shake hands. Next, I played a record of Guy Lombardo's Auld Lang Syne, and the children sang along, reading song sheets which I passed out with the New Year's whistles. The brief celebration was great fun, and gave my students a glimpse of what their parents had done while they stayed home with the baby sitter. After all the whistles and song sheets were collected, we discussed the meaning of New Year's Resolutions, and many of the children vowed to be more friendly, helpful, and kind in the new year.

That was a wonderful way to begin the new

year with my students every January. The rest of the lesson involved the way in which our months and days got their names, a colorful subject and fun to share with children.

After visiting Stonehenge, in England, in 1971, I used a poster of Stonehenge to teach how the sun rose above the "heel rock," outside of the saracens and lintels on June twenty-first, the day of the longest daylight every year and why December twenty-first has the shortest hours of daylight every year. The spiritual priests who were in charge of Stonehenge 5000 years ago gained much power by their ability to predict an eclipse by moving two rocks from hole-to-hole around a large circle of holes outside of Stonehenge.

The children that I taught were always amazed to learn that wishing someone "Happy New Year!" is a very old tradition and that it was not always celebrated on January first. The various ways in which different cultures have measured minutes, hours, days, months, and years is a very interesting study. We can all be grateful to our ancestors who developed the system that helps us plan our schedules today.

A Christmas Memory

The Korean War took place between 1950 in 1953. It was first time Americans saw our boys getting killed on TV in our living rooms. By 1950 most Americans were watching the five o'clock news on twelve inch black-and-white TV. screens. While my sister, Lesandra, and I were in grammar school, we had learned about W.W. II by reading newspapers and Life magazine, and by watching news films in movie theaters. It all seemed to be happening "over there," in faraway countries. Our mother worked at Douglas Aircraft in Long Beach as a riveter all through W.W. II. When the war ended, she was laid off and returned to the only other job she knew, cleaning houses. For five years, the three of us lived on a very tight budget. We didn't even own a car. Our mother rode to work on a bicycle. When the Korean War began, she went back to work at Douglas Aircraft. For the next three years we enjoyed a more comfortable level of prosperity. It was a very special time for the three of us, the culmination of our 15 years of living together as a family. We were so used to being a part of one another's' lives, I don't think that it occurred to any of us that we might soon marry, move away, and drift apart emotionally. We were so used to hearing each other's familiar voices every day, sharing one another's joys and hardships, we more or less assumed that we would live like that forever.

The Korean War blessed my mother with a man sized salary. The second most unique feature of those pivotal years is that all three of us were beginning to date. This was a predictable chain of events for Lesandra and me, no surprise for two girls attending high school, but my sister and I were not used to the idea of our mother dating. We had become very accustomed to our mother as a grieving widow. Few men had entered at our house during our grammar school years. That is why Paul was such a fanciful curiosity to Lesandra and me. Our mother met him at Douglas Aircraft. He smoked a pipe. That introduced a new fragrance into our humble rebuilt garage. Paul was quite handsome, with dark wavy hair and large brown eyes. He was robust, well groomed, well dressed, warm and friendly. Lesandra and I liked him right away, and were thrilled with the idea that our mother might marry again, that we might actually become a normal family, and move into a real house. We sensed that it would be wise to be on our best behavior when Paul came to visit. We smiled from ear-to-ear while he was there and no one complained about anything.

Before Paul came to take out our mother for their second date, my sister and I decided to get involved in this promising situation by helping our mother get ready. Lesandra set her hair in pin curls. When I combed it out, we were both pleased with the results. We had never seen our mother looking more glamorous. I applied mascara, rouge, and lipstick. "Look in the mirror, Mom!" We both encouraged. We felt like Cinderella's fairy godmother, getting her ready for the ball. It was a new experience for all of us, exciting and fun. Hopefully, it might be the beginning of a whole new era in our lives.

Before Paul arrived, we had time to wrap a few Christmas presents. We made a grand mess on our kitchen table with scotch tape, ribbon, boxes, and brightly colored paper. Suddenly, Lesandra yelled, "Here comes Paul!"

Determined to make a good impression on him, we all grabbed at our mess, stuffing the wrappings into the closet, the presents under our tree, and the scraps into the wastebasket. Paul was still getting out of his car when our mother yelled, "I can' fin' my teeff! Help me fin" my teeff!"

"What did you do with them?" Lesandra asked.

"I pud dem on da table while we were wrapping gifts because dey hurt. You girls keep

Paul busy talking while I fin" dem!" she instructed desperately.

The next half-hour was one of the most comical the three of us had ever experienced. While Lesandra and I involved Paul in polite conversation, we avoided one another's eyes, afraid we would explode in laughter and give away our mother's secret. She did not want Paul to know that she wore false teeth. Later, Lesandra and I agreed we were terrific actresses, acting as if nothing was wrong. At last, our mother emerged smiling broadly, her near-perfect teeth gleaming. It was not until she returned that night that Lesandra and I learned where she found her false teeth. In her rush to hide the clutter, she had swept them into the wastebasket, along with the scraps of wrapping paper.

Our mother and Paul only went out a few times together. Eventually we forgot Paul's last name, went on with our lives, the Korean War ended, and other Christmases were very different as each of us married and moved away. But each year, as I sit at my kitchen table and wrap presents, I have to laugh as I remember the time that we looked at our gifts and wondered if one of them was hiding a pair of false teeth. It is a memory that always makes me laugh.

Herb Farmer

Lavender makes me feel young.
Purple buds blooming among
Yellow curry, sages green,
Oregano crowds between.
Yarrow umbels, brilliant gold,
All that my baskets can hold.
Artemisia, mint, and thyme,
Spicy fragrances divine.
I pick each magical stem,
Tie raffia around them
For my friends, afar and near,
Handmade little gifts that cheer.
Dried bouquets are fun to make,
Sunshine, seeds, water and rake.
Gentle dance of rainbow hues,
Reds and purples, greens and blues.
Thirty years I've planted there,
Blessed by herbs
I love to share.

Helen Saulman

Helen Saulman is the real name of Helen
the Felon, an obsolete child who writes true stories
of juvenile misadventures. Most of these felonious
non-fictions happened during the 1960's

Near Death Experience, tick, tick

In the summer before I entered Kindergarten, I had a unique experience. The woods surrounding our summer cabin bloomed with Sierra wild flowers – brodeia, clarksia, mule pareds, sunflower and sneezeweed. Wisps of smoke from a control burn drifted uphill to our mining claim. The combination of pollen and smoke was too much for a child, so I began to have my first life-threatening reaction. My eyes and throat stung. My breath grew raspy.

What could a child do? I sat alone in the cabin while my family ranged out into the woods to prospect for gold ore. I clung to the east window and whispered, "Help me," when the idea hit me.

"Of course, idiot. When those all-all-allergy things attack, Mommy and Daddy give me Benadryl." Sniffing my runny nose and wheezing, I shuffled over to the corner shelf where the medicines were. I took one and a half tablespoons of the syrupy liquid, and began to pass out.

Overdose! The muscles of my throat numbed out and over-relaxed. Unable to swallow my own spit, I hung onto the window sill to breathe, cough and drool. Breathe, cough and drool. The painful lack of oxygen made my ribs and shoulders sore. Lead-like limbs kept me from leaving to seek help.

The clock ticked away every half-second. At less than six years of age, I could still count to twenty-two between breaths. Eleven full seconds before I could breathe again! Count them, another twenty-two ticks of the old clock and another breath was dragged painfully into my lungs. I panicked and lost count, then struggled to cough and clear my throat. It was as if I were a marathon runner who'd just hit the wall. I relaxed and prepared for death. "I'm shot by a bad guy," I guessed, falling back on TV westerns, "I'm a dying cowgirl." I closed my eyes and just "stopped" everything.

Or so I thought. Why was I suddenly outside peering past the manzanita bush toward Daddy and our nearest neighbor? Daddy seemed to feel a sudden breeze as I approached invisibly, because he vigorously rubbed his right arm. Goosebumps. But how could I see them if my ailing body was still leaning on the window sill?

"Daddy!" I shouted without making a sound, "Daddy, I'm in trouble!" I forgot all about the notion of being a dying cowgirl, and just wanted my father's arms around me.

"Come back," I heard from the cabin, yet I knew no one was there. As if startled out of a deep sleep by the source less voice, a mist congealed above the surface of a nearby open well. It retained the loose shape of an animal as it drifted away from Daddy and me.

The voice from the cabin said, "Don't follow it." I ignored the voice to follow the retreating mist.

"Don't follow it – it doesn't know anything."

"Find God for me," I told the mist. It hesitated, and then retreated faster. I lingered near my father.

"Helen Rebecca," an obviously angry patrician male intoned," I was responsible for your mother and now I'm responsible for you. You will obey me." I knew that tone, and rapidly returned to an inert body that was still alive and breathing. When I chanced to look at the reflection in the window glass I was astonished. I saw the form of an anxious blue eyed man with short brown hair who staring at my back. He shifted his focus, and for an electric second our eyes met. He vanished. I'd just seen my mother's father who had been dead since Friday the thirteenth, July 1917.

"It's called Asthma, a male voice said from nowhere.

I saw Mommy outside the cabin on a long dirt trail. She was the center of my heart.

"God," I pleaded," please don't let my Mommy catch this As-As-Asthma thing." What I heard then is very private, but what I felt was joy.

The family made no outward show of sympathy for my condition, probably to keep me from getting hysterical. I was better, but Mommy put me into a nightgown and spoon-fed me tea.

"It's only an upper-respiratory infection," Daddy said. My Mother and Raymond went out to pound gold ore in the mortar and pestle. The noise gave me the opportunity to tell my Daddy where I went and what I saw.

"But you were 100 yards away "He said, "Still, we're Catholic and we don't chase ghosts!"

Dad's word was law, and the subject was

closed. As promised, though, the male voice came back about every six months to tell me encouraging things or to show me a vision. These special visits ended when I was a pre-teen of eleven or so.

I've never had another experience like the near death happening. It enriched my private life while isolating me from everyone who hadn't been similarly "blessed." Thanks to my NDE, I have the courage to go on through life without fear of the last journey.

"Find God for me," I told the mist. It hesitated, and then retreated faster. I lingered near my father.

"Helen Rebecca," an obviously angry patrician male intoned," I was responsible for your mother and now I'm responsible for you. You will obey me." I knew that tone, and rapidly returned to an inert body that was still alive and breathing. When I chanced to look at the reflection in the window glass I was astonished. I saw the form of an anxious blue eyed man with short brown hair who staring at my back. He shifted his focus, and for an electric second our eyes met. He vanished. I'd just seen my mother's father who had been dead since Friday the thirteenth, July 1917.

"It's called Asthma, a male voice said from nowhere.

I saw Mommy outside the cabin on a long dirt trail. She was the center of my heart.

"God," I pleaded," please don't let my Mommy catch this As-As-Asthma thing." What I heard then is very private, but what I felt was joy.

The family made no outward show of

sympathy for my condition, probably to keep me from getting hysterical. I was better, but Mommy put me into a nightgown and spoon-fed me tea.

"It's only an upper-respiratory infection," Daddy said. My Mother and Raymond went out to pound gold ore in the mortar and pestle. The noise gave me the opportunity to tell my Daddy where I went and what I saw.

"But you were 100 yards away "He said, "Still, we're Catholic and we don't chase ghosts!"

Dad's word was law, and the subject was closed. As promised, though, the male voice came back about every six months to tell me encouraging things or to show me a vision. These special visits ended when I was a pre-teen of eleven or so.

I've never had another experience like the near death happening. It enriched my private life while isolating me from everyone who hadn't been similarly "blessed." Thanks to my NDE, I have the courage to go on through life without fear of the last journey.

The Christmas Dilemma

Macy's, Los Angeles, 1962

"Just the kind of thing someone would do," grumbled the old gentleman, "load two kids onto my arthritic knees."

Since this story is true. I admit I wasn't so happy to be on Santa Claus' lap myself. He wore old people's prescription shoes. Maybe he was not the real deal and I was off the hook.

My problem began when my folks loudly discussed our Christmas surprise one gray December afternoon.

"They will be open, Elbert," Mom asserted

"They won't be by the time we get through the uptown traffic," Pop groused. "Blasted city! Mumble, mumble!"

"Oh Elbert- not in front of the children."

Yeah, she never let us hear the good stuff.

"Here's the telephonc book. Call and see if th' muffle-mum-mumble.'

"What's everybody sayin'?" I shouted. Daddy said I should go sit in front of the TV until I was called.

"I need privacy to make a phone call," he said. Pop pulled the cord as he carried the phone into his office and shut the door. I walked into the tiny kitchen.

"Are we goin' somewhere?" I asked Mom and my big brother Raymond He was four and a half and went to kindergarten.in the morning and in the afternoon gave tours of the Little General Nursery and Hardware. He was so in the loop he'd know what Daddy was planning. "So, Raymond what's the big secret?"

"Don't tell 'em I tole you, but we're goin' to see Santie Claus."

I shrieked. "Santie!"

He shushed me. I looked down at my white leather Buster Browns in embarrassment. "Hey" I whispered " who's Santie Claus?"

"He's that Christmas guy. Here, take a look at the front of this card."

I saw a picture of a rosy-cheeked Grandpa type who wore a fuzzy red coat and hat with white trim. Raymond grabbed the card from my dirty little mitts and with an air of self-importance, put it exactly where our Mom had left it:

"If yer good, he'll leave ya presents. This is WA-AY bigger than yer birthday."

"Huh? Why?" I gasped.

"You dummy," he snorted, "'cos Santie Claus asks ya if ya were good all year an' I know that ya weren't! Anyway," he continued, "be sure to say 'yes' or ya won't get a toy 'er nuthin' But if ya lie God hears ya an' ya get hit by lightning."

I edged toward Mom to tattle that I was being threatened.

"If ya tell," he said ""I'll tell Mom and Dad that yer ear was on the door when Dad was on the phone."

In a panic, I ran back into the living room. As I sat by the cold picture-less TV I wondered what was a lightning and what would happen if it hit me.

No good, I was sure. What should I do? I hoped like mad that the Christmas guy was too busy to rat on one little girl.. Yes, I'd be one of those wall flower things that Mom called our big sister. If I were quiet when Santie asked the question, maybe his friend God wouldn't hear me lie.

The ride to uptown LA was tremendously long, maybe forty-five minutes, whatever that meant.. Pop grumped as he looked at his watch and felt for change in his pocket. at the same time, The parking meter was like a steel balloon and ate dimes. But it didn't fly.

Eventually we found the big store , but lucky me, the Christmas Guy was off getting coffee somewhere- I was SAVED! Daddy decided to leave everyone standing outside the open glass doors as he went to talk to the guy call the "manger of the store", or somethin'.

"Maybe he's in charge of delivering hay to the reindeer department" I wondered aloud.

"No, dummy." Raymond laughed, "Dad's going to see the MAN-A-GER. That's the man who runs the store."

Our Mom brought us inside to warm up. We saw a really old boy of about nineteen behind a counter. Mom gabbed to him about this an' that until Dad came out from the secret room in the back, towing a big guy in a red suit. The big guy sat in front of a window with some fake presents. He spread his arms wide and asked if we wanted to talk with Santie.

I didn't.

"Look," my Daddy whispered in my ear. "You wouldn't want your brother scared to be by himself, would, you?"

I decided to be brave and help my brother in his time of need.

"I haven't got all night," the big guy complained. He smiled at me. "Here," he patted a kid-less knee, "you sit here and your brother can sit on the other one." He lowered his voice, Your old Dad is cheap and only wants to buy one photo, so you both have to be in it."

We looked at Dad in amazement. Screw Santie Claus? In later years Dad's miserliness would be well known, but tonight it came as a shock.

The very big man – I don't care what C. Clement Moore wrote, this guy was NO elf- asked Raymond what toy he wanted. "Maybe a nice train set?"

A Lionel," Raymond smugly answered.

I pulled a bit off the so-called Santie Claus' beard. It came off in my fingers! I was startled when he turned his attention to me.

"So, little girl, have you been GOOD ALL YEAR?"

Oh no, THE QUESTION! I could hear my heart or somethin' thump harder in my chest. My breath came faster. I had to cause a diversion: "Hey! Is that the store guy aiming a camera? Ever' body CHEESE!"

Raymond and the erstwhile Santie preened and I stared at the drift of white beard bits around the big guy's orthopedic shoes. I was probably safe.

"Have you been a good girl?'

"Yes," I squeaked. Huh, no lightning. Another Raymond lie One of his stupid stories was to blame for the day I played Superman with a baby blanket tied around my neck. I fell off the table and broke a collar bone that time. At least, I wasn't hurt tonight

"Time to go" Daddy crowed. "Let Santie get warm before his flight back up north."

Sadly, we got off the nice ole' guy's lap. He groaned, rubbed his bent knees and hobbled back into the depths of Macy's. Whoever he rally was, he'd left dozens of soft white bits of fake beard in his wake. I was still a bit confused.

"Why does Santie Claus have to warm up, when he wears those fuzzy clothes and all?"

"Altitude and wind chill." Daddy answered" It's much colder at the top of Town Hall than it is down here."

"Why?" I repeated "Why?"

"Oh, forget it," Pop mumbled around his pipe stem.

The trip back home was long and cold in the heater-less green Chevy truck. The radio guy said there were snow flurries somewhere in Southern California.

"I hope my avocado tree don't freeze," Mom said and wrapped all of us in tan pink and blue blankets

"Where'd ya get these?" I asked sleepily.

"A nice lady up North," Mom answered

Ah! Maybe Mrs. Claus gave us the snowflake printed blankets. I snuggled into the pink and white fleece dreaming that Mrs. Claus herself had tucked me in.

Debbie Croft

Debbie Croft is a columnist and correspondent for a newspaper in California's Central Valley. Her column, Over the Back Fence, features insights about history, happenings and the fascinating people of the Sierra Nevada foothills. From the frog that took a spin in her washing machine and tarantulas traipsing through her house, to hungry gophers, escaped cows and rattlesnakes sunning themselves in the garden, she presents a light-hearted look at how this city girl is ever so slowly adjusting to country life. Visit her blog at: debbiecroft.wordpress.com.

Married to a pastor for over 30 years, she is a chaplain with the local sheriff's department, teaches Bible studies and speaks for ladies groups. At a small private school junior and senior high school students improve their communication skills in her Creative Writing class. Two grown children, a son and daughter, call her Mom.

When finding spare time and extra money in the same month, she and her husband enjoy renovating their older home. Nestled among rose bushes, bearded irises, hydrangeas, and voo-doo lilies, the house sits beside a creek and along a winding country road in a forgotten ghost town of the historic Gold Country. There she enjoys reading, writing, home arts, music, gardening, watching the seasons change, and spending time with family and friends.

Baby Bird Day Care

One spring afternoon my husband and I worked in the yard—both of us on our knees. While pulling weeds Ron heard a *thud* beside him. He looked, and there on the ground was a baby bird. Somehow it had survived the fall. Its nest was two stories above in the rafters. Picking it up, he handed it to me, and very carefully I carried it inside to show our daughter.

She was in awe.

"First we need to find a small box to put it in," I told her.

Finding one, we promptly filled it with dried grass for a makeshift nest. I placed the bird inside.

Back outside Ron found two more babies, but they had not survived.

Emily took them for a quiet burial somewhere in our yard.

An hour later two more birds fell. Because they were still breathing, they too went in the box.

There on our kitchen table the three babies huddled together, breathing hard, shivering, and probably wondering what had happened to their safe, secure little world.

I covered them with a soft towel, put the lid on top of the box, and went back outside. Every once in a while, though, I'd slip back in to see how they were faring.

In my mind a battle took place. *What do we do with baby birds? We can't just let them lie there*

*on the ground to die, can we? But... we don't know
how to care for them What do we feed them? How
do we raise them? And if they actually survive
today's trauma (and our human ineptness with tiny
feathered creatures), what then? Our lives can't be
put on hold to raise these birds.*

I kept musing...

*They're common songbird, I told myself.
Most likely thousands just like them fall to their
deaths every year without our knowledge. They
have no eternal value, and the world will continue
just fine with or without a few baby birds, more or
less.*

Yet, these birds fell literally at our feet. And
because I value life, and try to live by honoring the
Creator of life, I spent the next three days fighting
for their lives.

Between Ron's experience raising pigeons
and my maternal instincts, we came up with a
recipe: mashed banana mixed with water,
administered with eye dropper.

Every thirty minutes those three starving
babies demanded to be fed. All my plans for the
weekend were set aside. But before you think me a
saint, you must know I was only a partially willing
participant in this experiment. There were a whole
lot of other things I would rather do on a gorgeous
spring weekend.

As with human babies, the smaller they are,
the more often they need food. And being so tiny,
these babies required *constant* care. As I continued
with their feedings, I tried to squeeze in a bit of
yard work and meal preparations for the rest of my

family.

According to our calculations, if they made it through the first night, they might be okay. Then we'd have to think seriously about what to do with them on a permanent basis.

The next morning we peeked in the box. The one orphan, whose breathing had been the most irregular, did not survive. But we still had two left!

Time to do some serious research on their diet. With lots of robins in our neighborhood, we looked in books, made some phone calls, and checked online for the nutritional needs of baby robins.

Ugh! I should have known. Earthworms. And *lots* of them—as in two or three earthworms every hour!

They also eat fruit. I know that, not just because I read it, but because we have grape vines. We rarely get any grapes, because every year the birds know exactly when the grapes are ripe. They strip the branches bare before we have a chance to pick them.

Earthworms, though, are the most vital part of their diet, for the protein. And as everyone knows, strong muscles need protein. Without it the birds can't fly. Which is exactly what I was hoping these birds would do before long, so I could go back to living my life.

Because in our neighborhood, besides having an excess number of birds, we also have an excess number of cats. And I wasn't about to scrimp on their diet and end up with crippled birds.

You think I was sacrificing my precious weekend so two weak little birds could hobble around our yard and become cat food? No way! If I was gonna feed these birds, I was gonna do it right.

This meant, of course, I needed to get busy and dig up some worms.

I don't know much about gardening, but I know that in our vegetable and flower beds, there are plenty of earthworms. So that's where I went, armed with my digging tools and a small bucket.

But... before I continue, you must understand: I am not a tomboy. I'm not a farmer. I am not a lumberjack. I do not enjoy getting dirty, nor do I enjoy living with mess, clutter or critters. My mother raised me to be a lady, and I happen to like it that way.

I believe earthworms belong in the ground, under the dirt, and out of sight, doing what God designed them to do. Yes, I appreciate their industry as they tunnel through the soil, helping my herbs and vegetables and flowers grow. But I also believe that's where they should stay. (Unless some mama bird carries one to her babies for breakfast. In that case I'm willing to make a concession.)

Yet, on that particular Saturday morning while my neighbors were still in bed or lounging in their recliners with the newspaper, I was outside on my hands and knees—looking for worms.

Now... I thought there was an over-abundance of bugs above the ground where we live... flying in the air, spinning their webs in every corner of my house, and building their little mud nests under the eaves.

159

I had *no* idea how many creepy, crawly things there are *under* the ground! Literally *millions* of bugs spend their days excavating and constructing subterranean tunnel systems below the surface! I'm talking about bugs I've never seen before. Strange looking creatures! And to think— most human beings live their entire lives completely oblivious to their existence.

But I digress...

After selecting a few choice morsels, I took them inside, and added mashed earthworm to the mashed banana mixture, with just enough water to make it soupy enough to work with the eye dropper.

I felt nauseous, but the birds loved it!

Every half hour I fed them. Religiously. And by the end of the day they seemed to be doing well.

Thankfully, nighttime brought a reprieve from the continuous feedings. When the sun went down we said, "Nighty, night." I covered the box, and breathed a sigh of relief.

The average modern American cannot imagine how much work is involved in caring for those tiny creatures. Their little tummies can only hold so much at one time. And just as quickly as I filled their bodies at the one end, they were just as quickly expelling what they had previously eaten, from the other end.

By this time the whole earthworm thing was getting to me. I decided to mash cooked egg yolk for protein instead.

As soon as the sun peeked above the horizon the following morning, birds started chirping outside. Then there came the sound of chirping from inside. Faintly and hesitantly the two babies sitting in their dark shoe box nest begged for attention.

As soon as I lifted the lid, they immediately looked up and opened their mouths as wide as they could, to let me know they were ready to eat. And the chirping continued.

For being such tiny creatures, those beaks were big! One beak, completely opened, covered half the bird's face. As the eye dropper came near, they opened wide and lifted their long necks, so I could fill them.

These baby birds had come to depend on me, because it was my face they saw peering into their box throughout the day. From that point on, whenever I checked on them, they instinctively opened their mouths, whether it was time to eat or not!

Amazingly, besides the fact that they were still alive, these baby birds were growing. They were stronger than the day we found them, and their downy fluff was disappearing. In just two days' time, tiny feathers starting covering their bodies.

Being that the next day was Monday, I got on the phone, calling every veterinarian and wildlife organization listed in the yellow pages.

"I have these birds. They fell from our roof, and there were three, but one died. We've been feeding them—bananas and worms—the typical diet of birds, I think... but we can*not* keep them..." I said to anyone willing to listen.

"Sorry, ma'am. We don't take songbirds. Try Fish and Game or..."

Nobody wanted the birds. Including me.

Finally I found a place in the valley.

"Well, we don't normally take in birds," a female voice explained on the other end.

But I insisted. I copied the address, put the box in the car and took off.

Shortly after arriving at the wildlife care center, I found a caretaker. Repeating my story once more, *and* insisting I was in no position to raise them, I could see her resolve beginning to weaken.

Then she opened the box.

"Oh, they're starlings!" she exclaimed. "Starlings will eat anything!"

The Sacred Calling of Motherhood or Love for the Long Haul

(Advice to a mom-to-be)

This journey of Motherhood you're about to embark on will be filled with unexpected surprises and strange emotions, daily struggles and challenges, continual thrills and delights, joys and sorrows, repetition and monotony, plus a myriad of other things you've never before experienced.

As a mom your patience will be tested, your character refined. Your faith will be tried in ways you never thought possible. But through it all, if you ask, the Lord will show you how to love like He does. Even with our human feebleness and frailties, remember the goal of parenting is: making the relationship we have with our children a reflection of the relationship God has with His children.

All of humanity and all of history is based on the family. Civilizations do not survive without the family. Family relationships were designed, fashioned and instituted by God within the first week of Creation—since the beginning of time.

When your dad walked his girl down the aisle and presented you, the beautiful bride, to a very nervous and adoring groom, it was a picture of God's presentation of Eve to Adam. (I imagine it as the high point of Adam's life, after having only animals to hang out with...) Adam and Eve... you and your husband... two unique human beings, made in God's image, especially for each other.

The reason we're here today is to celebrate the sacredness and the wonder of this miracle of life. All the little pieces and parts of the tiny baby growing inside you are seen and known by God (Psalm 139). But the reason I'm telling you these amazing truths is because, one of these days motherhood won't feel so sacred, and your baby won't seem miraculous. Instead, you will feel like you're drowning in messy diapers, crusty dishes, snotty noses, dirty laundry, and over-stretched budget woes. As a mom you'll be over-worked, underpaid and on call 24/7. Did I mention overwhelmed and feeling totally and completely inadequate and unprepared for the task? But when you're feeling at your lowest, that's the time to remember the miracle of life and blessedness of family.

Your mother is a wonderful example of a devoted wife and mom. She's a pattern you can follow with confidence. And she's only a phone call away!

Today we shower you with baby gifts to welcome this newest member of your family: little diapers, tiny onesies, even tinier booties, adorable outfits, the softest blankets, lotions and powders and oils and gels, and lots of other necessary items.

At my first baby shower almost 28 years ago, I very carefully opened each gift, folding and saving the wrapping paper to line my baby's dresser drawers with. Each time I opened a drawer I remembered the wonder of knowing, I would soon be a mom.

As you open your baby gifts, to take them home with you and prepare the nursery (or a corner of your bedroom) to welcome your new little one, spend some time reflecting on what God is doing and how He's working... This time of pregnancy and motherhood is not only sacred, but precious. Once children start coming and life gets swarmed with responsibilities and demands, there won't be much time for quiet reflection (like none actually). Which is why now is the time to allow yourself the luxury of making memories. Enjoy every simple preparation that's part of becoming a new mom.

If you haven't started already, keep a journal... Write about God's blessings in this new adventure, write about your feelings, your concerns, your hopes and dreams, and all the ways He's answering your prayers.

Remember the vows you made: for better, for worse, for richer, for poorer, in sickness and in health,
(and when the baby won't stop crying at 2:00 in the morning)...

And remember God's goodness when the problems pile up. Psalm 106 tells us, God was disappointed when Israel forgot about the miracles and wonders He performed on their behalf. It's the same with us... God's fingerprints are everywhere—all we need to do is look for them—and remember to praise Him.

As you demonstrate your love for your new baby—by feeding, and burping, and wiping, and cleaning, and cuddling—remember how God cares for us. Someday you'll be bandaging skinned knees and drying tears; And through the years you'll be instructing and disciplining and correcting and advising, just as God does with you and me.

God tells us whatever we do should be done for His glory (I Cor. 10:31). Day after day, week after week, year after year, every task done, every word spoken, every prayer whispered, from a heart full of love and based on the foundation of God's truths, will be rewarded by your heavenly Father.

Unexpected Rendezvous

It wasn't yet eight o'clock in the morning when the phone rang. In the middle of a project enjoying the quiet, the interruption annoyed me. I ignored it. But after several rings, decided to pick up.

My husband's voice greeted me at the other end. Hesitantly he admitted to having forgotten his keys and watch. He asked if I would bring them. But his workplace is half an hour away, and I had things to do.

I stood holding the phone, not wanting to answer.

After the silence stretched on, he begged, "I'll meet you half-way."

"I'm still in my bathrobe," I said, a feeble attempt to find any justifiable excuse to stay home.

"Just come," he said. "You'll be driving in the middle of nowhere, and no one will see you."

And that's just the time the car would die or there'd be a flat tire.

No way would I leave the house in my pajamas.

He sounded desperate. "I've got to have those keys for the cabinets, and if I come all the way home, it'll be an hour's trip," he said, still trying to persuade me of the inevitable.

I knew other people would start showing up who needed access to his cabinets. I also knew this wasn't the first time he'd forgotten his keys.

"You really need to have duplicates made," I insisted.

Still, as it couldn't be avoided, I agreed to meet him.

"Just drive and we'll meet in the middle," he said. "Can you leave now?"

"Yes—after I change into sweats. I'll see you soon."

A few minutes later, with my husband's required items in hand, I drove off through our sleepy town. The frosty winter morning dawned crisp. Once I got going I didn't mind the drive.

It's taken a while, but I think I'm finally learning to be flexible when disruptions come.

Keeping the speedometer close to where it should be, I wasted no time and enjoyed the passing scenery. After turning on the old toll road I knew it wouldn't be long till I'd see his car. A few minutes later I began watching, wondering where the "half-way" point might be.

While navigating the uphill and downhill turns, I spotted him and found a place to pull over. He slowed and turned around to pull up behind me. I stepped out of the car and walked over as he rolled down the window.

Handing him the keys and watch, I joked, "Well, dear, another cheap date!"

With a smile he thanked me and said something about having duplicates made, so this wouldn't happen again. Then he leaned forward and pressed his lips against mine.

"I just wanted a second kiss this morning."

As he drove away I stood beside the road, lingering beneath the brilliant expanse of blue sky. Our unexpected early morning rendezvous happened to take place near the top of one of the many oak-covered hills overlooking a beautiful Sierra Nevada foothills canyon. I breathed in deeply, longing to take an impromptu hike. But with our young daughter still sleeping soundly at home, I needed to get back.

Fifteen minutes later I pulled into our driveway. I couldn't help but smile as I unlocked the front door and entered the quietness. Then I whispered a prayer of thanks, realizing the unwanted interruption had become a memory I'll always cherish

George A. Tuthill

The first of my two stories is about several traumatic moves of my belongings from Ohio to Mariposa. The second is the story of tragedy in the birth of a lamb and my coping with its mother. I thought these two cautionary tales would inform and entertain.

I am a retired Aerospace Engineer who worked for The Boeing Co. in the field in Montana on the Minuteman project and North America/Rockwell International on the Apollo project and the B1 bomber. I completed my aerospace time with the Shuttle at VAFB for Lockheed and in Ohio for the FAA.

Interspersed with Aerospace was work as a Patent Examiner, a Dow Chemical Co. engineer, a Construction Manager in Palm Springs and Hollywood.

I completed my active life when I directed the demolition of a steel building in Long Beach and the re-erection of it here in Mariposa

The desperate political; and economic situation in the US prompted me to write a novel called "The 120." This novel required that I learn how to write. To learn how to write requires that you do a lot of reading and a lot of writing.

Adventures in Moving

Our move back to Mariposa from our twelve year-long residence in Wellington, Ohio had to be accomplished in several phases because of my inability to give up the mass collection of books, antique furnishings, tools and god only knows what else.

Our first haul was made using the services of a *drive-away* company who loaned us a G-20 Chevy van provided we eventually delivered it in Los Vegas for them.

I picked up the van from the Agency. My first mistake was in not having the agent thoroughly inspect the van with me. When I opened the drivers' side door to get in I noticed that it was very stiff but I just forced it a little and drove off. Back at home we started loading it up and I realized that all of the doors stuck badly. After more than an hour of applying DW-40 to the hinges and locks I was able to use them if I employed considerable force and more DW-40. When I tried to open the short hood to check water and oil I couldn't find the inside latch lever. Later I felt like a damn fool when I asked a lady in a market lot who had the same van if she knew how to open her hood. At first she said yes and then when she tried to show me she really didn't know! Finally in looking under the dash of her van I realized that it was centrally located and so she and I both found out. Mine was also in the same location but it also required lubrication. This problem is peculiar to Ohio where heavy rains and humidity are hard on automobiles.

The van had apparently been in storage for a long time. I noticed that the longer I drove it the better it ran. One thing never improved, the right rear brake gave me problems the whole way, especially the hills on Hwy 49 as we came toward Mariposa from the North. But we pressed on.

We had left late from Ohio so after unloading the van on Ashworth Rd. we pressed on for our delivery of the Van in Las Vegas. It was evening and dark when we entered Vegas and to say the least we were beat when we finally found the new owner. They were a young couple who had got the van from their uncle back in Ohio.

I told them about the sticking brake and then had the man take me to a service station where to his delight I filled it up with gas and oil and paid the bill.

He was more than happy to drop me off at a hotel from which we expected to leave by bus to Santa Barbara in the morning. For the first time in history, I expect, there was not a single room available in the whole town!

"Well I guess we will have to take the bus tonight I said," unenthusiastically.

At the Bus Depot came the start of our worst mistake. The last bus had just left a half hour before; so for the next seven hours, until six thirty in the morning we tried to sleep in the lobby with a very strange assortment of passengers. We really felt bad when we finally got on the bus we slept like logs all the way to LA and then to Santa Barbara where we were met by my Brother and his

173

wife.

After a great visit my brother gave me one of his three Cadillac's and we headed back to Ohio. The check engine service light came on shortly after we got under way but I could see no problem except for the stress it caused.

I later found that it was a burned out oxygen sensor and replaced it myself.

For our second move we rented a Dodge van and removed the seats so that we could haul a load.

Our first heavy truck adventure was in May of 1998 using a 21 ft. Ryder moving van. The truck was a Ford with a gasoline engine and only 2100 miles on the odometer. We drove out in the summer on hwy. 80 and made it to Lincoln, Nebraska before the transmission lost its seal and we had to spend three days getting it fixed. After unloading the truck in Mariposa we took the train back to Wellington

Our next trip to Mariposa was in the fall of 1998. I had retired from my job at the FAA in Oberlin, Ohio and though unable yet to sell our house in Wellington we decided to finish construction on our living quarters in Mariposa and hope for an improving housing market. I was driving a heavily loaded Chevrolet van that we bought in Ohio. Fearing weather reports of snow on Hwy. 80 we detoured south on Hwy. 15 at Salt Lake City. Bad move, the storm missed 80 and joined us on 15. After some hair-raising adventures we eventually made it to Mariposa. We spent the winter and part of the summer in construction and then returned to Ohio by plane in August of 1999.

Sharon finally sold our house by "creative financing' and cutting the price of course. Sharon was ready to go back to Mariposa, Calif., I was not. That fall I had experienced a disability in my right knee which put me on crutches. With a steroid shot, *Viox* and other pain killers which had no effect, and physical therapy which did I was a staggering wreck. I wanted to look for a better buyer in the spring but Sharon would not be detoured she wanted to move, period. So on January 23 of 2000 Sharon and I prepared to leave Wellington, Ohio, in a snow storm, driving a 24 ft. Ryder Maxi Moving van. Sharon, her daughter's husband and others would take two days to jam the truck full. RYDER was desperate to return this diesel truck just in from Florida to warmer climes such as California, so they had made Sharon what appeared to be a good deal. When I arrived at the Ryder dealership the temperature was below zero so the hard starting diesel truck was running out front. On the way from the dealer to our house I found the truck to be a real bear to drive. In the two days it took to load the truck I assumed a fatalistic attitude. I knew that Sharon would not be dissuaded from what I believed was a trip we may not survive. On the day we left the temperature was down around zero and I could not start the truck. Using Ryder's emergency number I had it jump started. The old man who answered my call gave me a few pointers. He showed me how to get to the battery-tray which held three huge batteries and pulled out. With his jumpers in place he got behind the wheel and went over the starting sequence.

175

"George, when the glow plug light comes on push the starter button down and keep it down, even after you think it has started."

He then turned the engine over while I watched the starter continue to be engaged until I was sure that it would be destroyed. Finally he let off on the button.

"I know what you are thinking but if you don't follow this procedure she will never start and even if you do it may not start in this cold weather. I have three other big batteries giving you a jump, good luck, you will need it. "We started out late in the day with a light snow falling. Empty the truck was ungainly; heavily loaded the truck was downright scary. Getting on the Hwy. 40/70 freeway was difficult and required hunting for the entrance on slippery narrow country roads. I got lost and had to turn-around, a maneuver which scared Sharon badly for the first of many times. Finally I found the freeway entrance ramp and pulled on into heavy slow moving traffic. My knee was killing me and the truck was jumping like a bucking bronco down the increasingly slippery Hwy. To ease the tension I started chewing tooth picks. I would have smoked but I was rationing my small quantity of cigars. The snow got even heavier when we reached Columbus. By the time we approached Springfield, Ohio, highway 40/70 was covered with wrecks. Sharon saw a particularly tragic scene. I was keeping my eyes strictly on the road. A truck had struck a car and the police were in the process of removing the bodies. My memory of the incident was of a highway littered with the wreckage of many vehicles and many trucks in the ditches. Sharon was warning me of hazards she could see while my eyes were focused straight ahead on the slippery roadway.

Later in the Motel room Sharon described the scene which explained her expressions of despair at the time. "I saw a wrecked compact car on our right. It had been smashed by a large truck which was parked off the road in front of it. The truck driver was crouched down by the side of the car he had hit. Projecting through the rear window were the heads of two dead children. Their mother's body was in the driver seat and her arm was jammed limply through the broken window of the ajar car door. Snow flurries blew the arm back and forth.

"George," said Sharon, "It was as though she was beckoning us to join her in death." After this we wanted only one thing, to get off the highway and into a Motel for the night! After creeping along for many miles past many more wrecks to the next exit we found it blocked by an enormous wreckage pile up being cleared by the highway patrol. So on we went, hoping to get to the next exit and hoping it was clear. Finally at Springfield, Ohio we found a clear exit and crept off it and into a Motel parking lot. I parked behind a moving van entitled something like "Poverty Stricken College Students Moving Co." The truck, also a diesel, was running in the cold and snow, I guess because he was afraid it wouldn't start if he turned it off! I pulled in behind him and thought a while before I turned off my truck's diesel engine. Our room was next to the two trucks and Sharon and I could hear the student's truck running.

Sleeping fitfully I more than once thought I should I have turned off my engine. Twelve hours later I followed the old man's truck starting instructions and, thank God, it started! As we continued the trip we noted that the Student's moving van was still there and still running!

The roads were still very icy and a light snow was falling as we left Springfield. Ice and light snow followed us on hwy. 40 to Villa Ridge, Mo. where we spent the night and worried over the weather reports, all bad. My right leg and arthritic knee had been killing me since the start of the trip and the leg was swollen hugely. With ice packs and rubbing Sharon brought me back to life. We knew we were in Oklahoma when our bucking bronco truck combined with heavily pot-holed roads shook us out of our seats. Having to pay a toll for the use these terrible roads really angered me. Will Rogers must be spinning in his grave as these poorly maintained toll roads are named after him. Along with my painfully and swollen leg the tension and rough ride had given me a terribly painful neck which Sharon rubbed as I drove along chewing my tooth picks. I am getting a sore neck just writing this story. We arrived just east of Tulsa at quitting time so we had to drive out of our way to stay in Claremore, Ok. Will Rogers home town, what a dump.

The next morning back on Hwy 40 we paused for fuel at a "Flying J" truck stop. On the whole trip stopping for fuel was always a problem. We had to use truck stops because they had diesel and enough height clearance at the pumps for the tall truck. Maneuvering the big rig around other big

178

rigs and backing up was hairy.

We reached a sleety, windy Flagstaff, Az. in the evening of January 26. My leg was now twice its normal size and the pain was continuous. We pulled very slowly into our Motel parking lot just off Hwy 40 which was coated with ice. Facing into a cold wind Sharon helped her crippled husband slip and slide to their room and then put ice packs on his terribly swollen right leg. As Sharon rubbed my leg and neck she expressed her worry that I might be contracting a blood clot. Tossing and turning with my huge leg gave me very little sleep. Though the night brought more sleet and the morning was brisk, the highway was passable. After breakfast I tiptoed across the icy parking lot and went through the truck starting procedure and again it worked! When we left Prescott the icy roads and storms always stayed a day behind us. From then on it was all down-hill to the Mojave Desert. There the sun was out and the weather was almost balmy so, at a crossroads, I pulled the truck over and we walked up a little hill to a diner for lunch and a rest. After a pleasant lunch we sauntered back to the truck. All the tension seemed to leave me and thoughts of maybe surviving this trip entered my mind. I got into the truck and pushed the start button of what to me was now my "big rig diesel." As the truck started a tremendous explosion enveloped the truck on Sharon's passenger side!

"Are you all right," I croaked.

"I guess so," she said in a shocked tone.

Strangely relaxed we got out and *calmly*

checked everything. I could find nothing wrong and the truck engine was running smoothly.

"What are we going to do", groaned Sharon.

"Hell, get in, let's go for it," I said.

And go for it we did, mile after mile filled with tension and wonder.

At Barstow, Calif. We stopped at "*Denny's*" for coffee and when we came out to the parking lot I noticed liquid dripping on the ground below the fuel tanks. The liquid turned out to be battery acid leaking from the adjacent battery box. Having seen the old guy jumper the truck I knew how to slide out the box. The outside battery, one of three, had exploded in the Mojave!

Sharon asked a friendly truck driver for help. He looked it over and said, "Since you have come this far I would just go on," and so we did! He also said that the front and rear tires on the truck were mismatched which explained the bucking bronco ride.

From Barstow we drove to Fresno, had coffee, and in even more pain we encountered a foggy night all the way to Mariposa, Calif. At about midnight with the truck roaring loudly we drove down Ashworth Rd. and then through the open gate and up to our big steel buildings front door. Looking down from my high perch in the truck cab I saw our faithful caretaker Dirk Ellis who had heard all the noise and had run up from his trailer. He was at the front door shaking his head in disbelief.

"You guys are crazy."

I turned off the engine. In the sudden quiet I sat dazed; I was still alive, how about that? Sharon and I staggered out of the truck and made our way inside the building while Dirk barraged us with questions. I don't remember what Sharon told him I was on my way to our Queen sized bed where I slept the sleep of the dead.

The next morning dawned beautiful and warm. Sharon sent me to the Doctor in Mariposa while she and others unloaded the truck. The Doctor couldn't find any evidence of a clot and the leg swelling went down. When I returned to our home on Ashworth I got the bad news that the contents of the truck were heavily damaged.

The following day, Jan. 29 we turned in the truck at Merced. I guess the battery that blew had been bad all along and that's why it was so hard to start the truck in Ohio. After driving the diesel that long a distance my confidence level was so high that I literally screamed around the streets of Merced to the Ryder agent and then back into town to fill the fuel tank! After filling the tank and handing over the keys to Ryder I finally knew that the nightmare was over.

Ryder didn't get away completely for damages when Sharon collected insurance payments from them on her broken furniture

A Lamb's Life

January 14, 2013, eight in the morning was the third of a series of freezing nights. My wife Sharon said that it was the coldest winter we had seen in Mariposa. I told her several times that week that 2007 was even colder but she continued with her refrain again and again. I was feeling sorry for myself about a required trip to see my eye surgeon in Fresno.

Before we left I had to let my sheep out of their pen and into their pasture. As I slipped and slid down the steep and slippery hill with my artificial right knee and my bad left knee I remembered in my youth when I could run down a mountain like a goat. I was brought back to my pathetic present when I heard a familiar but now rare sound, the bleating of a new born lamb. My flock of twelve was down to three sheep and thought that my new Ram *Balls* was sterile. Since the death of my old Ram, *Rambo*, no lambs had been born.

I started my flock with the purchase of three sheep from John Boldroff, my neighbor, across the road; one Ram and two ewes. During the past six years the flock had topped out at twelve. One year I had sold six lambs and during a three year period, before I built a shed and an impenetrable fence, I had lost five sheep to mountain lions. My worst time was when a pack of dogs ran my prize Ewe; I called *Black Beauty,* to death and maimed *Rambo*. With his back leg damaged Rambo stopped butting me and it also interfered with his service of the ewes.

The bleating of the lamb brightened my spirits even though I knew Sharon was set on my getting rid of the flock which tied us down to the property. Every morning and evening they had to be let in and out of their enclosure to prevent attacks by an all too present mountain lion. Every night we had a predator visitor and a huge mountain ran by Sharon within arms-length.

I walked down to the pen and unlatched the top and bottom locks of the ten foot high gate. *Balls* and the still sterile ewe rushed by me while the new mother held back, protective of her offspring. Both she and the new lamb seemed to be in good health as they followed the other two sheep through the gate. The thought came to me that I should lock them up for the day because of the intense cold. The lamb turned away from its mother and came up to me. This was a very rare occurrence; until they had been tamed they avoided a human's touch. I bent down and stroked its tiny head.

I could have easily picked it up and taken the lamb and its mother back into the shed and laid it down in a bed of old wool fleeces. Foolishly I hardened my heart. Even under the worst weather, I had never lost a lamb when I had let it follow its mother out into their dangerous rocky pasture. I had carried many a lamb back to the shed after it had been born out in rock piles and gotten stuck but I had never lost one. I wasn't really in a hurry to make the trip to Fresno; another of my despised chores of getting old. Normally I would have had time to watch out for the lamb but I was off to

Fresno.

With two bad legs and a sore back, the drive to Fresno and the 2:30PM appointment which didn't start until 3:30, the return to Mariposa wasn't until almost 5:00. The first thing I did was rush down to the sheep shed. Ominously the mother was not waiting outside with her companions; she came alone from inside the enclosure. She started to call out and run around in a panic. To speed-up the process I placed grain in the feeder which they attacked in a rush while I unsuccessfully searched for the lamb. I locked the three in while I searched outside listening for the lamb's characteristic bleat. The cold air remained unearthly quiet. Usually a lamb bleats continuously when he is seeking his mother and in the enclosure its mother was calling out for her lamb and running around the inside perimeter.

Then, Sharon found me in the pasture.

"I came down when you took so long to come back to the House. George you have to let the mother out to find the lamb."

I agree but we might lose both of them; and the mountain lion is probably already waiting now that it's dark."

We let her out and she started scouring the immediate area screaming bloody murder. I had never seen such a display of motherly love. For some reason she went around the perimeter of the outside of the enclosure again and again ending always back on a rock pile? I went on top of the rock pile and looked around; I could see nothing.

"Let's take the truck around the property's

184

perimeter fence; maybe we can see something," I said.

I locked the mother back in the enclosure. We drove around on all the property roads; later in the evening we tried again and I also walked down and looked to see if the lamb had come up to the enclosure; no luck.

"Relax George we will get up early in the morning and walk the property. I think the lamb is dead."

All evening and early morning when I let the sheep out, and watched the distraught mother run up to the pile of rock and return to me and I walked the area alone while the mystery deepened. Why the complete silence? I went back to the house where Sharon agreed that we walk the property when it warmed up. At 11:00AM I told Sharon per her request that I would take her into town after I took one more look around without her. Down at the sheep shed the distraught mother was still screaming and running up to the pile of rock. Was I missing something maybe a look in the rock? On top of the rock I looked down into a cozy nest and there was the lamb lying stretched out perfect and untouched. The lamb showed all the signs of having died before I came home from Fresno and the mother's strange behavior was no longer a mystery to me. I gently lifted the little cold body, carried it into the sheep shed and set it down on a pile of old sheep fleeces. When I walked out of the enclosure the mother had quieted and looked at me quizzically; then she turned away and ran up the steep rocky ridge to join the flock at the front of the property. What did it mean? Why had my finding her lamb and putting it in the shed stopped her insane search? Was she doing it so that I could have closure? Apparently it gave her closure as she joined the other sheep. Even when I put them into the pen in the evening she was with them as though nothing had happened?

Motherhood is not for us mere men to understand.

Juliana Hill Howard

Following study at The Goodman Theatre in Chicago, I graduated from the University of Iowa.. My compass pointed West, where I have found my "sense of place." The preservation of wild rivers, wild critters and Redwood trees has been my passion for many years.

These stories are simply bits and pieces from my life. I hope something in one of them will strike a note of recognition or remembrance for the reader.

Building or Planning?

About ten years ago we decided to inquire about the feasibility of building an additional dwelling on our fifteen acres. My partner, Susan, decided to go to the Planning Department for the county to inquire about zoning regulations and learn what we could or could not do on this land. Before the new county complex was built, Planning and Building shared the same structure. The sidewalk split out in front of the building and one went to the right to the door for Planning and the other went to the left to the Building Department door. This building was a ranch style design with a front porch across the front. There were two doors on the front porch; one for each department. Across the front of the porch was a fence about three feet high, which also extended up the middle of the porch between the two doors. In other words, if you got into the Planning office and wanted to go to the Building office you had to go outside, step down off the porch, walk to the other sidewalk and follow it to the stairs which led to the Building office door. Inside the building had been split in half and a wall of sheet rock installed to separate the two offices.

Susan arrived at the Planning Department and explained to them what she wanted to do and asked for information on the codes and rules that apply to our property. The woman in Planning, behind the tall counter explained that the information she desired was available at the Building Department, not Planning. She told Susan to go to the Building office on the other side of the building.

Out the door and down the stairs and along the wall she traipsed. Then up the other walk, climbed the three stairs on that side and opened the door to the Building Office. She stepped in and approached the counter, which was identical to the counter in the office she had just left. There was no one in sight. Finally she spied the bell to ring if you for service. She pushed down on the bell. At the sound of the bell, a door opened midway down the common wall and in walked an employee. She stepped to the counter and asked Susan if she could help her.

Needless to say, Susan was speechless. Of course, it was the same woman she had spoken to a few minutes earlier in the Planning Department who had sent her to Building. In shock and amazement, Susan once again explained why she was there. The woman went to some drawers, pulled out a copy of the county codes, presented them to Susan & told her this would answer all her questions.

Susan left in total disbelief. A major "Only in Mariposa" moment.

Down The Rivers, Oh Down The Rivers

The impact of the raft bouncing against the rocks threw me into the water and the beginning of the worst rapid on the South Fork of the American River. Its' name is Troublemaker. I could see the rocks below and the swirling souse hole just beyond the big drop. It could grab me, hold me and take me under forever. If the whirlpool caught me, I would have to find enough reserve strength to push out of its' hold, into the eddy beyond the rapids below. The water temperature was in the 50's, which is way too cold for the human body to survive for more than a very short time, perhaps fifteen minutes at best.

Larry (my former husband) and I got the "bug" for running rivers in the early 1970's. The only people out there at that time were commercial rafters and they stuck primarily to the really big waters of The Grand Canyon, Yampa, Middle Fork of the Salmon and one outfitter on the Rogue River in Oregon. We first met Vladamir Kovalik at the Sportsmen's Show at the Cow Palace in San Francisco in February of 1972. This meeting changed our lives forever. He had been an engineer and scientist at Stanford University and also worked for the Department of Defense, designing classified water craft for secret missions. The boats he designed became the top of the line craft for river runners. Initially he designed boats for Campways; the Havasu, eighteen and a half feet in length, with 23 inch tubes, for the mighty waters of the Grand Canyon and the Miwok, fourteen feet, with 17 inch tubes for rivers such as the Tuolumne and Rogue, with a little less volume. As the word got out, Avon Boats contacted him and he designed their Adventurer for commercial rafting trips which set the standard for all other craft.

Today at the age of 86 he is designing self-baling boats for Sobek and Avon.

Obviously, after conversing with this charismatic, knowledgeable man we decided that not only did we want to run rivers, but we wanted to travel in a raft designed by this expert. Kovalik invited us to meet him in Angel's Camp the following Saturday, where he had a base camp for his rafting company, Wilderness World. Larry and I already had a good deal of water experience from running municipal swimming pools and teaching life saving and water safety instructor courses, canoeing classes and trips of our own on lakes and rivers in northern Wisconsin and the Quetico/Boundary Waters in Canada. However, Class IV & V Rivers were not in our inventory of competency. We would gather the necessary books to learn about this sport and the equipment we should have and then explore rivers in the West starting with Class II & III. Although our children were still quite young, they swam like fish. Ulaine was ten, Sabra was eight and Brent was almost

seven when we began running rivers. Swimming in a pool or lake is a very different thing from knowing what to do in cold, swift moving white water. We headed home to begin our boat, river, and skill research.

Monday morning found me at the local

library. No internet access in those days. After an hour with the card catalogue, I approached the reference librarian.

"I am trying to find books on running wild rivers," I explained to her.

"Wild what?" She exclaimed to me. "I have no idea what subject you are inquiring about or what you mean."

"Do you have any guides to rafting California Rivers?"

The only thing she could come up with was the accounting of John Wesley Powell's legendary trip down the Colorado River. Well, that voyage took place in May of 1869, under arduous conditions, with home made equipment. It is a wonderful piece of exploration and history, but would not help with my quest. I finally bit the bullet and went to the local B. Dalton Bookstore. That was the only bookstore out there in the early 70's, in the Central Valley of California. The clerk began his search at the store. It came up with nothing. He told me he would do an advanced search and make some phone calls that evening and get back to me tomorrow. I headed back across the Mall parking lot to my old VW and headed home feeling disappointed, frustrated and puzzled. If people were doing this sport, there had to be information out there about it.

"Julie?", the voice on the phone asked at ten the next morning. "I have some good news for you." I learned that Kovalik had written a book and Bill McGinnis had the definitive guide book and Jim Cassady & Fryar Cahoun had several books out there.

I excitedly exclaimed to the bookseller: "Order them all!"

Saturday proved to be a sunny, warm day for the middle of the winter. We packed the VW Bus with lunch, kids, sweaters and my list of questions for Kovalik. After several trials and wrong turns, we did arrive at his camp to the north and west of Angel's Camp. He used this camp for his guides for the Stanislaus and Tuolumne Rivers. There was a

house for respite, as well as an enormous barn in which to store river equipment. At the

close of each year's rafting season, he sold all his rafts at half price or less. He explained that he only ran trips with brand new rafts for liability reasons, even though the craft would last for many years. As we walked and he talked, we began to learn about types of rafts and their uses and rowing frames and why we wanted ten foot oars and how convenient a 156 qt. icc chest was for a rowing seat. He told us we should only use the old May West type of PDF or life jacket. "You must have the roll around the neck to support the head in case the person has a head injury and it is the only vest that will give that protection. The head needs to float if the person is unconscious." We eventually bought the Havasu Raft because of its stability, forgiveness, eight separate air chambers and ability to carry lots of people and their stuff for extended trips. The Colorado was not on our immediate list, but we did plan to raft for a week or so at a time which would include the Rogue, Klamath, Salmon,

Yampa, John Day & Grand Ronde. Some of these we would not attempt until we were sure of our skill level and after reading guide books for the particular river. A Miwok, a smaller boat, would offer the opportunity for both smaller rivers and big water, but it did not have the same track record and the 23 inch tubes of the Havasu. Kovalik & his guides cooked dinner for us and then we loaded into the VW Bus a Havasu, giant Carlton foot pump, 156 qt. cooler, and 8 life jackets. Strapped to the top of the Bus was the rigid one piece rowing frame and three 10 ft. ash oars. Although Kovalik had already designed the break-down rowing frame that you could pack inside, it was too expensive for us to purchase at that time. Down the road, we lined up to get one and simplify our life. I drove and Larry had his long arms out the passenger window going down hills to be sure the oars stayed tight to the roof.

Arriving home after dark, we were still so full of excitement and anticipation for this new adventure that we rigged lights in the backyard and took the raft out to an open area on the grass. The pump was set up and we began to inflate the craft. This was not a 5 minute operation. It had 8 separate air chambers and each took about 15 minutes to fill with an adult pumping. But, finally the boat was up and we were all in it and sitting on the tubes. My son Brent, was on the front thwart watching for imaginary rocks heading down the Grand Canyon. The girls went inside to get pillows and sleeping bags to spend the night in the back yard in the new Havasu. It was the night before the beginning of the most exciting and adventuresome years our family shared.

In the weeks to come, Larry & I read every guide book we could get our hands on. We learned about eddies and souse holes and pool and drop rivers. We figured out cfs or cubic feet per second. This gives you an idea of how fast the river is running and how high the volume of water is at any given hour. This is vital information you must have if running a river with rapids of more than a Class III. Rivers are classified on a system of I-V. If it rates more than a V, it should not be run by anyone but a very fool-hardy expert with some kind of death wish. There are a few rapids on the Colorado & the Middle Fork of the Salmon with Class V designations, but very few other rivers in this country have rapids over that rating. We would start with Class II & III Rivers such as the Stanislaus and the South Fork of the American. With experience we would move on to the Tuolumne, the Klamath and the Rogue. River permits were not yet required for river travel by private party boaters. That would come some years later.

We began our river adventures at the same time as our environmental friends were trying to prevent a new giant dam on the Stanislaus River, called New Melones. We had worked to defeat Proposition 17 with a campaign to "Deliver the River", but the petition had failed and the dam was going ahead. After two trips on the lower section of the Stanislaus River which is Class I & II, it was time to move up. Larry had completed a guide school and we were all accustomed to traveling on the water in the raft, holding on, picking up our feet and using the cut off bleach bottles to bail out the excess water in the bottom after passing through a bouncy rapid. We would move up to a Class III & IV section of the same river. This was the run from Camp 9 to Parrot's Ferry. I had been told that if you survived the road trip along the edge of the canyon to the put in place at Camp 9 that the river trip would seem like a drop in the bucket in comparison to the ride.

One vehicle was left on the river bank at Parrot's Ferry and all the equipment and people loaded into the VW Transporter truck. This wonderful vehicle was a double cab pickup truck with truck bed sides that folded down all the way around. We could pack most anything on this truck. Off we went, spirits high, full of excitement and great anticipation mixed with a little insecurity about what we were about to tackle. The trip up the Camp 9 Road took an hour on a one lane dirt track with a sheer drop off to the canyon below on the south side. If you met anyone, one of you had to back up to find a place where both vehicles could safely pass. Finally, we arrived at the designated starting point. It was full of exposed rocks and did not look passable to me. Larry said," They must be holding the water at the Camp 9 Dam later in the day than usual…it will be coming up shortly."

Under present conditions, we could not run the river. There was barely enough water for a kayak. It was 2 o'clock in the afternoon in July in the foothills of California and the temperature hovered around 105 degrees. Finally, when 5 o'clock rolled around and the water was still not forthcoming, I said to Larry, "It's time to deflate the raft and pack up. We can return another day."

Larry was having none of that kind of talk, "We came to run the river and run it we will!" he shouted.

"No, I told him. It will be dark before we get to Parrot's Ferry and it would be a suicide trip, even if we had run the river previously and knew the rapids. It is not a safe thing to do."

I made no further protests. The children piled into their respective places and we pulled the raft out into the middle of the river to catch the current. They had finally increased the volume of water being released. Larry got in and up on the rowing seat while I held the boat and then it was time for my scramble to get aboard. Twenty three inch tubes are not easy to pull yourself up and over, starting from the water. I rolled into the bow and we were underway. Sabra & Brent sat on each side of me on the front thwart. Ulaine, our oldest child, sat on the back thwart which is like riding a roller coaster. You want to place the least amount of weight in the rear of the craft to decrease drag on the rocks. Larry sat in the middle on the giant igloo cooler, a 10 ft. oar in each hand. Darkness would be descending in another two hours and we had a four hour trip ahead of us. I was outraged at the decision I had allowed him to make and fearful of the hours ahead. It was a recipe for disaster and could have easily been avoided.

I hung out over the bow with a large red "floating" lantern of the 70's era. I continuously moved it in a sweep from side to side, like the searching headlights move on a train. As it became pitch black, Larry consented to one request.

"Please stay close to the left side of the river the remainder of the trip," I said to him through pursed lips. "We may hit more rocks & a few overhanging limbs but we will be out of the main current if disaster strikes."

Usually, you want to run with the strongest current in whitewater because there will be less obstacles. It requires more skill to keep your craft in that spot, but it saves lots of work and avoids many problems that are much more likely in slower water. The Havasu is a forgiving raft, with twelve layers of Kevlar to protect it from puncture, as well as eight air chambers. It will stay upright if four of the chambers are compromised. So we were aboard the safest raft made, if not being rowed by an egotistical man, using very poor judgment. Larry's rowing skills were first class, but his ability to change course when the conditions warranted it, such as darkness coming on, were adolescent. Down we went, our speed increasing because they had begun to release more water from the power house at Camp 9, our river put in. More water means less rocks to maneuver around or snags to catch the bottom of the boat, but with the increased velocity comes more possibility for hitting something with the likelihood of dumping someone in a large drop or flipping.

The Stanislaus River is a small Sierra River, only about fifty yards wide and narrowing to twenty five in chutes. However, it packs a lot of water between its banks and offers a wonderful trip. The rocks reveal wonderful petroglyphs, painted by the Miwok Indians and their ancestors thousands of years ago. The limestone canyons of the Stanislaus were honeycombed with caves used by the Miwok and prehistoric, pre-Miwok people. Archeologists believe the designs carved in the rocks are connected to fishing rituals at the river. Many of us fought long and hard to save this river and protect this ancient history and lost, but that is not part of this story.

Branches were snagging in my long braids, but I managed to break them off to free myself until THE BRANCH caught me.

"I'm caught," I screamed as the branch embedded itself in the top of my left braid.

It must have been three fourths of an inch in diameter and green. It would not bend and I could not break it or free it from my hair.

"Larry," I screamed, "I am leaving the boat!"

He pulled up his oars, reached forward and put his long arms around my chest and held me fast. Something about his movement or the change in my position snapped the branch. He let go to bring the boat back around to head down stream, as it had rotated while his oars were out of the water and we were now headed down the river stern first. I broke more of the branch free, but soon realized that the sharp end was stuck in my braid & had given me a scalp laceration, as I could feel and see the blood running down my cheek in front of my left braid. I knew head wounds bleed like crazy, even when superficial, so I was not too concerned and resumed my position watching for rocks, snags and overhanging branches. It was nine forty five, the kids were getting cold and the wind coming up the river from the ocean was becoming more than a breeze. My calculations estimated we had about two hours to go to take out at Parrot's Ferry. Could we get there?

I was beginning to shiver like the kids. We did not have coats or blankets. This trip should have been run in the blistering heat of the middle of the afternoon. We had water, sun screen, hats and some dried fruit and nuts. That was it. It was time for the music to start. On cue, the kids started singing "Delta Dawn" and "Marching to Pretoria", "Tie a Yellow Ribbon" and finally "This Land is Your Land." We were belting out the songs at the top of our lungs with no pauses in between. Sometimes, over the top of this noise could be heard my voice screaming, " Swing left, left. Jagged boulder or ragged snag on right."

And so it went for the next two and a half hours in the blind darkness, shivering all the way until I finally spied the Parrot's Ferry Bridge and our pullout on the steep bank on the left. We had done it and arrived in one piece, with no injuries and little extra impact on our raft. I decided it was an experience for children to learn from and to talk about down the road. However, their father never spoke of this trip again and stopped any discussion if the subject was initiated. It was not his greatest hour and a very poor example to set for our children.

We continued to make this river run in the years to come before the New Melones Dam was completed which drowned the entire nine miles of the river, erasing petroglyphs, waterfalls and any hint of the beauty which is now hidden by the backed up water.

We moved further north in the Gold Country and began to run the South Fork of the American River. This is a Class III & IV. We were confident in our competence and eagerly loaded the raft at the put in at Chili Bar, just north of Placerville. It is an easy start, but within the first three minutes you are into one of the most challenging rapids of this trip. It is called Meatgrinder. The river widens out after the first curve and becomes what river people call a rock garden. It is shallow and lined with rocks. It requires skill and maneuverability to ease a large raft like the Havasu without getting hung up. If the river is running less than 1500 cfs (cubic feet per second), it is not passable. However, Larry's rafting skills were well honed and we always made it through with a minimum of hang ups and none that caught us, held us or damaged our raft. This rapid lasts for more than one quarter of a mile before the river narrows in and gathers more volume and once again, you are skimming the top of the water. There are numerous calm Class II & III

Rapids in the middle of this run and then as you approach the finish of the journey you begin to hear the sound of the most fearsome rapid on the river. Its' name is Troublemaker. As your ears begin to pick up the sound of this approaching rapid, the river makes a wide sweep to the left and then enters a narrow canyon. Once you leave the pool at the top, all the water is forced into this narrows, which is a series of three distinct drops. The first one is a drop of about ten feet. When you complete this you madly hold your craft is place, make sure it has made the sharp left and is lined up for the second drop of about fifteen feet. The oars are pulled into the raft so they are not broken by the rocks that enclose the river. There is a souse hole at the bottom of this drop that can catch you if you do not enter the drop straight on, bow angled to the right. If you make it through this section you grab the oars, right the boat and enter the final drop stern first as the velocity of the water will turn the boat around and head it facing down stream before you complete the last drop. This is a very long drop of another fifteen feet and you must be balanced and low in the boat to complete this section without flipping. When you hit the water at the bottom, you are in calm, deep water with a strong current, but no further rapids.

The impact of the raft bouncing against the rocks threw me out of the raft and into the beginning of the worst rapid on the South Fork of the American River. I could see the rocks below and the souse hole just beyond the big drop. It could grab me, hold me and take me under forever, whirling me around and around. If caught by the whirlpool, I would have to find enough reserve strength to push out of its' hold, into the eddy beyond the rapids below. The water temperature was in the 50's, which is way too cold for the human body to survive for more than a very short time, perhaps fifteen minutes at best.

As the boat entered the first drop, I was

already below it holding on to a rock on the left side. Larry shored the oars into the raft, and yelled to the kids to: "Tuck and duck. I am going to catch your mother on the way by and pull her in."

I could see what he was doing but could not hear his words above the roar of the water. When I saw him shore the oars, I realized what he was planning to do. I tried to get ready. He was a tall man, about six foot, three inches with long arms. Those arms were meant for today. He leaned left out of the boat to reach me, yelling to the kids to: "Lean right, lean right! Keep it balanced."

It worked. He got one arm around my shoulder and the other around my back & started the pull and lift. Somehow, the river did not win that day and he pulled me back into the raft, over the twenty three inch tubes and onto the floor, before we entered the second stage of the rapid. I felt the rocks beneath me as we completed the drops, but escaped with only bruises and two gashes from the rocks as he dragged and lifted me into the craft.

In the years to come, we had many adventures and explored other rivers, but our earliest journeys are the most memorable. I hope that our children will realize someday that they had unique experiences very few other young kids ever knew. No one was on the water in those days except two professional outfitters and a handful of families like ours. We knew these intimate places before the rivers became freeways for the hoards that followed. Today, many of our pristine rivers lie buried beneath giant dams, but a few magnificent ones have been saved for all of us to enjoy and take care of for eternity. There are permit systems to keep the amount of people on a river at a certain number per day. Equipment is checked by River Rangers before a trip is allowed to depart on a permit river. Hopefully, these safeguards will afford more serenity to river travelers, less impact on the river environs and considerably less rescues of ill-prepared rafters and kayakers.

As I write, the integrity of the Wild and Scenic Status for the Merced River is in jeopardy. Just when you think something has been set aside and preserved for all time, someone introduces a glitch. Like grizzly and wolf status, our rivers are not safe either. We must be ever vigilant to ensure their survival.

FIRE...........escape

The loud ring of the phone brought me out of deep sleep. I had been up most of the night finishing a final paper that was 70% of the grade for a course I was taking called "The Relationship Culture Plays in Future Activism." It was January 29, 1962, the middle of finals week at the University of Iowa. I was exhausted from the stress of all of it. The phone should not have been ringing at this hour of the morning on a Monday. I came completely awake and picked up the receiver. "Julie?", the voice on the line was asking.

"Yes, this is Julie," I answered. Fear began in my toes and worked its way up to my voice. It was my parent's best friend, Esther Binger. "There has been an accident. You need to come home," and then her voice broke. Our drug store in Ottumwa, Iowa was burning and my father had been in the fire. She told me he was still alive and I told her I would find a way to get there that morning.

Ottumwa is about eighty miles from Iowa City. There was no public transportation and I did not have a car. Under any other circumstances I would never have had the nerve to ask, but I had to have a ride this morning. I called my friend, Marge, and she immediately told me to take her car for as long as I needed it. I asked my roommate to contact my two remaining professors, tell them what had happened and ask for an incomplete or extension in their courses. That should be all that was necessary to do. My suitcase was ready in just a few minutes and I walked to Marge's to get her keys and the car. A little more than an hour had passed since the phone call bearing the bad news.

As I swung the car on to Highway 1 South, out of Iowa City, the sky looked as ominous as the news I had just received. We didn't have all of today's technology available in those days, so all I knew about the weather was that it didn't look good to the West and that is where I was headed. As the outskirts of town were all that remained in my rear view mirror, light flakes of snow began to fall. I turned on the radio. This was a mistake. There was nothing on any of the stations I could receive except news about the large, spreading fire in Ottumwa. At this time it had consumed half a block on Main Street and continued to move on down the block. The fire hydrants were not working, as they were frozen. In addition, the announcers kept giving updates on the condition of Charles Hill, my father. Some reports said he was clinging to life, others that he was still in the fire and one, that he had died. I needed the comfort of some music, but could only get news bulletins.

The snow flakes began to grow larger and thicker and began to blow at the car at an angle. Visibility was diminishing and the road was getting dicey. I had no choice but to continue. I had to get home….home…it was my only thought. As I slowed to make the curve at the Hedrick Y, that was all it took to start the car into a slide. I knew it was fruitless to try and correct. It was leaving the road and all I could do was stay inside for the ride. The ditch was not terribly deep and I was not harmed, but by this point I was close to hysteria. I could not open the driver's door as it required too much strength with the car on its' side. The snow was up to the window on the passenger side, but I was able to roll the window down. Pulling myself halfway out of the window, I pushed away enough snow to roll out and into the snow bank. As I made my way to the highway to try and find someone or a house or something, I became aware of a loud sound coming through the blizzard. It was a farmer on his tractor and he had seen me go into the ditch. He hooked some kind of fancy hitch and chain to the front of Marge's car and after six tries, the car was back on the road. I got his name and address, explained who I was and tried to show my appreciation. He said," My God, You're Charley's daughter? I will drive you to the hospital." I told him that I should be able to make it the remaining twelve miles. He followed me till I turned on to Highway 63 South, a main road and then he headed back home. I made it to the hospital by 3:30 that afternoon. My journey had started at 9:30 that morning. It had taken 6 hours to make the eighty miles. I was lucky to have completed the trip.

My father was alert in his room, swathed in gauze, in obvious pain. The hospital hallway was full of family, friends and people whose lives had been touched by my father. He was the old fashioned Rexall druggist who took care of everyone in town whether they could pay their bills or not. No one had ever gone without medication for lack of ability to pay for it. We even delivered to people at all hours of the night. On this day, the realization of what my father meant to this small community brought me full circle. I knew he was wonderful, but I had no idea how many other people loved him.

He did survive. He left the hospital six months later after many surgeries and grafts. Our business and income were gone. Mother was quickly given a teaching job, which helped. A classroom was divided to make a job for her in the middle of the year. That is how small towns take care of each other. We were so blessed. My father was never able to live in a cold climate again. I left college to take care of all the financial matters of the business and to sit with my father in the hospital. We had round the clock private duty nurses, but he needed the comfort of family close by. Eventually, I was able to return to college and finish. However, our lives were never the same. Before it was finally contained, the fire consumed half of the city block. The cause was a defective five gallon bottle of Naphtha. It was never distributed again in glass, following our fire.

I did return to the farmer's home later in the Spring with cookies and cakes and other goodies. One of my professors did not believe the story and gave me an F in his class. I eventually went to see him with a notebook full of newspaper clippings and a statement from my father's surgeon. It took an entire year to remove the grade from my transcript and a lifetime to forgive him.

Your Tax Dollars At Work

It may have been December, but I believe it was January when I first began to notice the pink and blue glossy announcements. There were posters at the library, smaller signs at the senior center and even business card size notices to take home, left at various public places around the county. "Join us! Help count the population," they boldly declared. Benjamin Franklin was the father of the first U.S. census in 1790. It became a constitutional mandate to deliver population counts by December 31 of each decennial year. That first census cost the taxpayers $44,000.

Short-term employment was offered at $15 an hour and $0.50 per mile. How could our government afford to offer this kind of employment, as the country implodes around it? Not for me to figure out, but I did wonder. A little extra spending money always comes in handy, so I signed up and took the test. I was a bit surprised to learn that I had passed, for although it was not difficult, it was tricky and I felt that I had failed it. Training was to consist of five days starting in two weeks. No one could speculate on how long the job would last. The statement given was, "as long as there is a need."

Then the phone began to ring. First, it was Angela informing me that I was in Daisy's group and we would be doing our training in Le Grand. That seemed a little far from home base, but the taxpayers were paying me for my time and mileage. "I will be there," I told Angela. About a week went by and Sandra called to tell me I had been moved to the Bass Lake group. I was to report the following Monday at eight a.m. I checked the mileage to estimate my driving time and found it to be about forty-one miles one way, so it would be a bit more than four hundred miles for the week's training, in addition to an extra two hours of drive time each day. This amounted to $150 in salary and $207.50 in mileage, in addition to my pay for working an eight-hour day. This seemed preposterous to me and a total waste of my tax dollars.

I called Sandra in Fresno and asked if I trained with this group would I then be doing my work in that area? She explained that the Bass Lake group would be working from Wawona to the northern outskirts of Fresno. Therefore, following the training, I would still be driving long distances to do my enumerating. I then asked if there was not a group in Mariposa or somewhere closer. Yes, there would be training in the Mariposa area. I asked for a transfer. She told me those groups were closed. However, I got a call several days later from Norm telling me that I had been transferred to his Mariposa group and we would be training and working in the Mariposa area. Finally, this made some sense. I thanked him.

Monday morning I drove the eight miles to the school board room to start training. As we introduced ourselves, I learned that three people had come from Chowchilla, two from Madera and one from Los Banos. They would have fat paychecks. The remainder of us were from the general Mariposa vicinity. Training consisted of my supervisor, Norm, reading from the script in his training book to all of us. This went on for five days. I could have just taken the book home, read it and been equally prepared for the task. It seems the supervisor had just had his "training" the previous week. People were nodding off throughout each day. At the conclusion of the week, I could only see the necessity of all of us gathering to simply pick up all of our census materials. The enumerating was detailed and had to be done properly, but going to the training did not increase our knowledge. We were each given black cordura bags with the census name on them and many, many forms and booklets. The amount of paper involved with the job is shameful. In addition to the black bags, each enumerator was assigned a black leatherette binder containing the forms and maps for their individually assigned area.

I worked the job as an Update Enumerator for four weeks, up and down the hills of Midpines. I knocked on friendly doors, empty doors, garage doors and tent doors. I had one encounter that nearly finished me. This man did not want anyone on his road and carried a gun to back up his feelings. He should have had a locked gate and no one would enter his property. He had a rifle pointed at me at all times. It was scary, but I managed to back out and get on my way. Needless to say, he will not be part of the count unless another enumerator returns to his property in the company of law enforcement. I completed my binder and decided that I was not the right candidate for this job. I have much difficulty bothering people in their private space; consequently, the job was becoming too stressful for me to continue.

Although I learned little from the week of training, I have gathered information on the enormity of this undertaking. The following list consists of the jobs I know exist: mailing preparers, schedulers, door hangers, recruiters, couriers, trainers, finger-printers, enumerators, update enumerators, information centers, and quality control enumerators. There had to be people to write the training manuals, print the materials, record the data and document it. More than 700,000 people have been hired so far to complete this project. One hundred thirty three million was spent on television ads. Ball caps, t-shirts and bags have been imprinted with the census logo and given out to the public for their personal use. Dr. Robert Groves, the Census Director, projected the whole project would cost around fifteen billion dollars. Apparently, it has already left those figures in the dust.

It is costing about $48 dollars for each person counted, compared to $16 in 2000. So many people have been hired that it has dropped the unemployment rate nation wide by three percent. Federal auditors designated this year's census a "high-risk area" of federal spending. Weak management of Census Bureau purchases, including computers and software, and inaccurate cost estimates were cited as some of the reasons. The Kansas City Star found that twenty eight million Census mailings will simply be thrown away. Bureau officials and the U.S. Postal Service both agree on this point. Of the four hundred twenty five million pieces of mail that began going out last month, as many as twenty eight million pieces, or about seven percent, will end up in the nation's recycling bins. "That is waste at its worst, and we could have avoided it," said U.S. Rep. Jason Chaffetz, a Utah Republican who sleeps on a cot in his office to save money. Census spokesman Stan Rolark agreed that as many as twenty eight million letters could be tossed, but said the mailings were needed to ensure that the census reaches as many respondents as possible. He had no estimate of the cost.

As a taxpayer in the United States, I find this whole scenario abominable and inexcusable. How can the Census Bureau possibly feel they have the right to squander the "people's" money? At a time when so many people are suffering financially, it is almost scandalous to realize that this is one more government department racing out of control. It is tragic because the platform and purpose of the Census is important work and determines representation in Washington for congressional areas, as well as making allotments for road repairs, education and senior services in local communities, based on the Census numbers. As I wrote this, the Bureau was tapping into its reserve fund of seven million dollars to buy ads in low-response regions with predominantly "non-English speaking households." Immigrants and minority groups traditionally do not respond to the Census, so more effort will be made to reach these groups. Ironically, they are some of the people who benefit the most from the Census. The Bureau is determined to fulfill the job assigned and plans to count every one of us no matter what the cost. How do you feel about your tax dollars being spent in these ways?

Murderers, Rapists and Diggers, Oh My

Or...... Sometimes the grass over the septic tank is not Green, just soggy.

The heavy motor of the backhoe roused me from deep sleep. It was Saturday, September 21, 1977, the weekend following our almond harvesting. As I began to awaken and focus, I realized that the heavy engine sound was coming from my back yard. What had he initiated now? I peeked out the blinds to the back and saw three disheveled looking men...scary looking men...not the kind of men I wanted in my backyard or around my children. One had a Mohawk haircut & goatee, faded black tee shirt with the words Folsom barely legible, cigarette pack tucked up in the cut off sleeve. His age appeared to be around thirty. Next to him, leaning on a shovel was an older man, hair graying and pulled back in a long ponytail. His tee shirt said Hell's Angels on it and had a picture of a Harley, with wings above it. The third guy was somewhere in his forties with a shaved head, moustache and speckled beard. The back of his shirt was emblazoned with the words: Bar Hoppers, Local 1322. Parked in the yard was a large flatbed truck to haul the backhoe and a pickup truck that was tri-colored, mostly with rust. I was wide awake now. No way, I silently raged to myself. You have done it again, Ted. My emotions ran from rage to grave fear and I got dressed.

We bought this wonderful home in the spring of 1974. All was well for about three weeks until one morning in late May, rounding the corner through the pantry to the master bath, the pungent fragrance of a sewer smell filled my nostrils. Glancing down at the floor in the bathroom I could see something brown oozing up from the shower drain, over the lip of the shower step and on to the carpet in the room. The toilet seemed fine. Due to my lack of experience or knowledge of septic systems I was puzzled. It did not take very long, however, to figure out what the problem must be. I remembered something about "the grass always being greener over the septic tank", and soon realized that my situation must have some relationship with this statement. I called a septic service that was recommended. They came out and pumped both liquids and solids and told me: "You're good to go." I'm not sure he realized the double entendre of his statement or not.

Things went along well throughout the summer months and we made plans to have both of our sets of parents for the Thanksgiving holiday. My parents lived close by, but my

husband's parents were coming from Iowa. I cleaned & got extra beds and planned the meals and our family all arrived. Thanksgiving morning I was up early to get the turkey going, as well as to peel potatoes and bake two more pies. I had taken a shower before coming into the kitchen and thought that the shower drained rather slowly as I finished, but dismissed that thought as there was so much else on my mind. Soon the rest of the family were up & ready for breakfast. About eleven o'clock, my sleepyhead daughter, who was eleven, called for me to come to the master bathroom for a minute. I

216

set everything aside, a bit irritated as I was really busy, to see what she needed. After about fifteen steps, my feet were squishing in the problem. It had happened again. Impossible, but true. I was standing in the backed up sludge and water. Who could I call on a national holiday and what would it cost? In the intervening months I had been reading about septic systems and how they work. I had started feeding it and carefully stretched out laundry over several days and cautioned the kids about bathing back to back. Well, my new knowledge did not save us. This time it filled the bathroom, pantry, down the hall to the kitchen and even out the door to the utility room. All the rooms in this house were carpeted, no bare floors to make cleanup easier. The oozing sludge continued to creep. We piled up towels and then sheets to try and contain it, but it kept moving forward. The drains were covered. We moved the dinner outside, adjusted the menu a bit and set up three tents in the backyard. I was unable to get anyone to service the tank until the following day and the smell had permeated a large portion of the house. My parents offered my in-laws shelter, which was a great help. The rest of us used the other bathrooms if necessary, with no flushing. I had also set up a camping toilet in one of the tents. It was a disaster. The septic service came the following day. They pumped and pumped. When the operator came to the door for payment he told me that we really needed new leach lines in order to make it work efficiently. "Thank you," I told him and said we would look into it. I had no idea what he was talking about, but bright and early on Monday morning I found out exactly what he meant. The replacement part of the leach fields would cost approximately $3000 and require four days of work. I thanked them and told them I would get back to them. We did not have an extra $3000.

The months rolled by and we put some money aside as often as possible for the renovation of the septic system. Before we could realize it a year had passed and it was Thanksgiving once again. This holiday, a local judge, his wife, and their three children would be our guests. The turkey was well on its way to done before the trouble began. This time the sludge was coming up in both bathrooms and the utility room sink. I

was overcome with frustration, disbelief and anger. We packed the entire dinner and took it to our guest's home for dinner. That evening we showered at my parents before returning home. I had set up the camp toilet again in the backyard. It was very private and hidden from any other homes or eyes. Ted promised me someone would be there to take care of the problem by Saturday. We limped along.

Sure enough, Saturday morning at six a.m. I jumped out of my sleep to the sound of a backhoe in the yard. Ted was already up and outside. I dressed and opened the drapes. The figure I saw on the machine was familiar, but I couldn't quite place him. An hour or two went by and Ted came in to get drinks for the two of them. The man seemed to just be digging a very deep hole east of the Redwood and the leach lines. "What is he doing?" I asked.

"He's digging a sump hole and we will divert all the water to the new pit until we can afford to do a whole new leach field."

By this time I was educated about septic systems and how they work and knew that the county code prohibited digging a sump hole. Ted told me: "Monte knows what he is doing. He did this kind of work for years before his troubles."

Troubles, I thought to myself? Then everything became very clear. The light bulb came on and I remembered where I had seen this man previously. It was in a courtroom. Ted had tried him for statutory rape about three years ago. Speechless, outraged and with some degree of concern (understatement of the year), I asked Ted if this was Monte Clark. "Yes, he said. He has been out of San Quentin for about ten days now. One of the first things he did after getting out was to come see me and tell me there were no hard feelings and that prison had given him a lot of time to think about his life and how to make it better. He can use some cash and the price is right. We will save money and he will have a little spending money."

The sump hole was completed, the septic seemed to drain and life went on. I was told there was no way he would come back and cause us any harm or worry. "He likes and respects me and would do anything for my family," Ted informed me. I was still in a state of shock and my anger had not dissipated.

The year kept rolling along and the septic worked most of the time. Sometimes it was a bit slow to drain, but it did not back up. Ted told me he had made arrangements to have

the entire leach field redone in September after we had harvested our almonds. Sure enough, the third weekend of September I heard the familiar backhoe sound in the yard once again very early on Saturday morning. When I looked out the blinds I did not see the local septic company. It was the new band of men I described at the beginning of this story. I stepped outside and motioned that I needed to speak to Ted. After we were alone in the kitchen, I once again asked the important question: "Who are these men? They seem quite familiar, but I can't remember where I have seen them."

The man with the ponytail was MauricVinson, the Mohawk belonged to his son Harry Vinson and the third member of the trio was Bobby Jones. Maurice had been tried twice for first degree murder and acquitted each time. Harry had just been released the previous evening at midnight from Folsom for first degree murder for the second time. In the few short years we had lived in this community my husband had prosecuted him twice for murder, gotten a conviction both times and he was once again out in society. Bobby was the adopted son of a local sheriff's deputy and a person of interest in the disappearance of two young girls that had been missing for some time in a small community to the north. He had been in and out of jail for burglary, spousal abuse and robbery. Charges for the removal of an airman's eye in an altercation had never been filed. He was the same man that had put out a contract on my husband's life one year prior to this time.

These 'good ol boys' all came from the same community in CA. They frequented the Wagon Wheel Bar in the small town which was a gathering place for Hell's Angels. Sonny Barger, the head man of the Angels was a regular visitor in this town. Johnny Carson stated on The Tonight Show in the early 70's that he had read some crime statistics and that: 'This town in California had the highest crime rate for any city of its' size in the nation.'

The reputation of these two families was known for miles around. The small town of Brookline was greatly influenced by their presence and the problems they created. All of them knew my husband or at least were familiar with his reputation. Ted was a district attorney with a personal calling. He was a man who believed in the law, and in order and

he would pursue that to the end of his life. He didn't take plea bargains or settle out of court. If your case was set for trial, that is where you would be headed. He was not popular...but, highly respected. Attorneys often came to sit in on his cross examination and his closing arguments, even though they had nothing to do with the case. Melvin Belli, of San Francisco defense fame, often sent one of his attorneys to listen to Ted in trial. He offered Ted a position in his firm, but Ted would never consider defense work. Two or three times a year he gave one day seminars for attorneys in the Bay Area or Los Angeles on cross examination or closing arguments. He was brilliant, articulate and determined to prevail, and defense attorneys often hoped their client's case would be assigned to someone else. I hope this will help you understand my extreme anxiety on this Saturday morning to find murderers in my backyard. Not only did they now know where we lived, but how far away the adjoining properties were, doors to the house, fences, dogs and a myriad of other things. They could tell from the bikes and toys that there were children in this household and no giant German shepherd dog to deter their entrance if they decided to return at another date. I got the kids up, dressed, out the front door, into the VW and away for the day. This was before cell phones. I left Ted a note to call my parents house when the work for the day was completed and the men had gone.

The crew completed the work in two days. We had a completely new septic system which was still working efficiently when I left that home in 1994. It handled crowds of ten or twelve at the house and their laundry and showers on a regular basis. It worked perfectly. The boys sent one of their wives to the house several Christmas seasons with a bottle of bourbon and we often came home to find fresh vegetables by the back door in the summer months from one of their gardens, but they did not bring us marijuana. Some years went by, Maurice passed away and Sonny Barger died. The Bar Hoppers are still a part of the Brookline scene, but not the whole scene as in years gone by. Harry has been tried again for murder and Bobby was in the paper just this past week for pedophile charges. The Hell's Angels have removed him from their membership, tied him down & blacked out the tattoo on his back that designated his membership in the organization. They draw the line at pedophiles. Bobby was tried for the murders of the two girls, murdered twenty one years ago. A DNA link was found. This trial ended in a mistrial and he was returned to Pelican Bay Prison for previous murder convictions from another county. These families are still a very large part of the fiber of Brookline, California, but they do not have the same profile they had when Sonny Barger & his right hand man, Maurice were running the club for California.

I never saw any of the men again. The rapist got our unlisted phone number somewhere along the line and would call to talk to Ted about once a week for a year or two. He got his life back together and found a job with Pacific Bell. My husband knew what he was doing and it did work exactly as he thought it would, but it certainly gave me cause for concern for the well-being of our family in the late 1970's.

Only in Mariposa

In the summer of 2007, we realized that we needed new asphalt on our private road and after calling several people, I made an estimate appointment with a paving company from a community nearby. Susan was still working in Tuolumne at that time and made arrangements to take the day off to be here when the paving contractor said he was coming. On Thursday night before the appointment, the phone rang at ten o'clock. It was the paving man confirming the appointment for eleven the next morning. I went over the directions with him, rechecked driving instructions and double-checked phone numbers. Susan drove down early the next morning. This would be an expensive venture and we felt it required both of us present before a decision was made. There was no sound of a truck on the road and finally at noon, we called the paving contractor. Of course, it was only an answering machine. I made lunch. We drank two pitchers of ice tea and called the company two more times. Our calls were never returned and to this day we have no idea why they did not want our business or what earth-shaking event prevented their arrival at our mutual appointment.

How many times have you called someone for some kind of service for your home or car and they did not answer the phone or come to the agreed upon appointment? I have had a plumber who did not show. A septic company would try to fit me into their schedule. Four propane companies never returned my calls and one told me they already have too many customers. I have had tree trimmers that never arrived. Three different handymen were no shows. PG&E and Sierratel are the only service people who have arrived when they said they would. What does this say about Mariposa?

Our unemployment rate is higher than just about any other county in California. People are short of food, have lost their housing, their cars need repair and they have no health insurance. Are they able to make the system work well enough for them to get by? Are they so "drugged out" that very few things matter anymore? Do they no longer see a future to hope for or work toward? I don't have the answers, but I have lived quite a few places in my lifetime and have never encountered a lack of work initiative like the one present in Mariposa County. Maybe there is something in the water?

Break Out the Oars!

Dawn was breaking as we quietly plied the waters of Sara Lake in the Quetico Area of the American and Canadian Boundary Waters. We were heading back to the island, hoping to find it unoccupied. Hopefully, the bears that had brashly entered our campsite last night had moved to the mainland & perhaps bed. We had fled the island in canoes after midnight when mama bear, with two cubs, interrupted our singing around the campfire.

It was August of 1961. I was leading one of the first women's canoe trips allowed into the Quetico, without a guide. There were five girls of high school age and myself. I had reached the ripe old age of twenty one. We were traveling in two canoes, for three weeks in this wilderness area. The girls selected to make this trip were highly skilled and experienced in the outdoors and knew about paddling a canoe, setting up a camp in the rain and had the stamina and skills necessary to portage a canoe or grubber pack upwards of two miles between lakes. My girls had been through rigorous competitive selection for this trip. They could start a fire after three days of rain, use a reflector oven & read maps. This was a roadless wilderness set aside for canoe travel only.

The previous evening we had set up camp, gone swimming, and cooked a freeze dried macaroni dinner, with fresh onion added for flavor. Lynn had baked a blueberry pie for dessert. (Somehow, she had managed to pick enough berries around the island to make a pie). After the dishes were washed and camp tidied up for the night, we built up the fire and I got out my baritone uke and harmonica. For most of us, it was our favorite time of day. After singing, swapping lies and letting the fire begin to die down it was almost time to turn in for the night. Suddenly Emily grabbed my thigh & put her fingers to her lips. Her expression looked frozen, as she pointed to the far edge of the clearing. Coming directly at us was a mama black bear with two cubs. I stood up and yelled," CANOES", to the girls. We ran in the dark, pushed the canoes into the water & rolled in and grabbed our paddles. Normally, we traveled three to a boat, but tonight it would be four in one and two in the other. Once I knew everyone was safely in a craft & we were moving out onto the dark lake, I asked the other boat to pull up close by.

Sara Lake was approximately two miles across and about five miles long. I felt sure that if we paddled out to the middle of the lake, mama bear would not follow us that far. We had camped on the only island on this lake & any large boulders above the surface of the lake were around the shore. We were safe for the moment. However, what would we do next? It would become way too cold to spend the whole night in shorts and shirts in an aluminum canoe drifting around on icy water. I would have to find a solution.

Thirty minutes passed and our campfire faded away and was gone in the distance. It was pitch black on the lake. We were on the dark side of the moon. The girls were shivering and huddled as low in the canoes as they could get. This kept the wind off, but their bodies were touching the thwarts along the bottom of the canoe. An aluminum canoe is the same temperature as the water, so their increasing cold was of some concern.

At first I thought I was seeing things & then gradually I realized there was a faint light coming from way down the lake. Distance was difficult to determine under these conditions, but it was not close. Canoe trips in this protected area were by permit only. All identification must checkout with the Canadian Customs officer who looks at your permit, as well as names & pictures of all members of the trip. In addition, all weapons must be relinquished. They can be reclaimed upon the return of the trip. It was almost unheard of to ever see other people when tripping in the Quetico, but tonight gave the promise of being the exception. After some soul searching, I decided we would head for the light. We paddled forty five minutes and at that point, I felt my voice could be heard on shore. "Hello", I called. No answer. We kept paddling. I called again. Finally, a reply came, "Hello to you." It was a man's voice. Although I had hoped to hear a female reply, realistically I knew how few women traveled these waters.

As we drew close, I could see ten to fifteen young men and three adult males. It was a dilemma. I knew my girls could not spend the night on the water and returning to our island before dawn was not an option. So, I asked if we could come ashore. "Of course, please join us", wafted out to us on the water. I thanked him and we headed toward shore. The girls were told to stick to me and be polite and get warm by the fire.

Several of the men waded out in the water to help us bring our canoes in without the risk of damage from rocks. We pulled the canoes up on the sandy beach, stowed our paddles and walked over to the group by the fire. I thought it was unusual to see such a large group traveling, but did not ask questions. The leaders were polite to us. Soon my girls had hot chocolate and sweaters or jackets to put around themselves. I explained our situation. Jack, the senior leader of the group, immediately put one of their tents at the disposal of my girls and had his boys double up. There was little grumbling or complaining. I had never seen this many young men with such developed muscles in one group. Who were these people? My girls went to bed and the young men got in the remaining tents. I had elected to spend the night by the fire, as I was uneasy and felt very responsible. Jack sat up with me and sent the other two leaders to bed.

Jack said that he was astounded to see a group of women traveling alone in this wilderness. I explained that this was the first year it had been allowed. I told him that we were affiliated with Camp Manitowish in northern Wisconsin. He then explained that he was a parole officer with the state of Minnesota & that all the young men were felons about to be released on parole. If they were able to do this wilderness trip without incident, they would be released to halfway houses throughout Minnesota to finish their parole. My jaw dropped! I had brought my girls to this environment! He assured me there would be no problems and there were none. At the first sign of light in the sky, I woke the girls and we returned to our canoes. Jack & I exchanged names and addresses, thanks were expressed and we paddled back out into the lake. The island was just discernable in the distance.

As we approached our campsite it appeared to be vacant. I left the girls in the canoes and went ashore making lots of noise. Our pots and pans had been scattered all around & one pack was torn. Mama had entered and collapsed one tent, but it was not torn. We were only missing some flour, a little sugar and some raisins. We had one week left & plenty of supplies to finish our trip. Needless to say we had true "Tall Tales" to tell when we returned. Many times in these ensuing years I have wondered if I did the right thing and try not to think about the things that could have happened that dark night so long ago on Sara Lake.

Somebody Light My Fire!!

The saga began in early September as I began to scan the paper, local bulletin boards and the classified ads on the internet at the Sierra Sun Times, in search of firewood for the coming season. There are always ads by Labor Day and often in August, but this year... nothing. We called three suppliers we had used in years past, but our calls were not returned. September seventeenth arrived and there was finally an ad. His name was Dan and he was advertising seasoned oak for $225.00. That is not a bad price including delivery. I dialed his number and left a message on his answering machine. Five days passed and finally the return call came. He would be happy to deliver two cords. They would be ready in about three weeks. Dan stated that he would call us in two weeks to update his schedule. This arrangement was not exactly what we had in mind, but at this date he was the only game in town.

October third I had a tire repaired in Bootjack. While I waited for the repair to be completed, I read the bulletin board. There it was jumping out at me: Seasoned oak, $200 a cord delivered. Holy Cow, that was an amazing price and a welcome sight. I called immediately. His name was Jeremy and he could deliver that afternoon. By five thirty that evening I could hear his truck grunting and grinding as it slowly made its way up our hill. He was pulling a trailer behind his truck and brought along a helper. They dumped the wood in record time. It was beautiful, clean, seasoned wood. Jeremy had split it into small lengths and it was just the size that I can use comfortably. Hooray! It looked like great wood. We thought it looked a bit short as we began to stack it; it was short by about one third of a cord. I came into the house and called Jeremy. No answer. The call was not returned the next day which was Thursday. No call was received Friday or Saturday or Sunday.

Meanwhile on Friday, October fifth, Dan called us. He would be delivering the wood on the following Monday, October 8, at 8:30 a.m. Things were looking up and we began to envision a comfortable, cozy winter. I went to the bank to get the cash and we set the alarm for 7:30 to be sure we were up and about by the time of the delivery. Eight thirty came and went. Soon it was ten o'clock. No phone calls and no sound of trucks on our mountain. Finally, at eleven o'clock a call was placed to Dan. You guessed it, just an answering machine. A fairly assertive message was left. About one o'clock the phone rang. Wonder of wonders, it was Dan returning our call from last Thursday, Friday,

Saturday and Sunday. He had been out of town for the weekend. He sincerely apologized for the wood shortage, seemed shocked about the error, but would be happy to bring us another third of a cord. "When?" I asked.

"Will this afternoon work?"

"Yes," I told him and the wait began again.

No wood that day and no wood the following day which was Tuesday, October ninth.

The following day I called Jeremy again. He was there and I once again asked about the remaining part of the cord and also ordered two more cords. The wood is excellent, if we can just get him to get it here, I said to myself. He would bring two ample cords and the missing wood on the weekend. He would call to give us the time. I decided to put my feet up for the day.

Saturday morning, October thirteenth dawned sunny and clear. We were up and ready for the delivery. I was still trying to be optimistic. However, I was beginning to feel a bit stupid. No wood and no calls. A call was made to Jeremy at 5 p.m. No answer. We told the answering machine that a return call was expected that day. At bedtime, the call came. He was having trouble with his truck and most likely would not be able to deliver until the following weekend. What could we say? There did not seem to be any other wood around and we needed at least four cords.

In desperation, we called a local establishment. They are in the business of brush clearing, tree trimming and removal. We have hired them in the past and knew they would recognize the name left on their answering machine. The woodcutters were called on Sunday, October fourteenth. On Wednesday, October seventeenth, Dan called to tell us that he would be delivering on Friday, the nineteenth. He would be here at ten a.m. that morning. Susan had an eye appointment at nine that morning, but planned to be back by the time of the wood delivery. She made it in good time, but no wood was here. At noon she called Dan. He answered the phone. "Hi, this is Susan. Are you delivering our wood this morning?"

"Right now I'm working on my clock business, so can't make it today."

"Dan, this is the second time we have waited for you for delivery and you have not called or shown up. The wood needs to be delivered."

We gave up, I started fixing dinner and Susan was working on stowing lawn equipment

for the winter. The phone rang at 4:30. It was Dan. He was on his way, but wanted to double check the directions. He estimated it would take him about fifteen minutes to get to the house. Sure enough, we could hear the truck grinding its way up the hill as it got close. Finally, he rounded the last bend and came into view. The truck was backed in and unloaded. The wood was split and larger than I like, but it was "well seasoned", according to Dan. He was only able to bring one third of a cord at a time in his truck so he would have to return two more times to complete one cord. It was dark when he left, promising to return at 7 the next morning with the second load. You guessed it, we were up and ready. All was quiet on our western front, just wild turkeys arguing and a few ravens debating among themselves, but no trucks or phone calls. At 11 that morning, he pulled in with the second load. He had no recollection of telling us that he would be here at 7. When it was unloaded, he looked at his watch and then up to the sky and said he had decided to bring the third load before dark. It no longer made any difference to us what he said as we didn't believe anything that came out of his mouth. Imagine our surprise to find him pulling in one more time at around 4 p.m. He did give us an ample cord. The wood looked beautiful, but I thought it felt very heavy for well seasoned wood. It was stacked and was a very generous cord. When he left he told us he would call when he was ready to deliver the second cord that we had ordered. We had decided we did not wish to deal with Mr. Dan any further. We had tried to have a fire only to discover that his wood was wet and not seasoned. It did not even catch with cedar kindling surrounding it to help it ignite.

Saturday night, October twentieth, we called Jeremy to see if he was coming the following day. He was still having truck trouble, but would have the wood here the next weekend, the twenty seventh.

Tuesday, the twenty third I found a new wood ad for seasoned oak. I gave a call to the number listed. That connected me with Bobby Joe. He was the woodcutter and he said,

"This will be the best wood you ever purchase. It has been seasoned for three years."

He could deliver the following day. That was hard to believe, but we told him to bring it on up. Sure enough, at the appointed time, Mike, his delivery driver called to tell us he was enroute. I nearly dropped the phone. This was too good to be true, we surmised. We had the money ready for him and he arrived in about ten minutes. Mike was driving a standard American pickup truck with wood boards stuck all around the bed to hold wood above the top of the side boards of the truck. He had it filled and we figured that by the time he brought a second load it would be a decent cord. Little did we realize that this was the load. He and Bobby Joe considered this to be a cord. Susan told him we would be talking to them after we had it stacked.

It is now Wednesday, October 24th and we are still short one cord of wood from Dan. We no longer want it, but he does not know that. Jeremy has yet to deliver the two and one third cords we are due and the wood cutting business has yet to return our phone call of just under two weeks ago. Winter is rapidly approaching and we are still short three cords of wood and they don't appear to be on our horizon.

This is truly an "Only in Mariposa" story.

Sunday Dinner

White linen napkins, spotless, starched and ironed, flanked each place setting. Olives and radishes sat in cut glass bowls. The iridescent pitcher sparkled with cold water and glasses for each diner were on the table. A steaming bowl of gravy, home made watermelon pickles and pickle-lily waited in their serving dishes, Mounds of swirled mashed potatoes, were piled high into the serving bowl for the table, from the roaster in the kitchen. Stacks of home baked bread, sliced and placed in baskets with butter by the side, sat in the middle of the table. The serving fork and carving knife, with boned handles, capped in steel tines sharp as hat pins, were in front of grandfather's place or one of the eldest sons. Stuffed celery, sliced tomatoes and fresh picked corn piled on plates ready to be passed, awaited the family. Roasted chicken or beef, falling off the bone, filled the room with wonderful aromas. Home canned green beans or fresh ones from the garden, depending on the season, were always part of the meal. Following this feast there would be homemade pies, at least one coconut cake, and coffee and ice tea. Cashews and butter mints, usually made an appearance on one end of the table, with a silver scoop to serve them, next to the dish.

From 1945 through 1960, Grandmother Hill served Sunday Dinner at her home at 1025 Boone Ave., in Ottumwa, Iowa. Her adult children arrived for this gathering no later than one p.m. The size of the group varied from a minimum of ten to as many as twenty-seven. We did not go every Sunday, but there was a phone call at my home on Monday morning to inquire what had happened if we did not arrive for dinner. My mother usually called to let her know if we would not attend, but occasionally she did forget.

The preparations for dinner began in earnest on Saturday. Grandmother invited me to come to her house to help her from about the time I turned eight. I could iron the napkins, set the table and polish the silver. I followed instructions for what flowers to cut for the centerpiece during the warm months. At other times of the year, nuts, fruits, pinecones or bare branches made up the decorations. She would turn me loose to design something for the table and always told me the finished artwork was beautiful and perfect. Looking back, I am not so sure they really were. We baked fifteen loaves of bread and five trays of yeast rolls on Saturday afternoon. I began the tedious job of peeling potatoes and plunging them into the salted ice water. They were ready for me the following day to do the mashing. Very late in the afternoon on Saturday, just before Orville Agee closed his neighborhood store, she would send me to get the meat for the dinner. I always carried a note to the owner requesting whatever he would be offering at a reduced price that evening because he would not carry it over for sale until Monday. Sometimes it was chicken, often pork roasts and almost as often, some cut of beef. I would bring home the small piece of meat, always purchased for about fifty cents and grandma would stretch it to

238

feed however many people came for dinner. No one left her table hungry. Extra gravy and mashed potatoes could always be prepared.

Underneath the layers of quilted fabric and oilcloth and sheets and then a tablecloth, was the beautiful table made of cherry wood. My grandfather, Richard B. Hill, made this table for his bride, Ida Swenson, in 1889. The round table extended with two leaves, to a very large oval. When the crowd became too large for the table, it was pulled apart and sawhorses were set in the open space in the middle. Sheets of plywood were placed on the sawhorses, quilts layered to make it the same height as the regular table and then this extension was covered with linens or sheets on top. With the table fixed in this manner, it would accommodate at least thirty people. Following dinner, the men gathered in small groups to set up Cribbage at one end, Pinochle on one side, Dominos at the far end and the fourth game varied from some kind of Rummy to Kings on the Corner to Hearts. When the women and children had finished up all the dishes, they retired to the front porch to visit or the kids to the side yard for games of Kickball or Kick the Can or Hide n' Seek. These activities continued until close to dark. Aunt Elsie & Uncle Ernie Schoech had to leave first because they were farmers and needed to head home to Blakesburg to do chores before dark.

My grandfather was an accomplished, creative woodworker and stained glass artisan. Most of the old churches in Ottumwa bear his imprint. He designed the windows and then carved the frames to fit around them. Today, that same beautifully hand hewn table with no screws or nails, sits in my dining room. There is rarely a reason to put in even one leaf these days, but how I do treasure the memory of so much family history and good times sealed in its' wood. If only that table could talk.

Purrfect Eliminators

The advertisement in the Mackay, Idaho weekly Gazette read: CATS NEEDED!!! Please bring all cats to the HP (Hewlett Packard) Ranch. We will carefully house and feed them and notify you when it is time to pick them up to return home.

The ad contained no phone number or address. Those items were not needed.

It seems that Sam Banks, ranch foreman of the HP Ranch outside of Mackay had gone to the main barn to check the roof and stalls in the early spring in anticipation of the cowboys bringing in cows and sheep that were about to give birth. If they were in the barn they would be safe from predators for the first weeks and accessible if they needed the service of a veterinarian. When he unlatched the wooden hasp for the first time since the previous fall and his eyes became accustomed to the darkness, the dirt floor was alive with rattlesnakes. It looked like there were hundreds. He closed the doors immediately and went back to the house to speak with Mr. or Mrs. Nelson, the Ranch Managers.

After some discussion with her husband, Lon Nelson, Eleanor Nelson placed the ad.

The newspaper was published on Wednesday. By suppertime, the cat deliveries had begun. The people came in Suburban's, F-150 trucks, and SUV's of every brand. The cats were in gunny sacks, pillow cases and carriers. When she retired for the evening the cat count was twenty. Thursday at bedtime she had fifty cats. The final

241

stragglers arrived on Friday morning and all the cats were enclosed in the barn, to roam at will. They were provided with plenty of water, the barn doors were latched and the waiting game began.

Sam checked on the cats and their prey three times a day for two weeks. When that time had passed he could only see three snakes still moving around in the darkness. The rest were dead. Some were partially eaten, others just lay on the barn floor in pieces, drying up. The problem was solved. Mrs. Nelson went back in the house on Monday afternoon of the second week and placed a new ad in the paper:

CAT OWNERS: Please pick up your cats at the HP Ranch. We will help you gather your cats. There is no further need of their services. They did a wonderful job. Thank you.

And so, in the summer of 1986, that is how the snakes were driven out of the barn at the Hewlett Packard Ranch just outside of Mackay Idaho.

Marcele Price

A poet at eight, I learned the craft rather late. As the mother of four and grandmother of seven, I'm blessed with an extra dash of leaven. My number one is my mother-in-law's son. The youngest of four by parents of two writing is what I like to do. Tickling the ivories or strumming a tune gives me pleasure morning, night or noon. A hike through the forest amidst a critter chorus with that deaf Dane of mine suits me fine. I've traveled the states from sea to sea but a California girl is what I'll always be.

Homeward Bound

Two tawny mountain lion cubs cross in front of my head lights. One claws up the red clay hill out of harms way. It's clumsy twin climbs up after. I proceed more slowly now. A gray mist is seeping into the forest. I roll down the window and stick my head out straining to see better. Enveloped by the scent of pine and cedar surrounded by damp silence, I continue on. The dotted center line evades me disappearing into the night. I drive on searching for it hoping that I'm still on the right side of the road. Fear is sweeping over me yet I continue. The smoky fragrance of wood burning somewhere comes wafting my way through the trees. I'm not alone. Picturing a fireplace, surrounded by chatting children clutching mugs of hot chocolate or perhaps an old woman sitting, rocking, knitting, remembering when her husband shared the winter evenings with her in companionable silence amidst the glow of the stone hearth.

Gripping the steering wheel thankful for the interlude of thought that has taken me away from this inescapable sea of gray I continue watchfully, listening.

Fred

Bear wandered in from the woods
Followed his nose
Clawed his toes
Opened cans one by one
Dug in had fun
Took snack home
Traced his roam
Trail of noodles, rice, pastry trays
Under sun's rays
We know you're out there
Fred bear

Camera Shy

Morning cool
Forest branch dance
Sunlight play upon limbs of oak/pine
Shadowy two step/country line
Footfalls awaken
Creatures aware
Snapshot taken

Do I Dare?

Do I dare dangle this participle in front of you?
Too late to hide it now
It's been seen I'm sure
Briefly
In a blur
There it hangs swinging to and fro
I hesitate to meditate on this any longer
Let sit upon the page
Relentlessly prickling the sage

Preponderance

Is it impolite to spit a little wit
Spray a little say
Voice a choice refrain
Cause a chuckle so loud
Wake up a crowd ?

Grandma's House

Grand kids
Whirlwind spin
Earthquake shake
Hop, Hop
Bubble pop
Scream
Shout
Pout
Cavort all in sport
Grandma tired
Worn thin
Time to turn in
Off the light
Appears little sprite
Hug so tight
Goodnight grandma
Goodnight

Dreaming

Yeah!
It's nap time
Granny nanny can get her groove on
Time for tapping computer keys or tickling ivories
Maybe a strum or two on that old guitar
Whatever the case
It's a race to have some fun while you rest little
one

Lowell Young

I wish I knew more about my ancestors. I long to know how they made their livings, and what they thought and dreamed about. I wonder why they left their country of birth and came to America. There are so many things I want to know but never will. With few exceptions, none left any record of their lives, other an occasional birth, death or marriage certificate.

Because I am colorblind, I have had many unique life experiences; experiences that are unimaginable for most people, and which I wanted to share with my family and friends. The problem was, I had no idea about how go about doing it.

Fifteen years ago my wife Sue, showed me an ad in the local newspaper about a life story writing class and suggested that I look into it. I did, and I have been writing about my life ever since. I hope you enjoy reading the following stories about my life as much as I enjoyed living and writing about them.

Phoenix The Swainson's Hawk

"Daddy, Daddy, you've got to come. It's been shot! A great big bird. It's been shot!"

I followed Sheila, my eleven-year-old daughter to where her brothers Brad, age fourteen, and Scott, age ten, stood by a large hawk. A bone protruded from its wing. I ran back to the house, grabbed a blanket and raced back. The hawk's posture, ruffled head feathers, and the way its eyes followed me indicated that it didn't understand what had happened, was terrified and prepared to defend itself against any threat. I wasn't sure how to proceed without aggravating its wound. Nor did I want to be injured by the raptor's sharp talons and beak. We spread the blanket, placed it over the bird, and gently wrapped it up, being careful not to cause it more harm. We left its head uncovered, so that it would not suffocate.

We took the bird home, and put it in our chicken coop where it would be safe. Our chickens and ducks panicked at the sight of their mortal enemy roosting in their home. They soon realized the hawk was not a threat to them and went about their everyday activities.

I phoned a veterinarian whom I had heard was an expert at rehabilitating injured birds. He said he would meet us at his veterinarian hospital as soon as he could. I found a box big enough to hold the 20" high bird and the blanket it was wrapped in. I put the box and its contents on the back seat of the car between the two boys and told Sheila to sit next to me. I then drove the two miles to the vets office. The doctor examined the bird and said, "Its wing is so badly damaged that I doubt I can save it. We should put it down."

"Daddy, don't let him do that." Sheila sobbed.

"That's not an option," I told him. "Could you amputate the wing so that the hawk could survive and spend the rest of its life in a Wild Animal Park?"

The doctor looked at Sheila intently and said "That's a possibility."

"I have heard how skilled you are and I have total confidence that you can repair the wing," I told him.

He thought about it for a few moments and replied, "The bones are terribly broken, but I think that I could put light weight stainless steel tubes on them for support and they just might heal. But he will probably never fly again."

"Do it," I said.

He did. After the operation, the vet told us that the hawk was doing well considering everything. We were elated. He also told us the raptor was a large male Swainson's Hawk.

The next day, the kids and I made the first of the many visits to see the raptor. We had decided to name him Phoenix. He had come through the surgery well and we hoped that he would rise, as the mythical Phoenix had risen from the ashes and fly again. Phoenix was kept in a cage that was just large enough to allow him to move around. His wings were wrapped tightly to his body so that the broken wing would be immobilized and have a chance to heal.

A strange thing happened when Phoenix saw us. He came to the front of the cage and looked at each one of us for a few moments. I had a feeling that he knew who we were and that he was grateful for our help.

Phoenix had been shot in the early April. As he improved, he was moved to progressively larger cages, giving him room to move about more freely and hopefully maintain some of his muscle tone.

It was obvious to us that he knew who we were. When he saw us, he pressed tightly against the cage and allowed us to touch him. We would take turns gently massaging him—he seemed to enjoy it. For us, it was a thrill. After a few minutes of gentle rubbing, Phoenix usually ran around the cage and leaped from perch to perch. It seemed to us that he wanted to show us that he was healing and doing well. He would then come back to us for more attention.

In mid June, the vet said it was time to put Phoenix into a large flight cage and remove the wrappings that held his wings motionless for so long. We went into the cage with him. It was about ten feet wide fifty feet long and six feet high. We were excited that our new friend had survived and appeared to be in good health. We were about to learn if he would regain the use of his wings. We were afraid of the worst and hopeful for the best. Phoenix seemed excited. "He seems to know what is going to happen," I said, The vet agreed.

Phoenix didn't move a muscle as the vet

carefully removed the wrappings. Finally the last of the bandages were off and Phoenix was free to move his wings. He just sat there—quietly. The air grew tense with anticipation as we waited.

It seemed an eternity had passed when suddenly, his wings dropped slightly. He let them hang for a bit. Then he pulled them back up and extended them a little. Over the next half hour or so, Phoenix stretched his wings in and out—ever so slowly. Each time he extended them a bit more. Finally, he extended his wings almost to their full 50-inch span and held them there. It became so still you could have heard a snow flake falling. Suddenly, he began to flap his wings ever so gently. We jumped up and down, raised our arms over our heads and shouted with joy!

During the next few days, Phoenix used his wings more and more, but no one had seen him fly. One morning, before we entered his cage, the vet told us that he didn't think Phoenix could fly, because he hadn't yet. We were disappointed, but accepted that possibility.

When we entered the flight cage, Phoenix, came to us as he always did, and gave each of us our greeting. During the three months of his captivity, Phoenix had become more and more friendly. He now expected to perch on our arm or shoulder. He would caress our cheek with his head—we loved it. I was always the last one to hold him and when we were ready to leave, I would put him on a perch that extended from one side of the cage to the other. One day, as we said our good-byes, Phoenix spread his wings, dropped off the perch and glided to the perch at the far end of the cage. We went wild—he could fly! To this day, I believe that he waited for us to be there for his first flight. During the next couple of weeks, he exercised his wings and flew about the cage frequently. His flights became longer and he would fly from one end of the cage to the other, flip over in the air, flap his wings, and fly back to the other end.

By late July, it became obvious that Phoenix was ready to be released and the Doctor set a release date. On the big day, the kids and I woke up early and we hurried to the vet's office. As we walked in, the receptionist said, "Oh! I forgot to call you, the bird was released yesterday, because the doctor had to be out of town today."

The kids and I were heart broken. The kids cried, I tried not to.

When we arrived home, we were all feeling very low. We sat in the kitchen moping around and felt sorry for ourselves. Suddenly, there was a horrible ruckus in the back yard. It sounded as if something was after the chickens and ducks. The dogs were barking excitedly. I yelled at them to be quiet. We ran to see what was happening. Our hearts jumped into our throats at what we saw. Phoenix was sitting on our back fence.

We saw Phoenix almost every day for the rest of the summer. He would soar and circle over our house. We loved him and loved to watch him. He had touched our lives deeply.

October came and Phoenix flew south as all Swainson's Hawks do during their annual migration. The next Spring, a Swainson's Hawk began to soar over our house every day. We were sure that it was our beloved Phoenix. Soon, there were two Swainson's. We believed that it was our friend and his mate.

We moved away that Spring. We never saw Phoenix, our friend, and his mate again. I have often wondered if he still circles over our old house? And if he does, does he know we are no longer there? And if so, does he miss us as we miss him? We'll probably never know.

On the conditions that my children would be able to release Phoenix, if he survived and could fly again, I agreed to pay veterinarian $1,500.00 for his work. When I received the bill, I sent it back to him with note written on it which said, "You did not keep your part of our agreement. Therefore I will not pay the bill. If you've got the guts take me to court and think that you can win, please do so. I never heard from the vet again.

Skinny Dippin'

My boyhood friends and I had a favorite swimming hole that we called Spring Run. It was located at 9th East and 45th South in Salt Lake, about 4.5 miles from my house. We went there several times a week every summer from the time I was about nine until I was almost out of high school.

There was a large marshy area upstream from the swimming hole. The marsh was created by many springs which produced copious amounts of water. That water was the primary source for the larger of the two rivers that blended together. At the confluence of these rivers, they had scoured out an area that was about 30 feet wide, 50 feet long and 10 feet deep at its deepest point. The swimming hole was wonderful to swim in for a number of reasons. Due to its size the current wasn't very strong. The water was crystal clear and we could go underwater, open our eyes and see fish, other aquatic critters, and even the other kids. It was surrounded by large deciduous trees and a small sandy beach.

It was about 10 feet from the bridge railing to the surface of water. We never tired of diving off the bridge railing and trying to touch the bottom at the deepest place. The other guys always said they made it, but I didn't believe them. Because of my big feet and long arms I could out swim any of them. I only reached the bottom at the deepest point a couple of times. It was really hard to do. When you dove in, you had to turn around and swim against the current to get there.

When we swam at Spring Run, we always skinny dipped. One of the nutty things we did, when we were younger, was to stand on the railing of the bridge and have pissing contests. I really believe the guy that pissed the furthest on any given day was the one that had to "go" the most urgently, because no one ever won the contests consistently. As cars approached, we waited until the people in the cars could see that we were naked. Then we jumped into the river – laughing.

Curiosity

From the time I was about 7, until I was in my late teens, I did one thing religiously every month. I went the drug store and bought all the latest model airplane magazines.

When I was about 12, I was perusing the magazine rack to be sure that I hadn't missed one of my target publications, I noticed a magazine called *Sexology*. I was oblivious to sex then, but my hormones had begun to flow. I was filled with curiosity and longed to learn about sex. But things like that were considered to be dirty and nasty in those days. I was afraid to even mention the word bra or anything that dealt with the opposite sex. One day I overcame my utter fear of having someone see me looking at that kind of material. After looking around to be sure no one was watching, I quickly grabbed a copy of *Sexology* from the magazine rack and put it inside a model airplane magazine. Then, when I was sure no one was around, I opened both magazines and read the one about sex while it was hidden inside the other magazine. I didn't understand a thing I read about until I had a health and hygiene class in junior high and I learned a bit about sex and how babies were made. I always wanted to know more, but was afraid to ask.

In retrospect, the material in the *Sexology* magazine was less informative than the advertising we see on TV today. I still have problems with some of the openness we experience now. But, I think the change is positive. I am adjusting to it slowly.

When I was young, I learned, in church, that sex was a terrible, filthy, sinful act. I grew up trying to figure out why the act that creates each of us is such a horrible and sinful thing. My grandkids are growing up knowing that sex isn't horrible or sinful. They have a better understanding of what it's all about than I did. And they deal with it in an entirely different way. They also understand the consequences of poor choices.

Personally, I like the changes that are occurring. I think that they are positive and will result in better relationships between the sexes; relationships based upon knowledge, understanding, equality and mutual respect.

I also believe better understanding and openness will result in fewer sex crimes. I have always felt that most, if not all, sexual predators began their misdeeds because of curiosity – curiosity that could be satisfied by a good education.

My Mud Hen Dinner

When I was in Junior High School, eating was often a necessary waste of time. I did what I could to get it over with as quickly as possible.- That usually meant taking big bites, chewing rapidly, and swallowing.

One day, about half an hour before our family's usual dinner time, I headed out of the house to meet some friends. Mom asked, "Where are you going?"

"I have to meet some of the guys." I responded.

"We'll be having dinner as soon as your dad gets home and you're not going anywhere—until you've eaten."

"Mom, I've got to meet the guys in 20 minutes and anyway, I'm not hungry." I protested.

Mom looked at me with her, *I know better than that look,* and said, "You're not going anywhere until you eat."

"But Dad isn't home yet, and if I have to wait until he gets here the guys will be gone." I moaned.

Mom thought a moment and said, "Well, I guess it will be alright if you eat dinner early just this once. But don't try to make a habit of it."

Mom put my dinner on the table. I shoved a fork load into my mouth and gagged. I spit it out and said, "Mom, this stuff is awful."

Mom was surprised by my comment. She gave me her, *Don't give me that line of baloney,* look, and said sternly, "I've slaved all day cooking the duck your Dad's friend gave him. You're not going anywhere until you eat everything on your plate."

"But Mom, it's the worst thing I've ever tasted. It tastes like a mix of marsh bottom mud and pond scum," I groaned.

"Don't "but" me. You're not going anywhere until you eat. That's final. I don't want to hear another word from you." Mom said angrily.

I groaned in protest and gulped down the duck. As I headed out the door, I hollered, "Honest Mom, there's something wrong with that stuff." As I ran to meet my friends, I couldn't stop thinking, That was the worst tasting crap that I had ever put in my mouth. Mom must be losing her cooking touch.

When I got home, Mom said, "Son, I owe you an apology. When your dad, sister, and I tasted that duck, it was as bad as you said it was and we couldn't eat it. Your dad called his friend and asked him about the duck. His friend apologized and told him that he didn't realize it at the time, but the ducks he shot were not ducks. They were Mud Hens."

Dear reader, I have a piece of advice to offer: If you ever have to choose between eating Mud Hen or death—choose death.

Male Mental Pause

Several years ago, while I was presiding over an Economic Development Corporation (EDC) meeting at the Red Fox Restaurant in Mariposa, California, an interesting event occurred. During a break in the meeting, I went to the Men's Room. When I returned, I took my seat at the head of the table. At the appropriate time, I stood and called the meeting back to order. As I was going through the next item on the agenda, Joyce Sterling raised her hand. I recognized her. She stood up and said in a very loud voice, "Lowell, your fly is open." Everyone in the room looked at my crotch and burst into laughter.

I looked down in disbelief. Sure enough, my fly was wide open. The sides of the fly couldn't have been any further apart if they had been propped open with a chopstick. I shrugged my shoulders, put an "oh well!" expression on my face and reached down to zip up my pants. As I pulled the zipper up, I said, "Now all of you know that I put clean shorts on this morning," and went on with the meeting as though nothing had happened.

A few weeks later, during another meeting of the EDC, Joyce raised her hand again. Knowing that she was a jokester and loved to make me the recipient of her pranks, I was reluctant to give her the floor, but I did. She rose to her feet with a big, sly smile on her face and said, "I would like to read something to all of you that I wrote especially for Lowell. (I braced myself and thought, *Good grief, what is she up to this time?*)

Joyce then read the following piece:

"There are four stages of male mental pause. The first stage of male mental pause occurs when you meet someone and you can't remember their name. This stages is mildly embarrassing, but not very serious. And everyone experiences it more often than they would like.

The second stage of male mental pause is similar to the first stage. It occurs when you meet someone and they say your name. You know you should know them, but you don't even recognize their face. Again, this happens to all of us now and it is more embarrassing and serious than the first stage.

The third stage of male mental pause is definitely more embarrassing and serious than the first two stages. Virtually all men experience it from time to time. It occurs when they forget to zip their zipper up.

The fourth and final stage of male mental pause has very serious and near fatal consequences. It occurs when a man forgets to zip his zipper down."

Who am I anyway?

Over the years, I have been known by many nicknames. Most of them, were earned. One of them taught me a great deal about life and people at a very young age. Most of them were just fun jabs. Others came from how people perceived me. At least one was a practical joke, and I was the butt of it. Some I took on for reasons that I will explain later on.

A couple of years ago, one of my younger granddaughters asked, "Papa, do you have any nicknames?"

"Yes, I've had several of them." I responded, and told her what several of them were.

"How did you get them Papa?"

That question got me thinking about the nicknames I've had and how I got them. That evening, I wrote down every nickname I could remember and wrote a few notes about how I acquired each them.

Over the next few months, I kept writing about my nicknames and the notes became short stories that if combined into one document would give my descendants a different view into my life. You will find those stories below.

When I was about seven, my friends started to call me Loco. Why, you might ask? I suppose it was because I gladly accepted any dollar bet that any yahoo offered. Anyone with a lick of common sense wouldn't consider doing any of them, but *I did*. I loved to climb to the top of huge trees and hang on to the thin branches as they bent down under my weight, and I would hang there almost upside down. I climbed sheer cliffs in the dead of winter. I dove into holes in the ice that covered a lake and swam around. I even borrowed an airplane and went for a flight. Did I mention that I had never taken an airplane off, or landed one?

Stolen Airplane

I spent much of my youth studying about building and flying model airplanes. I understood aerodynamics. I also had many hours of flying and handling the controls of several different types of small aircraft in the air and when preparing to land. I watched and copied every movement of the pilots as they took off and landed. I also spent many hours in the Link Trainer in the basement at Granite High School in Salt Lake.

One day in January of 1952, I was working at the Salt Lake City Municipal Airport with several friends who were also members of the Civil Air Patrol (CAP) unit that I was. We were washing the various CAP airplanes, checking oil levels, tire pressures, topping off fuel tanks, and making sure that they were ready if there was an incident that would require an air search and rescue effort.

We were finishing work on the last plane, a Piper L-4 "Grasshopper", when one of my friends said, "Lowell, I'll bet you a buck that you're afraid to fly this plane."

I said, without giving it a thought, "You're on." We pushed the L-4 out of the hangar. I gave the plane a pre-flight check, just like I had seen many pilots perform, and got into the cockpit. I told my friend to crank the prop. On the third attempt, the engine coughed, sputtered, and then jumped to life with a roar that only a 65-hp Continental flat-four engine can make. I checked to be sure there were no obstacles, taxied out of the hangar, and headed down the taxiway.

As I taxied on the tarmac, which I had done several times before, I was relieved that I didn't see any other aircraft moving around the airport. My main concern was fooling the guy in the control tower so that he would clear me for take-off. I put on the headset and taxied to the waiting-ramp. I ran the RPM of the engine up a bit and called the tower.

"Salt Lake Tower, this is Piper L-4 number 215271 requesting clearance for take off."

" Tower to Piper, you are a cleared for takeoff on runway 2 1 North."

" Thank you Tower."

I couldn't believe my luck. I had clearance to take off. This was the moment of truth.

Did I have the guts to do it? I just sat there until I was startled by the radio barking to life.

"Piper 215271 you have been cleared to take off on runway 2 1."

I pressed the mike button and said, "Thank you sir" Then I gave the engine some more fuel and began my taxi to the end of runway 2 1 North. I swung the plane's nose into the wind, and added RPM slowly. The last thing I wanted to do was a "hot dog take-off" that would attract attention. I kept the tail on the ground until I had enough speed for it to rise on it's own. As the tail came up, the speed increased and suddenly I was flying.

Holy crap, I'm flying. I'm soloing and it won't count. I can't tell anybody!

I had flown this very aircraft from this point of flight before. I knew what to do from here on. I kept my head in motion looking for other planes as I climbed to altitude. The lump of utter fear that had been in my throat melted away.

I headed west over the Great Salt Lake where there was a lot of flat land where I could crash-land if I had to. When I saw the white salt covered flats under me, I headed south to the small uncontrolled Midvale Airport about 15 miles south of Salt Lake. As I approached it from the north, I looked for the wind sock to get the wind direction. There was a north wind. I flew to the south end of the airport, lined up with the runway and made a slow decent flying into the wind.

Oh shit, I 'm dropping too fast. I'm not going to make it to the runway.

I added power and went around. On the next try I was too high so I went around again. On the next approach I was going too fast.

Man, I'm glad that I filled the tank before I took off.

After what seemed like a million tries, I finally floated over the end of the runway and made a perfect landing. Well, it was perfect after I stopped bouncing around like a dribbled basketball. I was ecstatic, exhilarated, and bursting at the seams with pride. I had done it. I made two more landings at Midvale and headed back to the Salt Lake Airport.

As I flew north, back to my final destination, a thought kept going through my mind:

My God, what if I get caught? They'll probably put me in jail and melt the keys to the cell.

That thought really scared me.

I lined up with the end of the runway and began my approach. Everything was going smoothly, except my heart, which was about ready to burst out of my chest. I got clearance to land and made a near perfect touch down. And I wasn't thinking about the old saying that any landing that you can walk away from is a good landing. I taxied back to the CAP hangar. No one was there, so I taxied into the hanger, parked ,the L-4, cut the engine and walked to my car. I was pissed. How was I going to collect my bet? I never did, even though I asked my friends to pay up. All they did was smile and shine me on with comments like, "What bet?"

Mt. Olympus

Another questionable thing I did on a dollar bet, was to climb the face of 9,753-foot high Mt. Olympus, during the winter. I took an old T-shirt with me and left it on the top of the mountain to prove I had been there.

I had been to the top of this mountain several times and knew the best route for going up in any season. I waited for a period of clear weather to do the climb. In the middle of January the Weather Service forecast a short period of sunny days. In a short time I would be on my way to win my dollar bet. I drove up the west slope of Mt Olympus on a muddy dirt road as far I could and parked my car. The sun was just peeking over the mountains. The sky was cloudless and the wind was resting from its labors of the previous day. The hike would be 4 ½ miles long with an elevation gain of about 4,500 feet. I figured that it would take me three hours to get to the top and a little less than that to get back to my car.

I hiked at a rapid pace on the crest of a long ridge that led to the south side of Mt. Olympus' rock face. In the winter, ridges are almost always easier to negotiate than the side slopes because the wind blows most of the snow off them and they get more sun. The south side of Mt. Olympus' face is the easiest way to ascend to its summit because it isn't as steep as the rest of the cliff. It also gets more sun than the rest of the face so there would be less snow, and I would be in the sun all day.

I reached the face in a bit under an hour and a half. From there on, because of the steepness of Mount Olympus' escarpment, the only place with heavy snow was on the many ledges. As with most climbs up steep inclines, getting up to the top is the easy part. I topped out in just over three hours. It had taken a little longer than I had thought it would, but still, I had made it in relatively good time considering it was winter.

The wind on top was fierce and the chill factor was unbearable. I swear, if I had been standing in that wind stark-naked, I couldn't have been colder. I needed to get going so I pulled out my old T-shirt, dug a hole in the snow, and stuffed the T-shirt into it. I put a rock on top of the shirt so it wouldn't blow away when the snow melted. I wanted to be darned sure that my friends would be able to find my shirt the following summer so that I could collect on the bet.

I took one last look at the valley and the mountains before I headed down the steep cliff. The Salt Lake Valley, the Great Salt Lake, and the mountains to the west were bathed in a golden light and glistened like jewels—it was breath taking. For me, going down a cliff is always more difficult than going up. On the way up, I can lean out and it is relatively easy to see hand holds that are above me. Coming down, that doesn't work as well because when I lean out, my body blocks most of my view. So, I have to feel around with my feet to find places to put them. And that can get down right scary because what feels like a good place to put my foot sometimes isn't, and could cause me to fall.

I was making good progress going down the sheer rock faces which were free of snow, but the ledges gave me a lot of trouble. They were filleted with concave junctions of frozen snow that were hard and slippery and I had a hard time securing a footing on them. About 2,000 feet down from the top on a narrow ledge, I put my weight on one foot; it went through the crusted snow, hit the rock below, and threw me off balance. I scrambled desperately to grab anything solid, in the hope of preventing a fall. I slid off the ledge and plummeted down from ledge to ledge. Finally, I hit a very wide ledge where the snow fillet was flat and deep. As I went through the snow, I hit something hard, rolled off and came to rest on my back. I was stunned and just laid there in the snow. I have no idea how long it was before a sharp throbbing pain on the left side of my stomach brought me to my senses and I became aware that I was injured. Because of the cold, I was afraid to open up my layers of clothing to see the severity of the injury. I reached under my clothes and felt a trickle of blood running down my side. I felt around very carefully to see how bad the injury was. I had a small cut that was about 4 inches long. It was bleeding a bit, but I wasn't too worried about it. I gently tucked my shirt back in and as I started to get up, a pain that was straight from the depths of hell tore through the calf muscle of my left leg. A five-inch shard of rock, a bit bigger in diameter than a pencil and shaped like an icicle protruded from my leg. I pulled the rock out of my leg and stuck my finger through the hole in my pants to check the injury. I wasn't bleeding much, but this injury worried me. If I couldn't walk, I'd have to crawl. If I had to crawl, the going would be very slow and that meant I would probably have to dig a den in the snow and spend the night on the mountain. I'd be damned lucky to survive the night. This thought scared the hell out of me.

I grabbed the rock outcropping that I had hit, and used it to pull myself to my feet. I gingerly tested my left leg to see if it would take my weight. Thank God, it did. I took a few short test steps to see if I could walk. Doing so hurt like hell, but I felt confident that I would be able to make it to my car. Now that I was on my feet and felt confident that I could walk, I looked around to determine where I was and which was the best route to take before I set out on the journey to my vehicle. The ledge I was on appeared to go all the way to the canyon on the south side of the shear rock face. If it did, I would be able to pick up the trail that I had broken in the snow when I came up the mountain. I decided to stay on the ledge and carefully work my way to its' south end—and hope. If I was right, it would be much easier, and far safer, to descend the rest of the way to my car. As I walked I led with my uninjured leg. To get a better footing on the slick, crusted snow, I stomped on it so that I my foot would penetrate the crust. It was slow going and painful. I cussed myself out and wondered why I let myself get into situations like this. Luck was with me once again. The ledge did go all the way to the canyon and I was able to find my trail.

It's hard to know for sure, but I believe there are a couple of reasons that I wasn't killed. The snow on the ledges formed concave fillets on them. When I hit a ledge, my body put a dent into the snow and that cushioned and slowed my fall. Because the snow was sloped, I slid off the ledge and fell to the next one. I bounced along like that until I hit a ledge that was wider, so the snow on it was deeper and softer. When I hit that snow, it absorbed most of the energy of my fall and I sank deeper into it and that stopped me from rolling off. Another thing that helped was that I had learned to relax when I was falling and to roll, as I hit the ground. In this situation, I wasn't able to roll when I hit the snow, but I was able to relax as I fell.

When I finally reached my car, the sun was setting behind the mountains. I opened the car door and sat on the seat with my feet still on the ground. I was exhausted from the strenuous trek. I just sat there for a few moments. Then, I reached down and pulled up my pant leg. I was relieved to see that the hole in my leg was barely bleeding. I opened my coat and shirt to look at my stomach. The injury was more of a deep scratch than a cut and it had stopped bleeding. I put my right leg into the car and lifted my left leg in. I shut the door, started the engine, turned the heater on, and just sat there resting while the car warmed up. I thought about what had happened that day, and I became acutely aware of how lucky I was. The fall could have killed me, or I could have been injured so badly that I couldn't have walked out, and I probably would have frozen to death. Instead, I was sitting in my car getting warmed on the outside by the car's heater, and on the inside by the joy of being alive and the exhilaration of having cheated death again. I put the car in gear and drove home.

I never said anything to my folks about what had happened, but years later Mom asked me if I remembered the day when I came home with the injuries on my leg and stomach. I asked, "How did you know?" She never said a thing. She just gave me that "wouldn't you like to know smile" that only a mother can give.

When I got home, I did something that was uncharacteristic of me; I went right to my room and went to bed. That probably made Mom wonder what was going on and I suspect that after I was asleep, she must have checked me over and had seen that I had been hurt. Knowing Mom, she probably watched me like a hawk for a week or two. If there had been a problem, she probably would have intervened.

This was another bet that I never collected. None of the guys who made the bet with me had the guts to climb Mt. Olympus and find my shirt.

Hole In The Ice

One beautiful day in December, five of my buddies and I drove to Echo Dam to see what our favorite swimming lake looked like in the winter. We were clowning around on the ice when one of my friends said, "Loco, I'll bet you a buck that you won't go for a swim."

"I would, but I can't because the lake is frozen over." I responded with cocky confidence.

"Would you do it if we made a hole in the ice?" A second friend asked.

Without a thought, I said, "Sure if all of you put a buck into the pot."

One of my friends walked over to the edge of the lake, got a dead tree limb that was about ten feet long and five inches in diameter. He stood the limb on end, lifted it up as high as he could and slammed it down. The blow put a small dent in the surface of the ice. It took a while, but they finally broke a hole in the ice that was about three feet across.

I thought about what I was going to do for a few minutes. I figured that the water under the ice would be above freezing and I had swum in water that cold before. So, I pulled the big pieces of ice out of the hole, stripped down to my socks, shorts and T-shirt, stood on the edge of the hole, bent over, put my hands together over my head and dove into the water.

I probably should have just jumped in. I dove in because it was quicker and easier. I deliberately didn't go very deep because I wanted to go in and out quickly. As I came back up, I opened my eyes so I could see the hole and go right to it.

Holy shit, where's the hole? I thought.

I couldn't see it and I didn't know where it was. As I swam around a bit looking for the hole, I began running low on air and a wave of panic crept through me. I had been in scary situations like this before and I did what I always did in predicaments like this; I began to talk to myself.

Okay, you're been in worse messes than this before and you got out of all of them. If you panic, you're not gonna get out of this, so be calm, keep your wits about you, and think about what you need to do.

As I swam around under the ice, I remembered that there were little pockets of air between the ice and the water. I went up to the ice, rolled over on to my back, put my lips up against the ice and exhaled a bit of air. I couldn't hear or see any air bubbles, so I sucked in very gently just in case there wasn't any air. Man, was I relieved when air, not water came into my mouth.

I stayed on my back and began to move around a bit, trying to find the opening in the ice. I was chilled clear to my bones and I needed another breath of air when I saw a shadow on the ice above me.

It must be one of the guys. I moved toward the other end of the shadow. As I moved, I saw another shadow and then the hole.

I bobbed up through the hole, grabbed on to the edge of the ice and stuck an arm out. My friends grabbed me and hauled me out of the water. As cold as I was under the water, I was even colder out in the air. As I took several deep breaths, I took my dripping wet underwear off, pulled my dry clothes on and then I ran to the car.

In the car, I started shaking violently. I don't know if it was caused by the cold, or the damned scary close call I just had, or both. I had been taught to always have a bag full of warm dry clothes and blankets in my vehicle just in case I needed them. Lucky for me, I heeded that advice. Now, I needed them. I wrapped up in the blankets, gave my keys to a friend, and he drove us home.

On the way home, I collected a buck from each of my friends. I swear to God, this was one of the few times I ever collected on one of my idiotic dollar bets. And now, you have a pretty good idea of why I got my first nick name—"Loco."

Loco

When my friends first started calling me Loco, it really hurt my feelings and there were many times, I ran home crying. My mother always consoled me and repeated the old saying, "Sticks and stones can break your bones but names will never hurt you." She always managed to make me feel better, but her efforts never fully removed the pain I felt. One day when I ran home sobbing, my dad was there. I was scared. I was sure that he wouldn't understand and that he would call me a sissy. Anyway, I knew that he hated me because he was always on my case for something. I tried to avoid him, but he put his big paw out and gently pulled me toward him and asked, "What's was the matter son?"

"Everybody calls me Loco." I sobbed.

Dad's face softened in a way that I had never seen before. He responded in a tone of voice that could have come from my mom or one of my grandmas, "Why do they call you Loco?

"I don't know."

"Are you loco?"

"No!"

"Then, why do you let it bother you? " Dad asked. He waited until I answered.

"I don't know."

Dad waited a minute, as if he was in deep thought or reliving an event in his life.

Finally he said, "Son, the only thing that matters is the truth, and in your heart of hearts you know what the truth is. If you're loco and you know you are, then accept that fact. If you're not loco, and you know you're not, accept that fact also. You need to learn to ignore what others say, because the truth is all that matters, not what other say or think about you." It took a while for what Dad had said to sink in, but after it did, I was never again bothered by what people called me.

That nickname followed me from my early grammar school years through my first two years of college in Utah. When I moved to California in 1955, I thought the nickname was a thing of the past and I actually missed it. It had almost become a term of endearment, and it was always a good topic of conversation at a party. Best of all, it frequently made me the center of attention, especially with the girls, and I loved that.

In my second semester at Fullerton J.C., a friend from Salt Lake showed up at school. Once again, I became known as Loco. I finally lost the name for good in 1957 when I moved o San Jose, California.

Lonesome Lowell

In 1957, I enrolled at San Jose State College and pledged to the Sigma Phi Epsilon fraternity. I moved into the fraternity house at the beginning of my second semester. One evening, there was a knock on door to my room. I opened the door and there stood three of my fraternity brothers with odd grins on their faces. They asked me to donate a dollar for an ad in the Spartan Daily, the school paper. When I asked what the ad was for, all they would tell me was that it was secret, and everyone else in the house had donated. Because of their grins and their evasiveness, I was suspicious of their motives and I said no to their request.

Three days later, I was very glad I had not

donated to my fraternity brother's project in the school paper. There was a full page add in the Spartan Daily, with an 8 ½ x 11 picture of none other than me in the center of the page. Under my picture, there was a caption in large bold capital letters stated, "LONESOME LOWELL HAS LOST HIS GIRL AND DOESN'T KNOW WHERE TO FIND HER." I was flabbergasted when I saw the ad. At first, I was pissed off at my frat brothers. Then, I realized that it was all in good fun and they meant no harm. There was a telephone number in the ad. It was the number of the pay phone in the entrance hall of our fraternity house.

During the next few weeks, more than 300 girls called the fraternity house and asked to talk to Lonesome Lowell. My fraternity brothers took turns answering the phone. They told the girls that *they* were Lonesome Lowell and made dates with them. I was working full-time, as well as carrying a full load in college and was totally unaware of what was going on.

Soon, there were several "I Hate Lowell Young Clubs" at San Jose State. Some of them actually met in the Student Union and had signs on their table that read, "We hate Lowell Young." I wondered why they hated me, when to the best of my knowledge, we had never met. But, knowing my frat bothers as I did, I had a very good idea. All I can say is I was totally innocent.

One day, just for fun, I went to one of the tables that had a sign on it and asked, "What's that sign all about?"

One of the girls responded, "He's a lying,

two timing jerk!"

The other girls nodded in agreement. I just about swallowed my teeth and choked on them. They were talking about *me* and I didn't know any of them.

When I had recovered from the shock of learning what a rotten guy I was, I asked, "What did this guy do to make you so mad?" After hearing several stories about how they had been taken for fools, I asked, "What does this guy look like?"

One of the girls described him, "He was slim, about six foot four inches tall with blond hair and blue eyes."

Another girl said, "No, he's about six foot, a bit heavy and has dark hair and blue eyes."

The table became silent and the girls looked at each other. Slowly, they realized they each had been out with a different guy. I could never understand how could they have been taken in like that. Surely, they had seen my picture in the ad. Thinking back, I wish that I had thought to ask. Finally one of the girls looked at me and asked, "Who are you?" The girls looked at me and waited for a response. I wasn't sure what to say, because I didn't want to get torn apart by a bunch of mad women. Finally, I said. "I'm Lowell Young." Their silence told me what they were thinking.During the next few days, I went to the tables of other "I Hate Lowell Young Clubs" and settled the issue in a similar fashion.

It turned out that not many had actually seen my picture in the paper. It was amazing how word of mouth gossip traveled on campus. It wasn't long before the "I Hate Lowell Young Clubs" disappeared. I was glad, but I have to say I missed them. It was fun having all that attention. I did get a lot of razzing about the whole "Lonesome Lowell" episode and there were very few people that believed that I was unaware of what was going on. For several years after I left San Jose State, I continued to receive mail from lonely hearts clubs.

Duke

In the early to mid-1970s, my wife Kay and I joined an organization called the Creative Initiative Foundation (CIF). Unknown to us at the time, this organization would have a dramatic impact on our lives. Two of the CIF's goals were to bring about positive change in the lives of individuals, and in how people interacted with each other world-wide. The focus of those goals was to end war and establish world-wide peace. Their motto was, "We Are One, One Earth, One Spirit, One Humanity."

While in the CIF, we met five families with whom we became very close friends. We spent a great deal of time together for many years. We went on many vacations together and celebrated various holidays of several different religions together. During this time, there was a resurgence of John Wayne movies, and the children of these families thought I looked like him. So, they began to call me "Duke", which was John Wayne's nick name.

Darth

In the 1960s and the early 1970s, the nuclear power industry was growing by leaps and bounds worldwide. The ballyhoo was that nuclear power was a source of abundant, cheap, safe and clean electrical power. However, some people began to question what we were being told as information about potential problems with nuclear power plants began to reach the public. It was also during this period that three engineers who worked for General Electric in top management, quit their jobs because of the dangers they saw in nuclear generation plants that no one in the industry or the government was speaking about.

Over a period of many months, I had numerous long conversations about nuclear plants with two of my best friends, Greg Miner and Dale Bridenbaugh. They were two of the engineers who had resigned their jobs because of their concerns about the safety of nuclear power plants. Greg and Dale and their families were also members of the CIF.

Their primary concern was the emergency core cooling system. This system had been designed as a fail-safe mechanism to shut down the reactor safely if there were an emergency. The problem was that the emergency core cooling system had never been demonstrated to work. As I understand it, not even the scale models that were built to demonstrate the effectiveness of the system ever worked. Because of what was learned from the GE engineers and the information that was becoming available, the CIF made several decisions. First, as an organization it would oppose the development of nuclear energy for the generation of electricity. Second, it would work to inform the public about the dangers of nuclear power plants. And third, it would work to end the use of nuclear power plants for the generation of electrical power.

The main focus of the CIF was truth in all matters. As a result, nothing was accepted at face value and this was the case with nuclear power. Every bit of information was checked out to be sure of its veracity. As I learned more about the dangers of nuclear power plants, my concern about their safety grew. When I became aware of the incidents at Browns Ferry and Three Mile Island, my earlier enthusiasm for the industry began to wane. What finally ended my strong support for the industry was learning that the nuclear power industry, and sadly, our government, were covering up what had happened at these facilities.

I was appalled and dismayed to learn that our government was lying to us. I expected that from any business or industry, but not our government. Suddenly, I became aware of and was shocked by how naïve I was. Rattled to my core, for several days I loitered in a deep funk. I felt totally betrayed. At that time, I was in my mid thirties, and I felt utterly stupid for having allowed myself to be duped for so long. I was filled with hate and anger. I had never been so angry before, nor since. Finally, I decided that I had wallowed in the shit long enough, and I made a 180 degree turn. I became a strong skeptic of our government and no longer supported nuclear power. For me, it was a pivotal point in my life. I would never be the same again. My focus would be to make life better for everyone, however I could.

I believe that if you see a problem then you have a responsibility to do something about it. I also believe that if you are opposed to something then you must come up with positive alternatives to it if you want to bring about any change. Therefore, I was very reluctant to get on the bandwagon and try to bring an end to the development of nuclear power, unless there was a positive alternative. So, I began looking around for viable alternatives to nuclear power.

I had been building homes and doing remodeling jobs for a few years. The first house I built as a general contractor had a number of solar panels on its roof. I didn't know a thing about solar energy, so I began to read everything I could find about it. As a result of this research, I became convinced that solar energy was the positive alternative to nuclear energy that I was looking for. I made it known to my friends in the CIF, that I couldn't, in good conscience, oppose nuclear power unless we could offer a viable alternative to it. I also made it clear that I believed that solar energy was the answer. Because solar energy was relatively new and untried, most people dismissed it as untried and unworkable. Still, I was convinced it was the solution. So I dug in and went to work persuading others to look more deeply into solar power and to back me in my effort to offer it as a viable alternative to nuclear power.

My refusal to get on the band-wagon and oppose nuclear energy unless we adopted the use of solar energy, and promoted it as an alternative energy source to nuclear power, irritated many people in the CIF. Some of them began to feel that I was a negative influence in the organization. All of this was occurring at the time when the first Star Wars movie came out and Darth Vader was the epitome of the Dark, or Negative Force. The group of families that we had become close friends with spoke openly with one another and with our children. All the kids in the group quickly picked up on the negative feelings about me, and began to call me "Darth." It wasn't long before everyone was calling me "Darth" with teasing, knowing smiles on their faces.

In response to this nickname, I had a license plate on my truck that read, "DA FORCE." Ultimately, I put all of my energy into bringing about the end of nuclear power. The CIF also got on the band-wagon by promoting solar energy, and Alton Associates was formed to develop and promote solar energy as a positive, viable alternative to nuclear power. Ronald Reagan ended all government support for alternative energy development, which in those days was primarily solar. A few years later most solar energy companies including Alton Associates closed their doors. As a result of President Reagan's action, development of solar energy moved from our country to China and Germany.

The positive result of the CIF's work was that the media and the public became aware of the problems that were inherent with nuclear power plants, and further development of them in this country began to subside.

Trouble

I have never fully understood how I got this nick name. People who know me, seem to think the name is fitting, for some reason. Frankly, I think all of them are a little bit nutty. It seems to have started when I was living in Tuolumne County, California. The first time I remember hearing it was when I walked in to a school recreation hall in Twain Harte, to go square dancing. As I walked into the hall, a gravelly voiced woman, who was sitting at a table selling raffle tickets, looked at me and said, with a big, playful grin on her face, "Oh oh, here comes trouble."

"Me?" I said, with a surprised, dumbfounded tone in my voice.

"Yes you!" She replied, with great enthusiasm.

The woman and I had a fun, and lighthearted chat for a few minutes and then I went into the hall looking for a single woman to dance with. The gravelly voice woman seemed to realize that I was single and from that moment on she was constantly trying to set me up with some of her single friends.

The name seemed to come about in a gradual manner. I would go to meetings of various types and every now and then someone would say, "You're nothing but trouble", in a joking,

good-natured manner. I took the comment like I take all comments of this kind, with a grain of salt. I even had a little bit of fun poking back at people who had made the comment.

When Sue and I began to travel the name "Trouble" seemed to pop up in the darnedest places, and times and more frequently. We could walk into a restaurant where we had never been before and the waitress would look at me and say, "Here comes trouble!" I'd look around and there wasn't anyone there but Sue and me. Then, I would point a finger at myself with an expression of disbelief on my face and say. "Me?" Invariably, the waitress would say, "Yes, you."

Sue says that I am trouble and that I have earned the name. I guess it's because I really do enjoy making people smile and laugh whenever I can. I especially enjoy doing this with people that I know receive a lot of flak from the people that they have to deal every day, like waitresses, receptionists and people who answer the phone for complaint calls.

Papa Mean, Uncle Mean and Mr Mean

Uncle Mean and Papa Mean are names that I took on myself. Our family spread out and it became very difficult and expensive, to spend much time together. As a result, the kids in our family didn't have a feeling of belonging to a family larger than their immediate family. I felt sad for my nieces, nephews and my own kids. They didn't have the opportunity to know their cousins, uncles and aunts as my siblings and I did.

When Lorna, my sister, and I were growing up, our cousin Garee's stepmother treated him much like Cinderella's stepmother treated her in the fairytale. Our folks became Garee's legal guardians and he lived with us for several years. The three of us were, as far as we were concerned, siblings. As we matured, and started families of our own we became separated by large distances because of where we went to school and/or had jobs.

I felt that having a relationship with, knowing about and having positive feelings for an extended family, was important. So, whenever our families were able to get together, I started telling the kids that I was Uncle Mean, in a playful way, because I thought that it would give them something to rally around. All of the kids loved the name and started to call me by my chosen moniker. They took great delight in coming together and ganging up on the meanest uncle in the world—me. And they gleefully introduced their friends to their "Uncle Mean." I took great delight in watching the reaction of the kids that I had just been introduced to, as I played the role of being the meanest uncle in the world. It took most kids a few minutes to catch on, but after that, there was another member in the gang of kids that were out to best "Uncle Mean."

Over the years, we had various articles of clothing made for them with "Uncle Mean's Team" printed on them. When we got together, the kids always had their Uncle Mean clothes on. As a result of my assumed character and name, they felt a strong kinship with and love for each other. Giving them this feeling of belonging was very important to me and as it turned out, it was very important to them. After all, they had a common enemy to tease, chase and wrestle with. To this day, all of my nieces and nephews and their kids continue to call me, with great delight, "Uncle Mean."

Sue and I have six kids between us. When they began to give us grandkids, I added the name "Papa Mean" to my list of nick names. I did this for the same reasons that I had adopted the name "Uncle Mean."

Sue and I wanted to be able to spend more time with our grandkids, so years ago, we began having grandkids week. In the first batch there were four of them, and we had them at our home for a week. Katie was the sole member of the second batch and she was with us for just three or four days. There are eight of them in the third batch and they are usually with us for a weekend. Having as many as eight kids between the ages of nine and eleven for an entire week, is just a little too much for us to deal with, now that we are in our 70s. All the grandkids still call me Papa Mean and so do their parents. I really love my "Uncle Mean" and "Papa Mean" names. They feel very warm and fuzzy, and they fit like well worn gloves.

PITA

I got this name because of something that happened to me during an annual physical examination. The doctor tore the sphincter muscle in my rectum when he checked my prostrate gland. When the pain didn't go away after a few days, I went back to the Doctor to have him check things out. After he had finished, he said, "I want you to see a Proctologist.

The following week-end, on my way to my parents home in Oakview, California, I stopped at the proctologist's office in Fresno. After examining me, he told me," You have a very nasty tear in the sphincter muscle in your rectum, and it is very unlikely that your injury will heal on its own."

"And what are your recommendations?" I inquired

"The best course of action would be surgery. I can repair the damage to the muscle. I can schedule you for surgery next week." The doctor responded.

"What do you do, put stitches in the tear?" I asked.

"No, I would go in and make 12 or 13 very small incisions in the skin that covers the muscle. That would allow the muscle to stretch out and take the tension off of the tear. And that would allow the tear and cuts to heal."

"And what is the downside of the surgery?" I asked.

"The downside is there's a 50-50 chance that you will be incontinent, and need to wear diapers the rest of your life."

"And what would you recommend that I do in the meantime?" I inquired.

The doctor recommended that I do several things until the day of my surgery, such as sitting on an inflatable donut, especially when driving, and taking a high fiber supplement that he would prescribe.

I told the doctor, "I have to go to Southern California to help my elderly parents move to a new home, and I am not sure how long that will take. "I'll get back to you as soon as I return home to schedule the surgery."

I wasn't too excited about what the doctor had said. It didn't make much sense to me to create what could be additional problems, by cutting slices into my sphincter muscle The doctor was a pleasant fellow, but I was more than a bit put off by the fact that surgery was the first thing that he recommended.

I stopped at the first drugstore, I came to, went in, got the prescription filled, and took the first dose of the cherry flavored high fiber concoction. I damn near choked on the stuff, it tasted like mud.

The next day my sister and I began packing all of Mom and Dad's belongings and getting ready for the move to Alhambra. Despite all the delays and interruptions, Lorna and I had everything ready for the movers who were coming the next day.

In the morning while doing my daily chores, I had an experience the likes of which I never want to have again. My stools were almost the size of tennis balls and were hard as rock. I could feel the tear in my sphincter muscle ripping apart as they passed. It was absolutely excruciating. I spent the next few days in utter agony.

I realized that the high fiber diet was the wrong thing for me and it had been a major mistake. I stopped it immediately. For the next several days, I popped an over-the-counter pain pill every four hours.

When I returned home, I called my Doctor to make an appointment to see him. His receptionist told me, "The Doctor is very busy and won't be able see you for several weeks. I'll call the

Proctologist and make an appointment for you to have the surgery he recommended.

"I'm not interested in the surgery. I want to see the doctor and talk to him about other options." I told her.

She responded, "I'll talk to him about it and call you back." I never did see my doctor.

Stopping the high fiber diet produced the results I wanted. My stools were back to normal and as a result, the pain that I was experiencing had lessened a bit.

Our daughter Carolynn who was studying to become a nurse, was visiting us for the weekend. She left one of her textbooks on nutrition with us to read to see if we could find a solution to my problem.. Sue dug into the book and found some very interesting things about the kind of rectal injuries like mine. The book stated that when there is a problem in the anal area the patient should be put on a very bland, fiber restricted diet. It specifically recommended poached eggs, milk, Jell-O and other low fiber foods. Sue put me on this diet immediately and pureed everything I ate. This was the exact opposite what the proctologist and my doctor had told me to do.

During this time, which went on for at least three months, I spent my days and nights lying on the floor in front of the television trying not to cry. Sitting was agonizing. Walking was all put impossible. Crawling was a bit easier. I couldn't lay on my back, and lying on either side for too long was painful. I made repeated calls to my Doctor. I got the same results from the receptionist. She happily made an appointment with the proctologist for me. The Proctologist's receptionist would call to confirm the appointment and I would cancel it. I called other doctors and hospitals. None would see me. I suspect that it was because when I told them about my problem over the phone, they were afraid that I was a law suit looking for a place to happen.

Finally, in desperation, I called the Urgent Care center in Oakhurst. When I began explaining my problem to the receptionist she interrupted me, and asked, "Why are you on the telephone? Why aren't you here?"

After Dr. Schaffner examined me, he asked, "What the hell did they use on you, a frayed ended flagpole?" I burst into laughter, the most painful laughter I have ever experienced. It was the first good laugh that I had had in months and it was worth the pain.

Dr. Schaffner, Sue, and I talked about my problem for a time and he said that the course of action we had taken was the one he would have prescribed. He saw me frequently over the next couple of weeks, and thanks to his help, my problem began to heal and heal well.

I am sure you can imagine how unpleasant and stressful this whole period of time was for Sue. It was during this episode that Sue began to call me PITA, which stands for—well, I'll let you figure that one out for yourself. Sue says that it fits me to a "T" and I haven't got the guts to disagree. But between you and me, I don't think that I am a Pain In The Ass.

Not long after this, I felt that Sue needed a nickname. A nickname that described her in every respect, and also told her what I thought of her each time that I used it. It didn't take me long to come up with "MEL." It means, Mighty Elegant Lassie and it depicts her perfectly.

Teresa Scott

Smoke is still rising from the Rim fire in Yosemite, My first evacuation experience occurred in another fire 6 weeks or so prior. I had to write about it of course. A plebian effort. How can anyone experience fear and acceptance at the same time? The current fire is still burning. Hail the heroes within the firefighter community.

Recently I fulfilled a wish in creating pieces on the Vietnam War, discovering a friend who was willing to talk about his experience. My thanks to Richard Perez of 11th Cavalry for his willingness to go there, in both senses- a soldier who enlisted and who still serves fellow veterans, and foremost for answering my questions. Errors are mine.

Mother's Day, 1974

August, 2013 the 93rd Anniversary of the 19th Amendment to the Constitution of the U.S. State

"The right of citizens of the United States to vote shall not be denied or abridged by the United

States or by any State on account of sex."

I had recently become involved with the National Organization for Women. We were scheduled to picket for the Choice Movement and would ride the bus back and forth from NJ to Washington, DC where we would peacefully demonstrate in front of the Iranian Embassy.

Finally some action! I was jazzed. So far the meetings had been very "housewifey": recipes, crafts, conversation, coffee and doughnuts. Before signing up, I talked with my Mom for her input. She supported my desire to participate, not quite enthusiastically, but favorably. Among the group that boarded the bus, were housewives, mothers and like myself, working women with and without kids. Basically weekend warriors for Women's Rights. Yes, indeedy, I was one of them. Not quite radical enough, however, to burn my bra. In 1973, Roe vs. Wade was passed, for better or for worse.

At the beginning of our ride to Washington, we had been instructed to think about slogans to put on the posters we would be carrying. What I came up with was "My body, my choice." That event was my personal high point in Women's Liberation. Although I continued to support the movement with my dues to NOW, I was far too busy with my career, another second job with Weight Watchers and night school at Rutgers University, to dedicate another night to solidarity with the sisterhood while I crocheted. But I did continue in small acts of activism.

I received reparations resulting from a consent decree between AT&T and the US government. I held a job in the Plant department at what was then NJ Bell Telephone, an AT&T company. When the parent company signed the consent decree, money was awarded to women on the basis that we were paid less than men in comparable positions. After thinking about it, I decided not to cash the $91 check. Eventually, my immediate supervisor asked me if I had lost the check. I told her no, I was keeping it for a souvenir. A few days later the next interview was with our 3rd level Department head boss who called us into the office and asked me to explain. I told him I personally never felt discriminated against, but if indeed, I were, it was certainly not to the tune of $91, as at that time I had 9 years of service. He explained that the books could not be closed until all the checks were cashed and I was holding that up. Such power! After reasoning with me for a while, I capitulated and agreed to cash the check. The argument that convinced me was "Put it on your phone bill."

One of my work assignments had been as a member of a four person team to validate, or not, findings of a study "Women in the Crafts" and to make recommendations for action, if indeed we found deficiencies. In due course, we found that physiology and peer pressure affected job performance and that with rare exceptions, women failed to perform to the same level as men. Women who were athletic succeeded. When my turn came, I was offered a field position as a Foreman in the installation department.

Job duties included supervision of a "gang" of between six and eight Installers who routinely climbed telephone poles. According to Bell System Practices, safety inspections were performed by the foreman on the job as well as after the work was complete, necessitating pole climbing at least 68 times a month. Expecting no special treatment I booked myself into pole climbing class at Plant School and purchased the required steel-toed work boots. I already had the OSHA (Occupational Safety and Health Act) safety eyeglasses and hard hat.

The preliminary classes took place in the rubber room where neophytes were taught the basics in as safe an environment as possible. To prevent injury should a fall result from cutout when the climber hooks slip, the room, walls and floor were lined with thick puckered rubber.

My instructor arrived a few minutes after me. He was shorter than I, dressed in a one-piece work uniform. He introduced himself and handed me a safety belt and a set of climbing hooks and told me to put them on. With his back turned to me he told me which pole to climb. When he turned toward me, he saw me at the top of the pole. "Get the hell down from there before you break your neck," he yelled. The pole was not as high as the normal pole found in the field and indeed had no telephone nor electric wires on it. Nor did I wear a tool belt, which I would have had on the job. "OK," he said, "we're gonna do this the right way." I was told to direct my efforts toward planting my hooks correctly, first one foot, then the other while standing on the floor. My instructor gave me closer attention and issued no further challenges. Exhausted, all I wanted at the end of the day was to go home, a hot shower and a drink. After relaxing I knew I had some thinking to do. And promised myself, later.

The 3rd level manager suggested that I might do what the older Foremen do, have a lead Installer actually do the inspections at the work site on the pole. Climbing technique I could observe from the ground. What I asked for and was told I could not have was a bucket truck. What's that saying? Hindsight is 20-20. I regarded my options and did not accept the position. Hindsight was that I should have bought my own bucket truck. Since I was identified as a likely manager in what historically was a man's world, I was assigned studies wherein I learned about various opportunities. Even when I moved cross-country from NJ to California, those non-traditional jobs were the ones offered.

Other acts of feminism were fun and sometimes produced unexpected results. I sent an editorial to the local IBEW (International Brotherhood of Electrical Workers) asking the labor union to think about non-sexist job titles. The letter was published in the paper with a cartoon depicting a Playboy Bunny in trademark ears, grossly overweight, unshaven and with long curly leg and armpit hair. The caption read "Won't these EEOC (Equal Employment Opportunity Commission) people leave well enough alone?" wasn't that a telling remark. My manager, a woman, accused me of fame seeking , of wanting my name in print. Me, I found it funny. And there was no other fallout from higher management.

In a show of solidarity with the other departmental women, secretaries, technicians like my self and 2nd level managers, we made a different point with the 3rd level. He was very fond of bragging about "his girls" and the Instructional Technology we produced. So we dressed ourselves in girly clothes and invaded his office. Some wore super mini-skirts, one wore her old cheer leader uniform, I wore a pair of blue shorts over thick black hose, a t-shirt, my steel-toed work boots and my hard hat. We draped ourselves around his desk and one "girl" sat on the edge of his desk facing him, legs crossed, as though taking dictation. The pictures back then were *Polaroid's* that developed instantly. Point made.

Ben and Jake

Two little boys, age eight and seven out of school for the summer, entertained themselves with train watching, something they learned from Gramps. Ben was eight, idolized by his younger brother Jake who was seven. By the time their mother, Dolly went to work at 12 noon, the boys were headed out to their favorite spot for a day by the tracks. Jake carried the brown paper lunch bag and blanket. They knew the schedule pretty well, when to expect the freight trains on long hauls, and the local shorter distance cars. Gramps had told them, before he went to Heaven that they should never walk on the rails and when they laid down the blanket, not to get too close to them. The boys found a spot where a tree leaned over the fence, providing shade. In the scorching summer days even the hot breeze the trains made was welcome, and would stir the leaves.

Ben felt important when he shared his train knowledge with his younger brother. Sometimes Jake would ask a question for which Ben did not know the answer and he would invent one. Jake never questioned the information exchange, believing every word out of Ben's mouth as though it were gospel. Being older, Ben was in charge, by dictate of their mother and Jake was ordered around, quite willing to comply. Also their Mom entrusted the front door key to Ben, who preened in front of Jake.

They played many games: estimating the length of the train was a favorite as was the number of cars the engines pulled or pushed, determined by listening to the sound of the rails. An ear placed on the track told them many things. Although just lucky, Ben would guess the engine function, push or pull or both, and how many engines were required to move the trains down the track. Not too far south of the blanket was a switch where trains would move to an inside track to give place for a train of higher priority, usually a passenger train. But by far, most trains were freight trains, hauling chemicals, food stuffs, automobiles, lumber, and some refrigerated cars identified by their compressor tanks. When a train pulled up and stopped on the siding the boys could take a closer look at the cars. Graffiti was colorful in both paint and language and the boys tried to decipher the messages.

"Let's race", challenged Ben as the slow moving train entered the switch.

"OK" said Jake. "But I'll draw the line", thus establishing where the race would begin.

"What's the prize?" asked Ben almost sure that he would win, given the year difference in age and his longer legs. Not willing to give up his cookies in the brown sack, Jake offered the plum.

As the train neared, the boys took their stance at the line, toes carefully lined up so that neither had the advantage. They were going to race the train. Mindful of Gramps' cautions they were not near the track, nor the sides of the train.

"Ready… set … " a pause, then "Go." Smugly confident Ben allowed his brother the slightest head start. Even though the train looked like it had slowed down, it was a real race to catch it.

Jake's head was bent as he poured on the speed, well aware that he had to stretch his legs if he were to beat Ben. Indeed, he was concentrating more on his brother than the train. Jake's speed accelerated and he began to feel weightless. Looking at his knees he saw his lower legs becoming train wheels. He had often dreamed about such a thing happening so that once, just once, he could beat his brother.

As Jake pulled ahead, Ben saw Jake's legs as each foot raised and lowered. It looked like he was moving so fast that his legs had become metal discs. Impossible that his little brother could beat him, he surged ahead. And his feet and then legs morphed into wheels as well. Excited, they continued gaining speed and soon outdistanced the train and each boy who was no longer a boy but a train engine was speeding down the tracks, Jake pulling and Ben pushing, an entirely new adventure.

Ben and Jake pulled into the next siding to talk about how to get back home. Not possible for them to just turn on their legs any longer, Ben explained that they would need to get to a turn around, but had to wait until the tracks were clear. The engines' computers put them in an idle state and both Ben and Jake began to doze.

Awakened by the metallic clanking as a train backed into the siding, Ben did not know it but he was being linked to the train and was unable to get a panicked computer message through to the engineer After his hookup he was pushed back to Jake where he was joined to the train. Realizing that Jake would be with him eased Ben's anxiety. There was really nothing he could do about it, Ben reasoned, so enjoy the new sensations as a kind of train-bot.

Slowing for a drop of two refrigerated cars at the chicken plant Ben was uncoupled also and left on the siding. Jake was still attached and went forward as the rest of the train went on toward Fresno. Worried now, Ben had to find a way to get back to the train where Jake was. And, he thought fearfully, how would they ever make it back home to Atwater.

An old diesel engine pushed the three of them toward a loading dock and men on forklifts began loading the cars. It was done quite speedily. FDA required certification of temperature in the car and paper work was completed, copies placed in glassine carriers and the metal seals applied to the locks on the side of the cars. In less than an hour, the two cars and Ben were pushed to the end of the siding to await pick-up on their way to the Safeway warehouse in Richmond, California. Ben knew that Richmond was north of Fresno. Oh no, he thought, the exact opposite direction from where Jake was going.

Ben sensed a change in the control panel Perhaps he could lose the cars and make a run for Fresno. Engineers trained many weeks to operate the trains. How could he, a mere boy of eight years hope to even start the engine, never mind drive it. Looking at the various gages and indicators, Ben found that indeed he had the knowledge he would need; it had come along with the rest of the transformation. He knew he had to act quickly before the northbound train arrived

His first task was to uncouple from the other two cars, called rolling stock. It was a completely automatic procedure. All he had to do was select the correct command from the menu screen. Brakes and hydraulics were all included in the activity, and no human physical interaction was required. He found himself visualizing and the computer responded. Ben saw the message "Complete" and moved forward tentatively to ensure freedom from the tether to the refrigerated cars. He continued past the manual switch control and stopped there. His engine idled with the most pleasant hum of anticipation.

From points north came the next train. Bound to what destination Ben could not determine. It didn't really matter as long as it was south, somehow he would find his little brother who was probably an engine, too. How would he recognize his brother? Maybe he could contact him over the train radio.

"Jake, can you hear me? It's Ben?"

No answer. He repeated the call with the same result, then checked the status of the Fresno bound train. Ben concentrated and the schedule began scrolling. He needed the arrivals. Ah there, he thought, arrived on time. Status of the engines showed all at the barn for regularly scheduled maintenance. Ben searched rolling stock schedules to find all the engines that had been assigned and found five engine numbers that had completed the run. Each piece of equipment had its unique number And all five were unassigned until the day after next. He knew he had to find Jake before the engines were sent on their various routes.

The primary engine arrived, moved onto the siding and prepared to couple with Ben. Hasta la vista chicken plant. Hello, Fresno. Ben found he could no longer access schedules or command any functions at all. He could work out plans for getting himself and Jake back to Atwater. His mother must be frantic by now- he thought guiltily. First things first, since his dependence on the primary engine prohibited researching alternatives, he would have to go with what he already knew.

Would they ever get to Fresno, Ben wondered, both miles and time dragging Just as they took that last sweeping curve Ben arrived at a simple plan: he had to get free of the lead engine and find Jake as quickly as possible. It was a big assumption that once free he could again command his engine as before.

The engineer skillfully navigated them through the rail yard and deposited Ben at the barn. Once loose, Ben successfully opened the link to his computer The slight noise of the motor starting and the sensation of latent power was pleasing. Many different engines waited and not all their equipment numbers were easy to read, obscured as they were with black carbon There were diesel, diesel-electric and liquid natural gas engines, the newest and cleanest power source Ben was diesel and electric as were most of them. Jake, he knew from the

306

records was the same. Turning on the radio Ben called out to his brother and got no answer. That, he thought would have been too easy. Jake's status still showed oos- Out of Service: He was here somewhere.

Moving along the sidings, Ben called out for Jake repeatedly until he heard a faint crackle in response.

"What happened?" asked Jake

"Where are you?"

"I'm being loaded onto a flat car," answered Jake.

Looking toward the barn, Ben saw Jake and realized he had to stop Jake's transport immediately The BNSF repair garage was in San Bernardino, many miles to the south of Fresno. Ben maneuvered himself until he was by Jake's side

"Jake, concentrate real hard, get your boy legs back under you and board me."

"But Ben where are you?" asked Jake in confusion.

"I am the engine right beside you. Hurry, Jake. We have to get out of here right now"

Ben began making the computer entries that would schedule himself en route with no other rolling stock to Atwater. If it became necessary he would have to show engine Jake as being delivered there too. He entered all the switches noting the places and times of siding stops.

"Let's go" said Jake and there he was sitting on the metal fold down seat.

Ben had a million questions for Jake, but he

wisely rolled himself to the round house and requested the turn around.

"Hey Ben, where are you?" asked Jake.

"I'm here." answered Ben unsure even himself where he was. Perhaps the computer, maybe the dead man's switch, maybe in the hydraulics. Ben didn't have time to worry about that now, he had to get them moving.

Ben entered the barn and mounted the turntable to turn them back to the North direction. The

attendant was able to turn the 400,000 pound engine around with just a push.

The plate that did the turning was on top of a pit where hydraulics lifted and turned. In less than 10 minutes, he was on the northbound track on his way to Atwater. Piece a cake. 45 minutes to an hour should find them there, barring further complications. Don't even think about that.

The Four Bears

Kori is 16 years old, the daughter of a Greek father and a South African mother. Indeed, her name means "daughter" in the Greek language. The family live together in a section of New York City called Harlem, in peace and harmony with all their neighbors. Gus, her father's Greek name is Constantinos and her mother's name is Ena, which curiously, in Greek means "One." The happily married couple met in South Africa after Gus' family immigrated there.

Kori was born in the US after the couple was forced to leave South Africa, which had become very dangerous to the inter-racial couple following the return of Nelson Mandela to the leadership of the country. Not that Mandela was anti-white but many of the citizens acted out their anger and resentments toward whites which built during the long years of Apartheid. How different were race relations here in Harlem in the USA from those days her parents had spent in Pretoria.

In February, Black History Month at her high school, Kori was assigned a term paper. She mulled over possible topics, as she was taking the family Doberman leashed and properly controlled down MLK JR on her way to Marcus Garvey, Jr. Park. Both men for whom the street and park had been named were prominent figures and possible subjects, perhaps a contrast between the two men would be interesting. Rather fitting, she thought, since she wanted, like Garvey, a journalistic career.

Entering the park Einstein, the Doberman,

began to walk a little faster and broke heel. He was so in tuned to Kori that the slightest of pressures on his leash returned him to heel. As they approached the statue of Marcus Garvey, Jr., she looked for her school mates, Dora and Diego. Some Thursdays they would meet there. Yes, the twins were there along with their two younger siblings, Santyana and Ricardo. As soon as Kori stopped walking, Einstein sat.

"Que pasando" said Kori. ("What's happening") in Spanish

"Nada pasando aqui," said Diego. "Alli" "Nothing happening here." "There?"

Switching back to English, Kori said "Everything's good"

"Hey, did you bring me some Baklava?" asked Diego?"

"Sorry," she said, "we sold it all." "Otra vez" ("Another time") "¿Y dóde estámi Arroz con Dulce? Hace mucho tiempo dijiste que lo traerí?"(And where is my Rice pudding: it's a long time since you promised to bring it.)

"Well, here you are," Diego said producing a styrofoam container with a flourish.

"That was mine," said Santayana, kicking at Diego's shoe.

Diego quickly apologized for his brother's rudeness.

"I better go now," said Kori. "Thanks for the rice pudding," instinctively knowing that to offer the dessert's return would add more embarrassment to an already awkward situation.

The next week passed quickly for Kori. The following Saturday with Einstein beside her, she walked to the park hoping to meet her friends. Six pieces of Baklava rested in the blue cardboard boxes she carried, one for each member of her friend's family. At $4.50 for each piece she had traded one morning's work at the caféfor thc famous honey syrup treats. Diego and Santyana waited for her at their meeting place.

"Hola," Kori greeted Diego who smiled in return.

Santyana, unable to control his anticipation, asked, "What's in the little boxes?"

Heartened that Santyana seemed to be in a good mood, Kori said, "What I promised you last week. Do you remember what it's called?"

"Baklava," he said and held out his hand greedily.

Kori glanced at Diego, who ever so slightly nodded his head.

"Let's go sit down over there," Kori suggested.

Kori took the end seat on the bench and Einstein sat beside her.

"Hey, that's where I always sit," grouched Santyana.

"Come sit here beside me," Kori invited.

She handed over the little boxes carefully tied with string, to Santyana.

He pulled on the loose sting and all six boxes tumbled to the pavement.

Kori thought, so much for the careful

311

packing to protect the delicate pastries.

One of the boxes flopped open and the contents spilled out. Einstein tensed, ready to avail himself of the treat. Kori leaned over to clean it up and Santyana grabbed it from her hand. Einstein did not like the sudden movement, rose to protect his mistress.

"That's mine. You gave it to me," said Santyana petulantly as he stuffed in into his mouth. Honey smeared all over his hands and face he bent to retrieve the other little packages.

Diego tried to correct his brother's behavior but Santyana persisted. He grabbed up another piece and bit into it. "Hey, that's supposed to be for someone else," attempting to correct him, said Diego.

Time for Kori to leave and let him deal with the mess.

As she stood, Santayana accused her " It's your fault. You spoiled it all."

No thank you—no acknowledgment whatever for her offering. Only blaming her for his own misbehavior.

"Well, see you in school, Diego," Kori muttered as she readied to walk back home. "I gotta work on my paper."

" I'll walk you back," Diego said.

" Naw," she replied. "Your brother would not like that at all. For some reason I can never please him. So, I'll see ya in class."

Kori never met them in the park again.

The Dark

The feeble flame flickered in the feared dark
Her candle, her hope held tight in her hand
Not a defense but to see the path's mark

Alone she stepped forward, could not stand.
Ghosts and ghouls from the past haunted her mind
O'ercome the battle of her fainting heart
One step and another victory find
Courage and strength unnamed but there in part.

T'was not the nature of the dark like night
Nor was the lighted candle like the day
Neither promised to end the other's plight
But stasis to remain and constant stay.

Farther down the path smooth and wider grew
Darkness less viscous and hauntingly cruel
Pitch dark yielding perhaps to purple dawn
Invigorated unbroken along.

Still grasping the candle the source of her light
Boldly exploring the new and unknown
No goal defined stalwart progress in sight
Impediments to become the keystone.

The Devil's Cotillion

His appearance both comely and neat
Carefully groomed in well fitted clothes
Tidy graceful and a bit too glib
Dance partners deliberately chosen.
The music itself a seduction.

Casual approach building trust
He selects the moment he will pounce
Forward mouth insinuating
Lifted brows in an unasked question.

In other times and other places
She steps away and reconsiders
Soothing respite of his warm embrace
The music tempo's repetitious
Lessons learned through reminiscence.

Nam

Where was the parade, where the accolade
The war was hated and when I came home
From doing my job, friends dead, bodies laid
In the jungle man from the boy was grown.
Fifty times or more on Ho Chi Min trail
A guide bearing supplies, we could not fail
Wounded the blood dripping red from my vein.
Onward I went never to be the same.
Oh soul conditioned to the violence
Take a life an automatic response
All my energy for reducing stress
Fear no longer do I have to suppress.
Home coming heroes made in foreign lands
A different life with its own demands.
Not even soldier's pride, I had to hide
Among the fifty thousand who died.
For Richard Perez, 11th Cav.

Nam Redux

Seas roll in and ebb away
Bloody wounds though healed still flow
War follows man every day
Difficult to let it go.

On victory heroes come
Startle response within the veins.
Rest of life what's to become
That fight is what remains.

The psyche knows violence
Labors render its burden
A flash and crash of penance
Quick moment of peace is won.

Foreign land so far away
War politics mixed not free
Cultures clash yet we must stay,
On another day to flee.

Anyone who by chance resembles
Good guy or an enemy
Unknown prejudice stumbles.
Warfare's fog a killing spree.

Ho Chi Men cavalry raced
Some riding metal horses
You are killed, killing faced
Shutting down your mind closes.

Greeted like enemy they
Pay and pay and pay and pay
By demons chased every day
Not able to move nor stay.

Some stayed in the foreign land
They thought they might fit in there
An ex-patriot not planned.
Quiet and calm they could bear.

Welcome back home heroes all
For true freedom's breath we owe
For you courage answered call
Your sacrifice we now know.

Green Apples

Little green apples on your tree
Survived the pests but will not me
Spiced and sugared a pie I'll make
A squeeze of lemon adds some tang
And in the oven you will bake.

My Word

Still, in God's embrace you will find me
Circumspect circumstances or not
Whither far places I may be brought
Freely surrendered to destiny.

He took me at my word when my life
Forever changed and though I would fight
My personal war through day and night
With only myself in hellish strife.

Such was His God love of willful me
Even my best woefully short
A ship upon a sea far from port
Never left nor ever will leave.

Fire

One AM early morning or late night
"Wake up, half an hour to evacuate"
Came the call at the window, "Fire is near"
"Gather what you will bring and you must leave here."

"Go where?" " The Red Cross shelter in town at school."
What would I take what must I leave for fuel.
To feed the all consuming inferno
Take pills and clothes family treasured photos.

Every load carried while scanning the sky
For flames over treetops the mountain dry.
When I have gathered all I'm able to take
Time to get my pets into their crates

Rain

The sky is dark. Rain rides the wind.

Clouds empty their water like blessing.

Washed clean leaves grow heavy and treetops bend

Quenching earth's thirst and flames devouring.

Gone is the smoke and ash from the air.

No heady perfume sweet as answered prayer.

Jim Lindstedt

Harking back to my summer days at my uncle's dairy farm in Wisconsin I always loved the country. So, when Mariposa needed a deputy DA I applied and got my first job as a new lawyer. I moved from Southern California and settled in and that was 40 years ago. For 25 years I was the public defender in both Mariposa and Yosemite, and after that in private practice. During that I amassed a catalog of many stories I hope the reader enjoys these true tales about real people and real conflicts, or just my musing, as much as I enjoyed putting words to paper.

Cowboy Lawyer

A bend in the road is not the end of the road unless you fail to make the turn.   Anonymous.

"All of my heroes have always been cowboys" Willie Nelson

If you want to be a lawyer, you go to law school, to be a doctor you go to medical school, and future ministers and priests go to divinity school.   The next logical assumption is that cowboys go to, "cow school"?

Good agricultural universities like Fresno State, Cal State Davis, and many others throughout the country have animal husbandry courses, and a myriad of academic pursuits to teach a person how to do what it takes to make a living using the land. They teach statistics, when to plant, when to breed cattle, when to harvest, but nobody teaches anyone how to become a cowboy. Being a cowboy is a thousand year old self-taught career that comes from the university I know best, the school of hard knocks.

My move to Mariposa was simple enough, because I had a horse, and along with all belongings and the horse trailer, I just moved to what seemed like a calm, serene, life in the foothills.

Once, a really smart cowboy said to me, kiddingly, "don't ever tell me cowboys ain't smart, and I never appreciated just what an educated comment that was until after it all happened.

Another one told me that horses live with

two forces, love and fear, and don't let either one of them get the best of the other.

All of the cowboys I knew, all told me the same thing, "The first rule of the cattle business is to get out when the gittin's good." I'm not sure which of those word's I didn't understand, could have been "out", or maybe "get." Whichever one, I was determined. I learned that determination and good equipment is never a substitute for naïveté

It was about that time that I decided that since I had horses, and since I had some acres that were doing nothing I could buy some cows and learn to herd cattle and join the big cowmen. Well, maybe not really a big cowman, but cows are cows, and owning a few cows makes you more of a cowboy than the folks who hang around a place like Mickcy Gillcys, drink beer, ride the mechanical bull, and spit tobacco juice in a paper cup.

So, I had all the necessary ingredients of my cowboy empire, I had two horses, the truck, a horse trailer, two saddles, halters, and all the stuff they call tack. I had two pairs of good Tony Lama boots, three pairs of light blue jeans, two Levis, one Wranglers, three denim western shirts, one John Wayne hat, and a genuine leather belt with a big buckle that said something about me being a cowboy. I was so into being a cattleman I got a registered cattle brand approved by the California Brand inspector.

Then I went to see the mayor of Bootjack Bob Bissmeyer, and asked Bob if he could weld me the brand. Bob said," I can weld anything but a broken heart and the crack of dawn." I thought gee, Bob, let me think about that. I said "OK Bob don't forget to let me know then next time you run for mayor so I can help out your political campaign. Bob's political slogan was, "Bootjack, love it or leave it."

Now I had all the cowboy necessities, plus a cattle brand. It was called the "lazy L', It should have been called the crazy L.

I even talked the very talented Yosemite wood artist, to carve me a wall hanging. It said "B & J Cattle Co", I thought I would mix up the letters to make everybody believe there was a new cattle empire in town.

My first good break in the cattle business happened, when I got a call from a real cowboy. He told me that he needed to move 300 head of cattle about 30 miles away, and would I like to come along as a trail hand. Naturally, wanting to glean all the cowboy knowledge I could possibly soak up said "sure." I didn't even ask what the heck a trail hand was, but showed up promptly at 6:00 am with my horse, saddle, lasso, and I was ready to ride. There were probably about 20 people ready to make this cattle drive. I watched and did exactly what they did. I rode my horse, slapped my rope and yelled "hey, hey, get along cows" with the best of them. About noon we stopped for lunch, and it was great, lunch, country fried chicken, homemade bread, with real honey, fresh garden salad, and rice pudding. I noticed that lunch was prepared from the back of a pick-up truck not a chuck wagon, but, oh well, modern cowboys have to keep up with the times.

I learned something that day that I would later come to appreciate, and was, that it is easier to herd 300 cows than six cows. The trail ride was a huge success, all the cows were delivered safely, and I was now a seasoned cowboy with important bovine knowledge.

The next Monday morning at court I showed up as usual with a handful of case files for the normal work day, and the law continued to occupy my professional life. By now I had eleven cows and a leaky fence. I would get calls periodically that my cows were out on the road, and I would have to go home, change clothes, and herd them back inside my porous fence. I was a lawyer and I knew the law which is that Mariposa County is not an open range county, meaning that the owner is responsible for keeping his cows inside his fence, so I was determined that none of my cows were going to get out. It was a minor irritation, and took away from my duties at the courthouse, but after all, now I was a real cowboy, I owned real cows, and had a real booming cattle business.

I found myself on weekends riding my horse with a saddle bag full of fence staples, and the very clever fence tool used by all smart cowboys. All you have to do is find a wire that sags a bit, and twist the fence with the fence tool to tighten it, pound new staples in the fence post and "presto", you have a solid cow proof fence boy, was I good or what?

I have no idea of what the intelligence level

of a beef cow is but I suspect it is just slightly higher than that of a nematode. One of the animals I bought was a large Angus beef cow who seemed to be the leader of the pack. She also produced the most beautiful Hereford calves you ever saw. Anytime the darn cows got through the fence she was always leading them, not too far away from the ranch, but far enough, for traffic to stop and the phone calls come in.

That summer wasn't too bad, however there were several episodes of cows on the road. By now at various times I had heard, or I should say my secretary Stella had heard from from the constable, sheriff's deputies, a county supervisor, and increasingly anti-cow angry neighbors. I remember one call that was left on the answering device with no name but in effect said, "Can't you keep those f*****g cows on your own property." I thought that was little crude, I mean, didn't they understand here that I was trying to be a good citizen, a useful member of society, a real lawyer, and a fledgling cowboy? I felt they all needed to be a little more patient.

Summer ended, colder weather blew in, and naturally the rains came.

I was in court that day, and the clerk handed me a message from my secretary which said, "Get back here now!" It was just before noon and it was pouring. The judge announced that now was a good time for the court to break for lunch.

Stella had been with me for about two years. She was a very pleasant woman, in her 50's and had a lot of experience working with lawyers, and so I was very lucky to have her, as my secretary in my small town single practitioner law office. Stella had very attractive eyes, they were a deep blue, and always seemed not to change much. Her eyes were very understanding eyes, until that day. Stella was p.o'd.

When I walked into my office I looked at her, and she said. "JIM, SIT. DOWN!" I noticed that the color of her eyes had changed to a steely gray with a kind of red fire coming out the sides. I sat down and said, "well Stella, what's up?'. I think I saw a wisp of white smoke coming out of her ears, but I can't be sure.

She took a big deep breath and let the air out slowly, her eyes never leaving mine. She said slowly as if talking to a mentally challenged human being, "your cows are out again, stressing the word again."

I said, well gee, Stella, I can fix that and be back this afternoon, for court no problem."

She paused and said, "you - don't-understand - do- you?"

I said, "well, yes, I think so, you want me to go out in this rain and get the cows back in right?"

Her eyes now were almost totally red, and there was a tiny bit of spittle on the corner of her mouth. She said again, slowly talking to me like I was a moron just released from, a state hospital, "NO."

I said, "gosh, Stella what do you want me to do?" I paid more attention to what she said next, than I ever in my life listened to, any judge, jury, lawyer, doctor or sermon. By now I was worried that she might be having a heart attack, because I had heard that people foam at the mouth when that happens.

She picked up a piece of Kleenex, wiped it across her mouth, and said in a crackly voice I had never heard, "either you get rid of those cows or I quit!"

I said, "wow, you are really serious aren't you?"

Her eyes may have slightly returned to blue, I'm not sure, but she said "you dammed right I am." Now, in all the time I knew this woman I never, ever heard her swear, it just wasn't like her. Then she said, "get rid of the cows Jim," and added, "your afternoon is clear."

I said, "OK Stella, Ok right now I am going to get the cows OK, don't leave OK, just stay, stay, don't go OK."

She said, "don't talk to me like I am your dog!"

"Ok Stella, I am going now, right now, to fix it OK?" I went out that door so fast, I didn't realize it was still pouring as I got into my truck, and noticed I was all wet, because I forgot to put my coat on.

The drive home, the change of clothes to the cowboy outfit, and the walk down to the road to get the cows, was a blur. Big black mama was leading them away from the big hole in the fence, and I made a mental note, "got to fix that one." My neighbor happened to be home and agreed to help me. I was on foot, and at that moment saddling my horse and lassoing the cow didn't seem like a good idea, so I decided to get that rope around the cows head and use the neighbor's truck to slowly haul that black beast back behind the fence. It was now raining harder if that were possible, so I was really soaked. Rain was washing down my neck, and my shorts and socks were soaked, and I felt my feet squish with each step. To put it bluntly, it was a bad, bad day. The crowning moment came when the cow with the rope around her head was bleeding from her eyes, and I said to my neighbor, "this will not work."

He looked at me and said, "I can tell you why she bleeding, go look at the side of my truck." I did, and that mama cow had rammed the truck door with her head so hard it did about $350.00 damage. I thought, do all cows do this?

My homeowner's policy had an exclusion that said, stupid lawyers, who own stupid cows in the same household are not covered under this policy for any negligence which might occur to truck doors. Great, what next?

At that moment I can remember looking up at the sky and feeling the rain pounding down on me, and said to my helper. "I have a better idea, just leave them." I got the rope off the big black mama cow, and squished and dripped the 200 yards to the house. I have never in my life been so wet, cold, miserable, or felt so inept. I got in the shower and took my wet, soaking cowboy outfit off, and got a huge dry blanket to put over me. At least I was now dry. I remember thinking, OK Hoppalong, what's next?" My dog looked at me, equally wet, but lying on his dry warm dog bed. As much as if to say, "and you were smart enough to pass the bar exam"? I looked at that smirking animal and said out loud," just shut up dog, not another word." He gave me a big yawn put his head down on his pillow and, and if dogs could talk said, "you idiot."

I went to the telephone, got out the phone book, and called my cowboy buddy. He answered the phone with that absolute calm mountain drawl of his and said "hi Jim." I said as slowly as I could, "please, please, come get these, these creatures from hell, and I don't ever want to see a piece of beef in front of me unless it is medium rare and on a plate with a baked potato." He never flinched, and replied, "Ok, let me get the dogs and the cattle truck, and I will be there." He had two Australian Shepard's that probably forgot more about cows than I ever knew. It was still raining really hard.

He got the cows took them to the market and I got a check, and I was, a happy literally washed up cowboy, Stella was still working for me the next day, and sometime thereafter, so a happy ending, well not quite yet.

I was sitting on my patio about six months later when my cowboy friend and his wife showed up. In Mariposa you don't just get down to business you must chat awhile about the weather, the news, and the future before you talk reality. After what seemed like awhile and two beers, he said, "you know, you have those fifty four acres that aren't doing anything." I said, "yes, what about it", and he said, " well how bout I put 12 steers in there and I will give you a 500 pound beef cow for payment?." I thought "Ohmigod, this again", and stammered, "I did that and it was awful." A light sparkled in his eye, and he said, yeah I know, but I will guarantee you no cow will get out of the fence, I will take care of it." What he should have said is Jim, "I have been doing this for a long time, and I know exactly what I am doing, and you don't, so I can handle it." So, I said, "Ok go for it."

His cows were there for maybe eight months, and not one cow ever got through that fence, not one angry neighbor, not one call from the constable, not one complaint, best of all a happy secretary,

The moral to this story is doctors should doctor, lawyers should lawyer, and cowboys are the smartest guys of all.

Dog Stories

I have always loved dog stories, among all the reasons is because dogs are the only creatures that adopt us, as much as we adopt them. The old joke about putting your wife and your dog in the trunk of a car for an hour on a hot day, and see which one is the happiest to see you, always brings a smile, except from wives.

Between 30 and 40 thousand years ago a definite split in genes took place between the wolf, and the dog as we know it. The Egyptians, Romans, Greeks, and many other armies' used dogs to carry loads, be a friend, seek out the enemy, and warn of intruders.

There are the kinds of dog stories that Albert Payson Terhune made famous. He wrote, great stories about the love of a dog for his master, and the valiant deeds the dog performed to show that love. There was a classic story about the master who left his faithful dog to watch over his infant child, and how a wolf jumped through an open window to snatch the child, and how the powerful, well trained and faithful dog fought viciously to keep the wolf from harming the child. He wrote, that when the master returned he saw the dog and the cradle covered in blood, he immediately assumed that the dog had killed the child. So, on the spot he slew his canine friend, only to find the dead wolf outside the window and the child safe from all harm protected by the dead bloody loyal dog.

In the spring of 2000, in Ontario Canada,

Steven, his dog Elmo, and a friend Ethan were hunting for frogs in a pond. They got lost in an area with quicksand and cold weather. Ethan became entangled in vines and branches, and two very frightened boys needed help, so Steven left. Instead of leaving with his owner, Elmo remained with Ethan. Steven finally made it home and a search party tried to find the other boy. As night was falling one of the searchers saw a pair of green eyes reflected in his flashlight. Ethan was almost dead from hypothermia, but the dog had huddled with him to keep him warm, and probably saved his life.

How do you explain the genius of dogs?

Great dog stories come out of wars, like the Marine Corps "devil dogs" so feared by the Japanese, on Guadalcanal, Iwo Jima, and Bougainville, The dogs, mostly Doberman Pinschers, and German Shepherds were trained as sentry dogs to warn the handlers if any enemy patrols were nearby. The dogs must have thought it was" a piece of cake", because they could smell the enemy a mile away due to the primary diet of fish, Japanese solders' ate.

Chips, was a USMC sentry dog who was a WWII dog very adept at sniffing out Japanese patrols as much as 2 miles away. He became the most famous dog to emerge from WWII, and the marines even got him a dog tag that read simply "Chips" mascot, USMC.

In Korea, dogs were used mainly as messengers between allied lines, and again German Shepherds, were the most common breed   It is important to remember that all of these dogs, donated by patriotic Americans came home, and usually were adopted by the handlers, but with the approval of the donating family.

It was about this time that the armed forces came to the conclusion that dogs were not only an asset to troops, but essential for pre-warned attacks that would come. The military also learned that many breeds, besides German Shepherds could do the job, Border Collies, Labs, some big terriers, and even Poodles.

Viet Nam was a place where dogs were natural soldiers. The jungle was a perfect place for a dog's sense of smell to warn a patrol that the Viet Cong were nearby on land, or hiding in the water There were about 5,000 dogs used in the Southeast Asia conflict, and a fairly accurately estimate was that they saved 10,000 lives. Soldiers and handlers openly wept when the army issued ordered that the dogs could not go home. These honorable canine soldiers were left in there, like a piece of broken equipment that wasn't worth the cost of taking. Viet Nam was the only war where the dogs did not return. It is no guess, to say that many of them ended up in a Southeast Asian abattoir.

Congress through enormous pressure from all kinds of animal groups passed legislation making dogs, not quite soldiers, but given names and status, so they get to go home at the end of their tour. Bill Clinton signed that bill, in 2000.

We humans operate with our eyes, what we see is most important to us then, after that, what we hear, and smell. Unless you are on a cruise ship stalled in the ocean, with leaky toilets, our sense of smell is not as crucial to our survival as sight.

A dog's world is a smell world, who smells like what, how does its owner smell different than Mrs. Owner, and how about all those great smells away from home that make up doggie smell heaven. My dog marks her territory every day, to warn the deer that, "hey, this is my home," and you better watch out for me," because this is how I smell Bambi."

Tests have been done where a single drop of human sweat (*butyric acid)* was placed somewhere within an area the size of city block. A trained Labrador Retriever, can find that spot within 30 minutes, as their sense of smell is that good. A dog's sense of smell has been estimated to be ten thousand times better than humans. It is no wonder why your dog greets your friends by putting a cold wet nose up the visitor's crotch, with a wag of the tail, and a look, that says, "you have a great smell there visitor."

In recent wars, Iraq, and Afghanistan dog use has become much more sophisticated and much more rewarding for the troops who use them. They are capable of sniffing out IED's, smell enemy patrols and find chemicals the Taliban uses to make bombs. What piece of equipment can see it, smell it, hear it, and then warn his handler that "hey, Bud, we got a problem."

When Seal Team Six went to Pakistan to capture Osama Bin Laden they took with them as part of the team, a Belgian Malinois named "Cairo"

Names like Balto, and Togo, the lead dogs

that took the life saving serum to Nome Alaska, when there was no other way to get it there but by dogsled, are justly revered.

Bud, Lassie, RinTinTin, Uggie, and Old Yeller, are just a few of the movie dogs we as an adoring public have come to know.

Hawkeye, was a Black Lab who would not leave the coffin of his Navy Seal owner who was killed when the Chinook helicopter he was in was shot down in Afghanistan in 2011.

Hachiko was an Akita, so loyal to his owner he went to the train station every day for 9 years, waiting for his master to return.

Squeak, a Jack Russell Terrier would not leave the body of his owner a Zimbabwean farmer named Terry Ford. Ford was murdered by roving mobs of thugs carrying out Robert Mugabe's land seizure edict. A photo of little Squeak by his bloody dead owner on CNN raised worldwide attention to violence in Zimbabwe.

Theo, an English Springer Spaniel handled by lance corporal Liam Tasker of the British Army was used very successfully, to sniff out roadside bombs. Liam and Theo were inseparable, and the two had just set a record for finding more bombs and weapons caches than any other team. Theo and Tasker were in a firefight in Afghanistan, in 2010, when Tasker was killed, by a sniper. Theo died later at a British base hospital from what friends said, was a broken heart. Tasker's body and Theo's ashes were returned to England where the family was presented with the Dickin Medal, Britain's highest award for animal bravery.

How do you explain the genius of dogs?

Great dog stories are the natural result of the thousands of years that have bonded dogs and humans. This article could go on forever, discussing the value, love, and treasured memories we have of pets in our lives, usually dogs. Today, dogs are used to tell if their owner is going to have an epileptic fit, has a certain kind of cancer, or suffers from a host of other illnesses, which are among the growing uses for canine genius. Reports show clearly that regular interaction between very ill hospital patients and therapy dogs, cause levels of curative chemicals in the body to rise significantly.

I can't leave you without one last dog story. George owned a Labrador retriever named Buster who brought home the most vile, smelly, rotten, awful dead creature he had ever seen. He tried to take it from the dog and bury it but the dog would not let go, and would run as soon as his owner came close. So Buster spent the day eating and swallowing this terrible mess. Finally after the canine dumpster consumed all of it, he started to flatulate, and run around the yard. These smelly horrible, gases coming from the dog was more than George could bear. He got 6 cans of room freshener and began spraying the outside. His wife said, "what, are you doing" and he answered," can't you smell it." She immediately closed all the windows and locked the doors.

The neighbors were looking over and holding their noses and yelling, "What is that smell." George just shrugged and put a red bandana over his nose old west bad-guy style. His

337

buddy Stan had a bath towel, over his face. They just watched the dog run in circles, and fart, while they drank beer. After what seemed like a long time Buster stopped and flopped down on his side and was motionless. Stan said, "George, is he dead"?, and George turned to his friend and said, "no Stan, I think he just ran out of gas."

Trouble, Trouble, Boil and Double

"There is danger from all men, the only maxim of a free government ought to be to trust no man living with power to endanger the public liberty."
                                        John Adams

Trouble seems to come in three kinds, bad, worse, and disaster. Trouble always seems to start, right now! It's very hard to plan for bad things to happen, because they just materialize from very innocuous beginnings.

Little did the people described in this story know what an unfair, disastrous day would take place before their collective eyes.

John Jones, his 83 year old father-in-law Jack Smith, and his 12 year old autistic son Jason all set out on that March day in the family car to go to Merced. Jack had an appointment with his cardiologist in the medical office complex very close to the Merced Mall. The trip to Merced was uneventful, and they arrived at the doctor's office promptly at 11:30 am. The receptionist informed the three of them that Jack's appointment was later at 1:30 pm. So, Jack and John decided they would go have lunch to take up some time. They decided to go to the Home Town Buffet, which was just down the block. John parked the family van and the three of them walked the restaurant, and down the narrow hallway to the cashier's station. Jason, the 12 year old decided that he was not hungry, so Jack paid for two meals with a twenty dollar bill and got change from the cost of $15.25. They each picked up a tray and selected the dishes of food they desired, and found a booth. While in the food line Jason decided he would like a piece of green Jell-O, so John put it on his tray.

After the meal was finished, they left the restaurant to proceed to the car.

At that moment a Pandora's Box opened and all kinds of really bad things happened.

Her name was Theresa Salazar, and she was about 20 years old, and to this day no one knows why she did what she did. The day after this incident she disappeared, or at least I could not find her. Did you know that the Merced Mall has eight security cameras on top of the building, and not one of them showed anything but straight down? A video of the Home Town Buffet parking lot would have been priceless.

She followed them out into the parking lot, screaming at John, "hey you m f, you owe me for another meal." John said, "calm down, it was only a piece of jello", and with this crazy woman yelling, he threw a five dollar bill at her. By this time they were at John's car, and the three of them got in. John in the driver 'seat, Jack in the front passengers seat, and Jason in the back directly behind John. This lunatic got in the car through the open van sliding door behind the passenger's seat All this time the ugly f m-bomb was being hurled from her foul mouth at John, the old man and the child. Jack was bewildered, and Jason was scared, and John did not know what to do. John yelled at her to get out of the car, but she refused to leave continuously yelling curses. The manager by this time was on the sidewalk in front of the restaurant yelling, "I told you to just get the license number" So, he started the car and drove about 20 yards and then stopped. All the time she continued to rant and rave over this unpaid jello bill. She finally got out of the car and ran back into the restaurant.

If John thought his bad day was over, he was mistaken, the nightmare was just beginning.

He thought that they had to get out of there and reach the safety of home, so the medical appointment was a distant memory.

He drove about six blocks when the sirens and flashing lights appeared. Not just one Merced Police car but two of them, and two motorcycle units appeared all using every electronic gadget they had, to stop this horrible criminal. This person who was fleeing the absolute power of law enforcement in Merced, California, had committed crimes, and he was going to pay the price.

John was handcuffed, placed into the back seat of a police cruiser, and taken to the Merced City jail He was placed in a holding cell given two phone calls. He called his wife, and a bail bondsman. His bail was $65,000.00 as he was charged with one felony, robbery, and two misdemeanors.

Most people understand that when crime is committed or alleged to have been committed someone must look at a chart and see how much the bail amount is.

Our Constitution guarantees bail in almost all cases, and is not up to some judge or cop to decide if a person stays in jail or gets out.

The bail bondsman is very much like an

insurance agent. He has an agreement with some companies that write bail bonds. He or she gets ten percent of the face amount up front, as in this case was $6,500.00. So the bond was posted and now John was at the hands of the justice system. I told him later that, in view of the law enforcement actions in his case he was lucky, he wasn't charged with the Kennedy assassinations.

Statements were taken from all the parties after John was on his way to jail, and Jack had to drive the family car home to Mariposa with Jason as his passenger. The two of them could only wonder about what had happened to make this innocent normal trip such a dreadful affair.

The term justice is a very elusive one, because it means one thing and one thing only, and that one thing is whatever happens is justice. Whatever a judge says, whatever a zealous prosecutor says, whatever a jury says, is what we know as justice.

Fortunately there is a buffer amid all this madness, and that is the defense lawyer. His job is to make sure his client gets all his constitutional protections, and make sure he isn't ramrodded into a plea or incarceration for something he didn't do.

The DA in Merced County filed a complaint charging John with misdemeanors. Count I a violation of Penal Code section 537 (A) defrauding an innkeeper with intent to not pay for services amounting to less than 900 dollars.

Count II a violation of Penal Code section 242 a battery, which means someone wilfully and unlawfully using force and violence upon the person of another. C'mon are you serious?.

So the legal process began in Merced County. In a case where a person is charged with misdemeanors only, he or she may appear through their attorney   In this case John never had to appear in person. I entered a plea of not guilty to all charges and we continued the case.

The case was on the docket four times and then I told the DA we ought to both interview Ms. Salazar in her office. I did not receive an answer, but at the next appearance the DA said, "I am not going to continue this case any longer, I am going to dismiss it."

Whoom-oh, this case was over, the bail was exonerated, and John was free.

All this for what? To prove police power? To show that law enforcement badge wearing officers can do whatever they want? To fill up the court system? To make a good story? I hope someone will tell me the answers to these questions, but while I am waiting, it is what we in our legal system term justice.

The Dark Side of Eden

Whenever something seems too good to be true it probably is,

No one would disagree with me if I said Yosemite National Park is a gem of our country. No one would tell me I didn't know what I was talking about if I said that YNP was a wonder of God's creation. We all agree that Yosemite would have been one of the ancient Seven Wonders of the World.

Nothing is perfect, and everything known to human mankind has a dark side, so let me tell you just one story of a dark tale about Yosemite.

Every national park has a U.S. Magistrate, a judge who hears three kinds of cases, petty offenses, which include throwing trash outside a car, driving on the wrong side of the road, and not following the rules of the road. Misdemeanors, which can be driving under influence, to smoking pot, possession of mushrooms, to a very serious crime which, in the opinion of the park ranger is less than a felony. Then the felonies, murder, mayhem, robbery, rape, that are only arraigned in the magistrate's court and then sent to the US Federal District Court in Fresno. The Magistrate in Yosemite gets paid about 150 thousand a year with benefits. He might work 2 days a week, and is provided housing amid the glories of the park.

The US park rangers are pretty much guys who got a 2 or maybe 4 year degree in botany, or maybe entomology, and who wanted to be in Yosemite. Phoenix University was unknown then, and there were no degrees for law enforcement. nor, the biggest oxymoron of them all, Criminal Justice. So they got a job, and were given guns, cars with multiple bright lights, sirens, badges, telephones, hand held radios, and the latest in domestic warfare. I likened them to Smokey hatted, well-armed, fern feelers.

Mr. Estas Macedo called me from Florida, and told me about his problem, which was that he was born in Brazil, and brought to the United States by his parents when he was 10 years old. He grew up in the US, went to school here, got married to a US citizen, bought a house, had a business, and had 2 children who were US citizens. Now in 2010 he was going to be deported by INS, (Immigration, Naturalization Service), now ICE Immigration Naturalization Enforcement because he pled guilty to possession of marijuana in Yosemite in 1987. I liked it better when it was called a service, like the IRS is a service.

He, and his lawyer from Florida inquired if I could do something, to keep him from being deported, and I thought I just might be able to do that.

In both state and federal jurisdictions, courts must have a preserved record, called a *BOYKIN/TAHL* waiver. What this means, is that each court must have a written or tape recorded admission by the defendant, and, it must have evidence that the person understood his constitutional rights, and gave them up willingly to satisfy the requirements of the law. The wording from BOYKIN/TAHL is that " a prior conviction may be challenged i,e, set aside, overturned, and/or dismissed when there is an inadequate showing that the defendant knowingly and intelligently waived his or her constitutional rights."

I knew full well what the policies were in Yosemite and I had a hunch they might not have it. I thought that if I filed a motion to strike a prior conviction, I might succeed, because of that lack of a preserved record. I told Mr. Macedo and Regina D. Morales, esq. his attorney in Florida that I thought we had a chance to set the plea aside, as long as the prosecution could not produce a valid waiver.

The magistrate at that time had a brass plaque on his desk that read TANJ. I said, "judge what does that mean." He said, "you don't know what TANJ means" I said "sorry I don't" Then came the classic words from a famed jurist, "they ain't no justice" The law just doesn't get any better than that.

The first good news was after I asked for a copy of the tape recording from the Magistrates clerk in Yosemite who then directed to the United States District Court clerk's office in Fresno, who then informed me after quite a delay that the tape was unintelligible. Surprise, surprise.

Just about at this time, a new supreme court case came down which held that lawyers **must** tell the client what the consequences are of entering a guilty plea in a case where there is even a remote chance of deportation. *Padilla vs. Kentucky* was even cited my papers, the prosecutions papers, and the judge in his 10 page decision. One would think with this that Mr. Macedo was home free, right?, not on your life.

After everything was filed stamped and done we finally had a court date for the hearing, and that day was August 28, 2010. It was a beautiful day in Yosemite and great to be there and, get paid for it. The judge set this hearing on a day when there were no other cases scheduled. The only people in the courtroom were the judge , the clerk, the prosecutor and me, and oh yeah, the federal Marshall, funny huh?. I told the judge that the prosecution and I agreed, there was only one issue before the court, and that was, does the prosecution have a valid waiver?

Then one of those surreal moments in time happen when you think you have been transported by a time machine to the land of the Eloi, or someplace where logic is gone. Your don't believe what you are hearing, it's utter nonsense.. The judge started talking about "presumed governmental fairness" and "presumed governmental honesty", and most appallingly, "presumed governmental correctness."

I didn't feel like going to jail for contempt that day, so inwardly I said, my God judge did you ever hear about John Mitchell, the US attorney general lying to congress, or have you heard about Oliver North and the Iran-Contra affair, or how about Bill Clinton and Monica L, in the "O" office. or John Haldeman, John Erlichman, and tricky dickie Nixon? Remember Watergate judge? Could I refresh your recollection about how Robert McNamara lied about Vietnam? Let's not even start on Iraq and Afghanistan because you will put me in jail, and the Yosemite jail really sucks, it

347

resembles a giant monkey cage at the zoo. In my time the menu up there was a baloney sandwich and a banana.

The petition was denied, in his ten pages of judicial nonsense. So I walked out into the bright warm sunshine and thought to myself, when all else fails, tell yourself something positive, and I mused, Whiskey, Tango, Foxtrot. That's a military acronym for "what the f**k", just happened?

This story gets even better, because after I helped my client file an appeal, and the time came to produce the tape of the "government can do no wrong" hearing. Would you believe it, the clerk's office informed me, "we lost it." I wondered at that moment if the government could take a few bucks from the war, any war, and spend it on some Chinese recording equipment for the court in Yosemite.

Cat Fishing

Lexicology means the formation, usage and meaning of words in a language. For example, when I was young the word cool meant something less than hot. Today cool has an abundance of meanings, everything from a good looking car, to, anything describing a copasetic atmosphere. So, words do a lot of things, they are the conduit by which we communicate orally and written.

An example of this is the word, or words shell shock, that's what they called it in WWI, and in WWII they called it battle fatigue, in Vietnam it was PTSD, post-traumatic stress disorder, same word, same meaning, just different lexicon, jargon, argot. The military has not yet figured out how to coin a new word for the same thing in Afghanistan, but I'm sure they will.

Words have always been an anathema of society, which is a good thing because words keep us alive, moving and vibrant.

Some words are born, live a life, and die out after few hundreds of years, but others gain a new meaning by idiom, jargon, and local usage known as argot.

Recently the TV, news media, magazines, newspapers, and every other form of mass communication have been filled with the story of a college football player from the University of Notre Dame, named Manti Te'o. He is obviously talented, big, and good enough for the pro football scouts to drool over him. No one becomes a Heisman Trophy candidate finalist (one of three) without being outstanding in College football. This award is given once each year to the best collegiate football player in America. He also is apparently very ignorant,, and or/very naïve, we really don't know which one or both yet. The total truth is emerging very slowly, as the media squeezes every drop of gut wrenching emotion from this truly pathetic story.

Manti's naiveté and an Internet scam is the subject of this story, and in which he played a disingenuous part. Because of his notoriety and fame,

He brings a much larger image of fraud and ignorance to the public eye, than had been previously imagined.

This story is about "catfishing "and In order to understand what "Catfishing" means you need to understand the history or the word, and realize that the does not mean someone sitting on a riverbank in Georgia with a can of worms, and a Coca-Cola in a cooler, trying to get food for tonight's meal of "hush puppies", (another two words which have had several unrelated offspring)

In 2010 there appeared on television a documentary called Catfish" in which a 24-year-old New Yorker named Yaniv Schulman told about his long distance romance with a woman he met on Facebook. Her name was Megan. She was 19 years old, beautiful, wistful, and far away. He told of trying many times to arrange a meeting, but was always put off for one reason or another, and became naturally suspicious after a while. She seemed too good to be true, which is exactly what she was.   There was no Megan, In fact she was Alice who was a lonely middle aged woman in Michigan who spent her days caring for her two severely handicapped children, and sought an escape on the internet, via Facebook.   When Schulman finally went to northern Michigan and saw face to face what wanted to see he instead, spent a long time talking to her husband, who knew nothing of the scam.   Schulman had been "catfished"

So, what does the word mean?   When fishermen started to ship live cod from Alaska to China, the fish arrived weak and listless, the result of inactivity during transit.   Some bright person came up with the idea of putting catfish in with the cod, to keep everything alive, and moving.   It worked because the Cod arrived alive, wiggly, and fresh as a daisy.

There are those people in life who are like catfish, and they keep you on your toes.   They keep you guessing and thinking fresh.

Thank God for catfish because without them it would be a dull life.   Everyone needs something to nip at their fins, and keep them wary.

This story mushroomed into a reality show called, "catfish", where Schulman tried to give would be Facebook romance seekers, tips on how to be aware of dangers lurking out there.   The show wasn't really a big hit until Manti Te'o and his make believe girlfriend Lennay Kekua appeared 24/7 on the media stage.

"Catfishing" is not new, in the 1980'a several big time celebrities were mysteriously seduced by a woman named Miranda, who it turned out was a thirty something social worker from Baton Rouge.

So, if you feel you've been "catfished" I suggest you go to the delete button, and then turn your computer off for at least 24 hours, and then send an e-mail to Dr. Phil asking what kind of mental exercises you can do to keep up with the would be scams in the world.